T5-AEY-618

"I Know What Your Name Is, *Red,*" Nick Gallagher Drawled, And Began To Close The Distance Between Them.

Lacey followed her first instinct and backed away, but a chair suddenly appeared behind her and she fell into it. Nick merely leaned over her, bracing his hands on the chair's arms, his face a mask of contradiction. His voice, no longer angry, purred huskily. "But *Red* suits you so much better."

Her green eyes were ensnared by his brown ones as they raked over her coiled, coppery locks. "My—my hair is blond," she countered breathlessly. Was her pulse racing? And why was her heart pounding so? "St—strawberry blond, if you will."

"In this light," he voiced softly, his gaze falling from her hair down to her emerald eyes and on deliberately to her full breasts, "it's fiery red. A man could get burned runnin' his fingers through it. That's what you do to men, Lace. You burn them with your fire. . . . Or do you freeze them with your coldness?"

She found her breath coming in short, labored gasps. She saw an unexpected gleam appear in the depths of his dark eyes. His mouth, wide and well chiseled, slowly came closer to hers. . . .

Dear Reader,

We, the editors of Tapestry Romances, are committed to bringing you two outstanding original romantic historical novels each and every month.

From Kentucky in the 1850s to the court of Louis XIII, from the deck of a pirate ship within sight of Gibraltar to a mining camp high in the Sierra Nevadas, our heroines experience life and love, romance and adventure.

Our aim is to give you the kind of historical romances that you want to read. We would enjoy hearing your thoughts about this book and all future Tapestry Romances. Please write to us at the address below.

The Editors
Tapestry Romances
POCKET BOOKS
1230 Avenue of the Americas
Box TAP
New York, N.Y. 10020

Most Tapestry Books are available at special quantity discounts for bulk purchases for sales promotions, premiums or fund raising. Special books or book excerpts can also be created to fit specific needs.

For details write the office of the Vice President of Special Markets, Pocket Books, 1230 Avenue of the Americas, New York, New York 10020.

Gallagher's Lady

Carol Jerina

DO NOT DESTROY . . .
RETURN TO:
BOOK BARGAINS
147 BANK STREET

A TAPESTRY BOOK
PUBLISHED BY POCKET BOOKS NEW YORK

Books by Carol Jerina

Lady Raine
Gallagher's Lady

Published by TAPESTRY BOOKS

This novel is a work of historical fiction. Names, characters,
places and incidents relating to non-historical figures are either
the product of the author's imagination or are used fictitiously.
Any resemblance of such non-historical incidents, places or
figures to actual events or locales or persons, living or dead, is
entirely coincidental.

An *Original* publication of TAPESTRY BOOKS

A Tapestry Book published by
POCKET BOOKS, a division of Simon & Schuster, Inc.
1230 Avenue of the Americas, New York, N.Y. 10020

Copyright © 1984 by Carol Jerina
Cover art copyright © 1984 by Harry Bennett

All rights reserved, including the right to reproduce
this book or portions thereof in any form whatsoever.
For information address Tapestry Books, 1230
Avenue of the Americas, New York, N.Y. 10020

ISBN: 0-671-52359-7

First Tapestry Books printing, August 1984

10 9 8 7 6 5 4 3 2 1

POCKET and colophon are registered trademarks
of Simon & Schuster, Inc.

TAPESTRY is a trademark of Simon & Schuster, Inc.

Printed in the U.S.A.

To my mother and father, Beth and Cecil
And to the men in my life,
Patrick, Jason, Daniel, Michael, and
my husband, Drew

Chapter One

November, 1899

DRIED LEAVES THE COLOR OF BURNISHED COPPER whipped through the air, blown aloft by the swift wind that buffeted the hill dotted with marble and granite headstones. High above, dark clouds lumbered slowly across the sky, promising the long-needed rain. One leaf, persistent in its journey, flew against the tall, black-clad young woman. It caught the tip of her veil before drifting past her to settle on the polished mahogany coffin, which rested above the gaping hole so near the edge of the old church cemetery.

Lacey pulled her veil back into place, covering the strands of copper-gold hair that had been momentarily revealed by the sudden gust of wind. Reclasping her hands, she listened patiently as the elderly minister's voice droned on and on. His seemingly never-ending verse of scripture had been chosen to ease the heavy burden she now bore. Her husband had died, suddenly and without warning, and now lay in the coffin before her.

Lacey didn't feel like the widow she was. She felt

1

more like an outsider, a stranger who was merely looking on at this solemn occasion, even though she and the deceased had known each other most of their lives. But they had been married for such a brief time, she reasoned, it was difficult to think of herself as a Gallagher, one of the select members of Dallas's wealthy elite and the widow of that clan's last male descendant.

At last, the minister bowed his snowy head, said a brief prayer and ended the ceremony with a softly spoken "Amen." He turned to Lacey and took her gloved hand in his. "If there is anything I can do to help, my dear child . . ."

"No, thank you," she intoned softly. "I've been on my own before, sir. I'm sure I can manage."

He nodded. "You know where I am if you should need me."

She turned then to the other mourners—all male —who passed in succession, giving her slender hand a squeeze as they offered their condolences. A few had the audacity to give her sly looks, looks that could be interpreted in only one way, since they had been old whoring friends of Chris's. The others, those who respected her and kept their comments brief and tasteful, were business acquaintances of her late husband's. Bless them, they had helped Chris turn his limited legacy into a tidy little fortune, one he had taken pride in accumulating.

Chris had died owning not only land near Dallas, but five hundred acres of farmland near Beaumont, as well as the mansion his father had built. He'd amassed shares in various companies and had purchased stock in railroads, all at the advice of these friends. And she, as his widow, was now an extremely wealthy young woman. *Not bad,* she told herself bitterly, *for the bastard daughter of Maxwell Gallagher's mistress. Not bad at all.* But the knowledge wasn't a comforting one.

The last mourner in line was Peter Thorne. An artist and close friend, he had been with Chris the day he died. He approached her and took her hand in both of his. "I want to drop by the house soon, if it's all right, Lacey. There are some things I think we should discuss . . . about Chris's death."

"Peter—" she began.

"No, listen to me, Lacey. It wasn't as sordid as the gossips have made it appear." Rolling his eyes heavenward, he sighed a ragged breath. "*I* should know."

An unbidden pain tore through her and fresh tears stung her eyes. "I don't want to talk about it, Peter. . . . Please! Maybe later, but not now. It's much too soon."

He patted her hand and gave her an understanding nod. "May I still call on you, though?"

"Of course. You're always welcome at Gallagher House."

As Peter followed the others, who were departing in their carriages down the cemetery drive, Lacey reflected on how kind he'd been to her through her recent ordeal. But her musing was interrupted by the low-pitched voice behind her.

"You gonna be awright, Miss Lacey?"

Turning, she looked up into the comforting black face and smiled tremulously. "I'll be fine, William."

Taking his proffered hand, she let him lead her to the shiny black carriage, now standing solitarily in the drive. As he handed her into the coach, he said,

3

"When we get home, Momma'll fix you up with one of her hot toddies. They can sure warm you up on a cold day like this."

Lacey paused a moment in her ascent to give him a long look. Having known William since childhood, she considered him to be like a brother, even though he was of a different race. They shared a protective camaraderie that was difficult to explain and even harder to understand. "You know something?" she queried softly. "I was feeling sorry for myself earlier, I guess because I was lonely. But I'm not alone. I have you and Hattiebelle, don't I?"

"Whether you want us or not," he acknowledged dryly and shut the door.

At twenty-four, William was five years older than Lacey, and a few months younger than Chris. But, at the moment, she felt as if she were the older one. The oldest woman on earth, to be truly honest.

Settling into the corner of the seat, she adjusted a blanket about her long legs. The cold outside, cutting through the tiny cracks in the coach's thin walls, chilled her to the bone. As the carriage tilted under William's weight, she pulled down the dark curtains at the windows, wanting to shut off the outside world from her view. People would be stopping and gawking as they drove back through town; people always did at the sight of black-plumed horses. But she was in no mood to suffer their pitying looks or their behind-the-hand whispers.

She removed her veiled hat and gloves and felt her puffy coiffure to see if any errant strands of hair had come loose. Assured that they hadn't, she let her hand rest next to its mate in her lap and frowned sadly at the gold band and small emerald that winked

4

back at her. Had it been only four months ago that Chris had given her the emerald? Oh, God! Yes, that's when it had been.

Shutting her eyes, the painful memory of that happier time flashed through her mind with a clarity that was startling. She could hear the band playing a rousing Sousa march as it had done that day in City Park. She could see the baseball game in progress on the diamond nearby, as the onlookers shouted and cheered. Children, and their parents alike, lay about the green, grassy embankments, replete after their picnic lunches; while above them, birds and insects chirped in the pecan and cottonwood trees. It was the kind of idyllic memory to cling to and cherish.

She had been sleepily listening to the music, her head resting against the shade tree's trunk, when she noticed Chris searching inside the pocket of his discarded coat. He extracted a jeweler's box and opened it, saying simply, "I want to marry you, Lacey." And without waiting for her reply, he placed the ring on her left hand, laughing at the amazed look which suddenly appeared on her face.

Recalling now that all-too-special moment, Lacey bit her lips to hold back her tears. The memories of those precious, happier times were much too painful. With every fiber of her being, she wished she could dispel them forever, but knew it was impossible. Seeing Chris as he'd been that day, lying beside her with the brilliant summer sun shining down on his fair, golden head, was much too easy.

The coach swayed dangerously to one side, jerking her out of her melancholy mood. Gasping, she reached out to grab hold of the leather strap by the door. But almost as quickly as the coach had tilted, it righted itself again, leaving Lacey stunned and shaken.

Leaning forward, she opened the window just behind the driver's perch. "William?" she called in a worried tone.

"We're awright!" she heard him growl. "Just some fool, ridin' like the devil was after him. He was headin' into the graveyard as we come out. Tried to get through the gate before us."

"Some people can be so inconsiderate," she mumbled nervously, settling back in the seat with an uneasy sigh.

A deep ditch, running parallel with the road, was just outside the cemetery gates. Had William not been adept at handling the horses, they could easily have overturned into it. She shuddered, remembering that it had been just that kind of accident which had taken her mother's life a year ago. Max Gallagher had died that night as well, but his passing hadn't been as painful or left the void in her life that Rachel's passing had. In fact, Lacey had been almost glad that Max was no longer around to humiliate her mother as he'd done.

It was just after the funerals that she and Chris became attracted to one another. One thing naturally led to another and they found themselves feeling emotions neither had ever experienced before. But she had been truly astonished when he had proposed last July. He had been enough like his older brother, Nick, to ignore proper convention and marry the daughter of his father's mistress. And though there had been a considerable amount of gossip about their sudden engagement, Chris had openly courted her anyway, taking her out as often as he wished to, while treating her with a respect few had shown her before. He had literally forced a number of society matrons to acknowledge her, and she loved him all the more for doing it.

When the sound of wheels and horses' hooves no longer clicked against the paved streets, Lacey knew they had left the city limits. Only then did she raise the curtains to look through the watery afternoon light at the passing scenery. The houses here weren't as grand as those closer to town were. Many of them were little better than hovels, unpainted and leaning sadly with neglect. But there were people inhabiting those hovels. She should know; she had been born into a neighborhood such as this one.

Rachel hadn't always been a rich man's paramour. Before she had given birth to Lacey, she'd been a poorly paid dressmaker, sewing for women who didn't always pay her. Maxwell Gallagher's wife, Lillian, had been one of her more thoughtful, conscientious customers. It was after Lillian's death that Max came and rescued Rachel and Lacey from their bleak, futureless existence.

William drove the carriage down the curving road, past the old wooden bridge that crossed White Rock Creek and up the slight incline of the next hill. Soon Lacey could see the tall, red-brick wall that surrounded Gallagher House, protecting its vast gardens from view of the road below. Max had designed the house for Lillian, but she hadn't lived long enough to see it completed. Instead it had been Rachel who had been the first mistress of Gallagher House, as well as mistress to its owner.

Shortly after their unholy alliance began, Max's oldest son, Nick, left home. He preferred to have his

father's displeasure than live with the woman who
had replaced his mother . . . or so Lacey believed.
But Nick hadn't forgotten his family. He had written
to Chris for a while, telling him of his adventures.
Then, shortly before Max and Rachel had been
killed, they received word that Nick had died at the
hands of claim jumpers in the Yukon. A sad ending
indeed for the Gallagher family.

As the coach reached the top of the hill, Lacey
glimpsed the tall, wrought-iron gate as it passed by
her window. A feeling of peace and tranquility came
over her, as it always did when she came home. It
was as though she had entered a safe haven, a world
totally unrelated to the real one outside.

William brought the carriage to a halt and hurried
down from the driver's seat to assist Lacey. Just as
her feet came to rest on the wide, gravel sweep, the
mansion's front door swung open and she saw
Hattiebelle emerge. Tall and motherly, the housekeeper took one look at Lacey and flew down the
steps, wiping her flour-covered hands on her apron.

"My poor little girl!" she wept, throwing her arms
protectively around Lacey's slimmer frame. "You've
done been through mis'ry this day, ain't you,
honey?"

Equal in height, Lacey looked levelly into Hattiebelle's warm black eyes and gave her a weak smile.
"Yes, but it's all over now." Thank God, she added
silently.

"Listen at me blubber," Hattiebelle sniffed, dry-
ing her eyes with her apron. "I been carryin' on like
this all mornin'. I can't help it, though; that boy was
like my very own."

William stepped up and placed an arm about his

mother's shaking shoulders. "Come on, Momma. It's startin' to get cold out here. Let's go in the house where it's warm."

Allowing him to lead her up the wide steps and into the warmth of the entrance foyer, Hattiebelle sighed. "I done thought the saddest time of my life was when Nick up and left home to traipse around the world, but with Chris a gettin' run over like he did, so soon after y'all married . . . well, this is ten times worse!"

Glancing at William, Lacey noticed how his full lips pressed into a thin, disappointed line. They'd tried—unsuccessfully, it now appeared—to protect William's mother from the sordid truth of Chris's death. She could only speculate as to how much of the story Hattiebelle actually knew.

"We gotta go on livin', Momma," William remarked tenderly. "We can't just give up 'cause a loved one was taken from us. You survived when Poppa died; you'll make out now, too."

"You two go on," Hattiebelle sniffed, wiping her cheeks again. "I need to be alone for a spell. I'll be awright after a while."

"Are you sure?" Wanting time alone herself, Lacey was nevertheless reluctant to leave her beloved housekeeper in case she should be needed.

Hattiebelle nodded and turned toward the back of the hall, where a shorter side hall led to the massive kitchen at the rear of the house. "I got supper to cook yet, so I'd best start fixin' it if we're gonna eat tonight. You two run on."

William watched his mother retreat to her domain, then turned and left quietly through the front door.

Lacey stood alone in the foyer, listening to the empty, echoing sounds around her. Even though others were in the house, she felt lonelier than ever before. She had no one really close to her now. They were all dead.

With a heavy sigh, she swept toward the curving staircase and climbed to the second floor and her bedroom at the front of the house—the bedroom she and Chris had planned and furnished together, and where she alone had slept. She tiredly dropped her things onto the chair and closed the door behind her. It was all hers now, God help her. Or it would be when the lawyers and the State of Texas made it so. Strange that all this wealth and opulence should mean so little to her; she felt like a hypocritical fraud.

She removed her dress and hung it on a padded hanger in her wardrobe, feeling the heavy black silk before closing the doors. While she looked only presentable in the somber color, her mother had looked truly beautiful. With her pale, magnolia white skin, black had been Rachel's perfect foil. And with her vibrant, dark red hair piled high atop her head and diamonds gracing her slender throat, she had been one of the most beautiful women in Dallas. But being beautiful hadn't been enough . . . not in Lacey's estimation. Because for all her poise and pleasing looks, Rachel had never been allowed into many homes in the city due to her embarrassing position as Max's mistress. Had she been his wife, it would have been a different story, but old Max had vowed never to marry again after Lillian died, forcing Rachel to accept her less-than-honorable position.

Lacey turned to the silver-framed photograph of her mother, resting on her bedside table, and gave her head a despondent shake. It wouldn't have been easy, but they could have made it without all the disgrace. Rachel had supported them adequately before Max entered their lives; she could have continued doing so until Lacey was of an age to help. But circumstances Lacey would forever remain ignorant of caused her mother to disregard her conventional Christian upbringing and align herself with Max.

Lacey shed the rest of her clothes and pulled on a wrapper. She felt disheartened and a bit guilty at her now-elevated social position. Oh, she may have all the money any one woman could possibly want, but she was still looked down upon by the decent women in town. She was still a part of that shadowy half-world of paramours and illegitimate by-blows that everyone knew existed but could never openly acknowledge. Though she had never descended to that degrading level herself, but had been given the finest education a woman could want and had married the scion of a renowned family, she was still part of that shadowy world. That, she admitted painfully, had been one of the reasons, if not the deciding factor, in her eager acceptance of Chris's marriage proposal. It certainly hadn't been her undying love for him.

She crossed the room and sat down at her dressing table, taking a critical survey of her pale features in the mirror. Except for the strain about her sooty-lashed green eyes, she looked no different from before. Her skin, though paler than normal, was still creamy; her nose still slender and tip-tilted; her mouth still naturally full and pink. Why, she wondered, if she looked no different, did she feel so evil and malevolent?

"It's your guilty conscience," she informed her reflection with a bitter laugh. "You're finally owning up to your guilt, my girl, and it's all because you want something you can't have."

More than anything she wanted to be a lady; a respectable, proper, well-thought-of woman. But looking as she did, would she ever be one? In the strictest sense of the word, that is? Unfortunately, she had the looks of a wanton; a trait inherited from Rachel . . . and her father, whoever he had been.

Emitting a muffled groan of disgust, she shook her head. Enough of this! So what if she *did* look like a wanton? Was it something to be ashamed of? She might look like a chippie, but she wasn't—and never would be, either! As long as *she* knew what she was, what did it matter what the rest of the world thought?

Lacey angrily pushed her critical thoughts aside and moved to her wardrobe, deciding to put her priorities in their proper order. First she had to dress for dinner, and afterwards she would begin answering all the sympathy letters she'd received. But when she heard the loud rumble of thunder roll through the darkness outside, she turned to see bright, jagged flashes of lightning over the tops of the swaying trees that surrounded the house. With a shudder, she closed the drapes and plucked a burgundy velvet gown off its hanger, needing the heavier fabric to add to her comfort and warmth.

As the sound of the door chimes floated up to her

room, Lacey frowned. Who could possibly be calling this time of night? She quickly finished dressing and left her room, seeing Hattiebelle's form appear at the top of the stairs.

"It's that lawyer Chris had dealin's with," Hattiebelle explained, slipping into her disapproving housekeeper's role. "You know, the shifty-eyed, rat-faced one?"

"Hattiebelle!" Lacey scolded, but smiled in spite of herself. For all her bluntness, Hattiebelle had an incredible ability to see through people's false exteriors.

"You gonna ask him to stay for supper? I need to know so's I can set another place."

"Would you? I'd hate to be rude to him on a night like this."

"He's awful edgy 'bout somethin', if you ask me."

"Well, I didn't!"

Hattiebelle caught the warning gleam in Lacey's eye and grumbled beneath her breath. Then she turned and started down the stairs, tossing, "I'll go set another place," disapprovingly over her shoulder.

"Yes, you do that," Lacey agreed.

She waited a moment until Hattiebelle had reached the bottom of the stairs, then descended the wide marble steps slowly, holding her head high. But as soon as she set foot inside the parlor, she knew Hattiebelle hadn't exaggerated; Jamieson Crawford did indeed look nervous.

Burly and middle-aged, he turned with a jerk at her entrance, wiping beads of sweat from his brow and the palms of his hands before accepting her extended one.

"It's nice to see you again so soon, Mr. Crawford. What brings you out on a night like this?"

"Business that couldn't wait," he admitted seriously.

"Would you care for a drink before dinner? Oh, you will stay for dinner, won't you?" She asked this en route to the liquor cabinet across the room.

"I'm sorry, I can't. My wife is waitin' supper for me back at the house."

"Then your business *must* be urgent."

Her simple speculation seemed to make him even more nervous. As she peered through her lashes at him, she saw him run a stubby finger inside his stiff, celluloid collar and pull it away from his thick neck.

"Is bourbon to your liking, Mr. Crawford?"

"Bourbon'll be fine."

She handed him the drink, noticing how he shifted nervously from one foot to the other while his hands continually pulled and tugged at his collar and tie. "Do sit down, Mr. Crawford. Make yourself comfortable."

As soon as he had settled himself beside her on the sofa, he suddenly remembered the drink in his hand and quickly tossed down its contents, not even wincing when the fire hit his belly. It was Max's finest sour mash, but Crawford hadn't noticed.

"Uh, I really don't know where to begin, Miss Doug . . . I mean, Miz Gallagher."

"That's quite all right, Mr. Crawford. Take your time."

"That's just it," he croaked, "I don't have much time! He said he was comin' here right after he went to the cemetery, and . . . oh, sweet Jesus!" Groan-

14

ing, he shook his head, then took a deep breath before beginning again. "You see, when your husband inherited his father's estate, no questions were asked because of the airtight way the will read. Max left everything to his sole surviving son. But now that he's turned up, it changes everything. All of this . . ." He gestured widely with his hand. ". . . *and* what Chris accumulated . . . well, the situation is just nigh on to impossible."

"Mr. Crawford," Lacey began impatiently. "You must forgive my ignorance. I think I understand some of what you're telling me, but not all of it."

"I'm not surprised," he muttered, whipping out his handkerchief to mop his sweaty brow again.

"Is it too hot in here for you?" she queried. "I'd be glad to raise a window if—"

"No, I'm all right . . . I think. Though, God knows what's gonna become of my reputation if all this gets out."

"I *beg* your pardon!" she stiffened defensively. She had fended off insults before, and from better men than Crawford, but never in her own home!

"Oh, no! I—I didn't mean it *that* way. I'm speakin' of my professional reputation . . . as a lawyer. I'd never insult you, Miss Doug . . . uh, Miz Gallagher."

Breathing deeply, Lacey reluctantly conceded her position. "Your apology is accepted. Now, suppose you try and explain about the wills again. And *please* do it without the legal mumbo-jumbo; I wouldn't understand a single word for sure."

"Well, old Max's will was very simple. His sole surviving son was to inherit all of his estate and it

explained what the estate consisted of at that time."
At the understanding nod of her bright head, he
continued. "Well, that will, as you know, was auto-
matically considered valid by the courts, because we
all knew Chris was the only living son. Nick was
dead, so there was no question of Chris not immediately taking control of his legacy."

"Yes," she agreed.

"All right." Crawford seemed to gather up all his
mental forces and took a deep breath. "The money
that Chris accumulated on his own . . . outside what
he had initially inherited . . . has to be considered as
his estate, and not a part of the inheritance he
received from Max. You got that?"

She nodded.

"There's quite a bit, too! One thing about Chris,"
he laughed harshly, "he didn't balk when it came to
taking a risk. If he thought he could make a profit,
he would put up the money. Lord knows, though, *he*
might raise a fuss and demand that Chris's profits
were made through investments made with his inherited money and therefore ought to fall under *his*
inheritance."

"Now wait! You've lost me again," Lacey protested. "Who is 'he'? Surely not Chris!"

"Nope," rumbled a deep voice behind her. "It
sure as hell ain't."

Lacey whirled around and glared up at the stranger, standing just inside the doorway. Damp and
windblown, he was taller than William, who stood
beside him, grinning. His full growth of dark-brown
beard glistened with droplets of rain, as did his
equally dark hair, which hung shaggily over his

frayed shirt collar. He wasn't handsome, but there was something decidedly virile and attractive about him; something clearly savage and half-tamed. His hooded brown eyes examined her with a mocking glint in their depths, and his nose, hooked like a hawk's beak, twitched as he sniffed his approval, giving him an even more disreputable, dangerous look.

She came to her feet in one graceful motion. "And who, may I ask, are you?" Her chin lifted to a superior tilt. "You've come barging into my home without invitation, and I—"

"And you'll sit down, Red, and keep your mouth shut while I deal with this thievin' little weasel. After our talk today, Crawford, I'm surprised you'd want to show your face around here. I'd advise you to get your ass back to your office and start diggin' around for them loopholes you made for yourself when you took over the widow's legal affairs. From the looks of her, I'd say she don't know a helluva whole lot."

"William!" Lacey flared as soon as the insult was uttered. "Escort this . . . this *person* out of my house!"

William's eyes darted back and forth between the stranger and Lacey. "Uh, Miss Lacey, I, uh, I—"

"William's workin' for me now, Red." The stranger tossed her this information as he tramped across the drawing room to the liquor cabinet, ignorant of the venomous look she shot him. He was stupidly unaware that the mud and horse manure clinging to his boots was dropping destructively onto the carpet's expensive fibers.

"My name is not Red!" she shouted. "And if

William won't throw you out, I'll telephone the sheriff."

"You can't. Telephone lines are down. Oh, I didn't cut 'em," he remarked innocently. "That little old Texas breeze outside's the one to blame." Giving her a bored, cynical smile, he jerked the stopper out of the brandy bottle and tipped the neck to his wide, well-chiseled lips. As he guzzled the imported French liquor, his eyes never once strayed from her.

Lacey's nostrils flared and her green eyes flashed before she turned sharply on her heel, leaving the arrogant stranger to stare after her bemusedly.

"Well, that didn't take long," he observed. "Now, back to you, Crawford. By tomorrow morning, I want a complete list of Chris's assets. After you're done with that, draw yourself up a modest bill for services rendered. You can bring it to me over at Jake Goldstein's office and if I think it's reasonable, I might give some thought to paying it. You savvy?"

Crawford mumbled something in a tight-lipped scowl and started for the door. Stopping just short of the opening, he turned back to face his opponent. "You have to understand how it was. We all thought—"

But the stranger wasn't listening. His hooded eyes were focused just to the right of Crawford, and he was grinning, lopsidedly, at Lacey, who was dragging Max's fifteen-pound, double-barreled shotgun clumsily up to her fragile shoulder.

"If you aren't out of my house by the time I count to three, I'll blow a hole clean through you. *One!*"

William came alive. "OhmuhGawd!" he cried and quickly dived for cover. He knew Lacey couldn't hit the broad side of a barn at ten paces, and should she

18

take the notion, she wouldn't hesitate in turning the gun on him.

"Two!"

"Aw, hell, Red. Put that damn gun down. Stop showin' off, or I'll have to turn you over my knee and paddle you again like I did when you were seven."

"Thr . . . What did you say?" The nose of the shotgun dropped, pointing harmlessly to the floor, as her eyes focused on him in bewildered confusion.

"You were a real scrawny little thing," he began, "but you lit into Chris like you was twice his size and fought him over a blasted can of worms. When I got fed up of listenin' to you bellyache about not gettin' your way, I pulled down your drawers and paddled your little butt. I gotta admit, it shut you up. Course, paddling it *now* might prove a different undertakin'." He eyed her graceful, curving hips with a blatantly sensual gleam. "You didn't know your place then, either, did you?"

Lacey's sooty lashes blinked as recognition dawned. "Nick?" In the dark recesses of her mind was a vague picture of Nick Gallagher as he'd been twelve years ago; a hazy, mental image of a young man nearing twenty who was leaner and lankier than the muscular individual who stood before her now. Then came the distant recollection of an acute, but brief, pain across her seven-year-old backside. Only Nick Gallagher could have known about that!

The longer she looked at him, the more he began to resemble Max. Without the scruffy-looking beard and mustache, and dressed in different, cleaner clothes, he might even look like Chris. He couldn't be anyone else but Nick.

"Nick!" Her acceptance voiced, she handed the heavy shotgun to William, who had come out of hiding. "Do put this thing away for me, please."

Breathing a sigh of relief, William eagerly complied and carried the gun down the hall to a safe hiding place where she would never be able to find it.

"We all thought you were dead!" Unconsciously echoing Crawford's words, she drifted toward Nick with outstretched, welcoming arms. A few feet shy of him, she stopped and wrinkled her pert nose at the foul odor coming from him. "Uh, would you like to freshen up?"

Nick's lopsided grin reappeared. "Oh, it might be kinda nice to have somebody scrub my back."

"Well, I'll see if William won't accommodate you," she retorted, her green eyes sparkling.

"You couldn't . . . ?"

"I most certainly could not!"

"Shame," Nick replied, turning a baleful eye on Crawford. "You still here?"

"I was just leaving," the man grumbled.

"Yeah, well, don't let us stop you," Nick indicated with open contempt. Turning to Lacey again, after the front door slammed behind Crawford, he said, "Lead me to the hot water, Red! I feel like I'm covered in half of the Panhandle."

"Nick, I do wish you wouldn't call me that. My name is not Red."

"It oughta be, with hair like that."

"Yes, well, it isn't."

He started toward her, but she moved back, wrinkling her nose again. "Nick, you smell like the inside of a dirty stable. Where *have* you been?"

"Inside a dirty stable," he drawled. "Last night I happened on a barn just outside of Denton and it wasn't too clean."

"You couldn't have taken the train?"

Nick hesitated, recalling the doubts he'd had about traveling accommodations before leaving Canada. At least on horseback he didn't have to worry about getting thrown off a fast-moving train at night.

"Uh, no," he answered finally. "I couldn't. And as it was, I was too late getting here."

It dawned on Lacey then that it had been Nick who had ridden into the cemetery as she and William were departing. A few well-chosen words of rebuke popped into her head, but she declined to comment on his carelessness and turned toward the stairs. "I'll have William draw that hot bath for you while I find you some clean clothes."

Two steps up the stairs, though, she remembered his deplorable boots and turned to face him, stopping him where he stood just behind her. "Would you please take off those horrible, smelly things? I don't want the rest of my floors to end up like the drawing room carpet."

"Your house . . . your floors . . . my, my, Red, you sure do take a lot for granted."

"I've been in charge of this house since my mother died a year ago," she bristled. "I've worked very hard at furnishing it and keeping it clean—harder than you obviously have."

He gave the stylishly decorated front hall a cursory once-over. "You mean, *you* picked out all this . . . this fancy stuff?" It reminded him of a bordello he'd once visited in Frisco.

"Not all of it. A few things were your father's, brought over from his old house. Chris and I chose the paintings and some of the furniture."

Nick's mouth twisted wryly as he nodded. "So you just naturally assumed it was all yours now, huh?"

"As I said before, we thought you were dead. Maybe if you had let us know you were still alive, I wouldn't have taken so much for granted."

"I *did* notify y'all," he replied, bending over to pull off his boot. "I told a friend. Leastways, I thought he was a friend. But he turned out to be a double-crossin' son of a bitch."

"Jamieson Crawford?" Lacey surmised with a frown.

Nick pulled off his other boot and stood upright. "The one and only, Red. But if it's all the same to you, I'd rather leave the rest of the explaining for later. I'm tired as hell. Where's the bath at?"

Lacey started up the stairs again, not knowing that he followed close behind her, openly admiring the gentle sway of her shapely bottom.

An hour later, Nick joined her in the dining room, looking more like a human being than a chain-gang reject. He wore one of his father's shirts and a pair of Chris's trousers, which were a shade on the tight side.

"You must see a tailor tomorrow," Lacey advised, uncomfortably aware of the bulging muscles of his thighs. Lord, but he could fill out a suit of clothes well.

"Among other things." As before, his eyes searched the room, mentally calculating the cost of such fancy appointments. "This sure don't look like the old place. It ain't nearly as homey."

"Your father didn't intend it to be. He built this house for sophistication and class, as other men of his rank have done. It wasn't built solely for comfort, though it has that, too."

"What happened to the old place?"

"A businessman from St. Louis bought it and turned the first floor into a dry-goods store. About two years ago, it caught fire and burned to the ground."

"And my mother's things? What happened to them?"

"They're stored up in the attic."

He sniffed. "Well, at least they weren't destroyed."

"Momma wouldn't have let that happen, Nick. She took great care of your mother's things."

"Mmm." Nick nodded, pouring a liberal amount of wine into his goblet. "Rachel was a nice lady; I gotta give you that. I didn't know her very well, but she always had a nice smile and a kind word for me, and she never pretended to be somethin' she wasn't."

Taking a long pull of the fermented brew, he emptied the glass and set it down. "So, how long were you and Chris married?"

A clap of thunder sounded outside and Lacey allowed the noise to fade before answering, "Not very long."

"How long was 'not very long'?"

"About a week," came her quiet reply.

"A week!"

She nodded sadly. "He was in Dallas . . . on business, and crossed the street just as a runaway team of horses broke loose. The wagon hit him and he died instantly."

"And y'all just buried him today?"

"You really should have come home sooner, Nick," she said, looking at him somberly.

As another clap of thunder reverberated through the room, Lacey looked up to see the chandelier vibrate, the crystal prisms tinkling. They were definitely in for a bad night, by the sound of it. Already the wind was whipping through the trees outside, rain blowing hard against the closed windows.

"Was there an investigation into his death?"

"Yes. The authorities discovered that the horses had been spooked; they didn't know by what. It was just one of those horrible accidents that couldn't be stopped."

Nervous from the strain she'd been under all day, Lacey literally jumped out of her chair when a brilliant flash of lightning shot just outside the dining room window, instantly followed by an ear-splitting crash of thunder.

Nick sensed her raw, emotional state and placed a comforting hand on her arm. "Hey! It's gonna be all right. Ain't no need to get scared over a little thunder."

The touch of his hand burned through her velvet sleeve and she withdrew her arm, feeling uncomfortable under the much too pleasant sensations his hand produced. Gulping deep breaths of air, she hoped to calm her ragged nerves and emotions. When she was at last settled again, she held out her glass. "I think I will have that wine you offered earlier. Not too much, though." As Nick splashed it into her glass, she added, "I do hope Mr. Crawford made it home before the storm got too bad."

Nick set the bottle down with a thud, gazing evenly into her clear green eyes. "Frankly, Red, I hope the thievin' son of a bitch drowned in White Rock Creek." Then he lifted his glass in a mock salute and downed its contents.

Chapter Two

"I THINK A CLUSTER OF DAFFODILS AROUND THE OAKS in front would be attractive next spring." Lacey peered down at the roughly drawn plan of the gardens she and Manuel Lopez, the gardener, were working on. Tall and slightly stooped, Manuel had devoted many hours to the care of the Gallaghers' grounds. "And I've heard there is a new tea rose out that is supposed to be quite sturdy and an unusual shade of pink. If we could get it, it would certainly be a lovely addition to the rose garden out by the solarium."

Manuel nodded his silvery head in approval. "I, too, have heard of that rose, señora. One of the farms near Tyler has it in stock, I believe."

"Oh, good! I was afraid we would have to send to Chicago for it. But if it's in Tyler, that's even better."

Just as she started to mention the spring kitchen garden, she heard the front door slam. Wincing, she knew that Nick had come home. It was getting so that she could almost sense what mood he was in by the entrances he made.

"We'll leave the rest of this until tomorrow, Manuel," she said, rising gracefully to her feet. "Thank you for helping."

"Gracias, señora." Manuel turned and left the warm, sunny morning room, pulling on his overcoat and gloves.

Lacey spent the next few moments adjusting the slim skirt of her black dress and running a hand over her brightly coiled hair before going in search of Nick. Not that she *wanted* to see him; she would rather avoid him, as he seemed to be avoiding her. Since returning home, he'd spent precious little time with her, and that annoyed her for some reason. After their first night of dining together, things between them sort of disintegrated. There hadn't been an obvious clash as yet, but there was something lying just beneath the surface whenever they confronted one another. That something was like a charge of dynamite with a long fuse that burned shorter and shorter each time they faced each other. Only God knew what would happen when that fuse finally burned out.

It wasn't as though Nick was avoiding her intentionally. Rationally, she told herself that he *had* been busy since his return. Why, on his second day home, he'd set up his office in the library, moving the heavy liquor cabinet into it so he could have freer access to it. And when he wasn't closeted in there, he was downtown at Jake Goldstein's office, going over all the books, ledgers and portfolios Chris had left. Both Nick and Jake had been working diligently, trying to find noticeable discrepancies, but if they had found any to date, Lacey was ignorant of it. Nick refused to tell her anything about

27

his business, and she, like the good, widowed sister-in-law she was, kept her questions to herself.

When Nick wasn't with Jake . . . well, she naturally had to assume he was spending his free hours with the so-called ladies in Frogtown, one of Dallas's more elite, but still notorious red-light districts. That was just a suspicion, of course, not a proven fact. Why it should bother her for him to go to those kinds of women, she didn't know . . . but it did.

The rain had continued for two days after the storm that heralded Nick's homecoming, turning the temperatures seasonally colder. Everyone was forced to adjust. As evidence of this, when she reached the front hall, she saw Nick, shedding his heavy topcoat. "Would you care for something hot to drink?" she asked, going toward him. "I can ring Hattiebelle for tea."

"Tea!" Nick snorted and entered the library. "I need something with more kick to it than tea's got, Red."

Assuming she was being dismissed, she turned to go back to the morning room, her unofficial office.

Nick, however, had other ideas. He called to her in a voice that held an undertone of sarcasm. "Ain't you even interested in how much you're worth now, *Mrs. Gallagher?*"

His curtness surprised her, and it should have warned her of the foul mood he was in. But, squaring her shoulders, she followed him into the warm, book-lined room and sat down on the edge of a chair placed near the roaring fire. "Not particularly," she replied honestly. "I don't really have any interest in that money." It hadn't been Chris's money she'd wanted; it had been the respectability he could have given her. Not that love hadn't been there, too. She *had* loved him . . . but like a brother.

Nick stood before the fire, his feet planted apart, as he looked down at her. "Yeah, well, as my brother's . . . *widow,* you ain't doing so bad."

What was wrong with him today? she wondered. He was definitely upset about something. She felt a curious mixture of unease and temptation at being this close to him. Dressed in a suit of dark brown with a heavy gold watch chain draped across the front of his vest, Nick looked every inch the proper Dallas businessman. His scruffy beard and shaggy hair had been neatly trimmed, leaving only a well-shaped moustache brushing his upper lip. He looked almost distinguished, in a rugged, half-civilized sort of way.

Lacey tore her eyes away and glanced down at her hands clasped in her lap. "Nick, I didn't marry Chris for his money. I don't know what gave you the idea that I did."

"What do you suggest I do with it?" he asked tightly.

"How should I know?" she frowned back at him in bewilderment. "Invest it, if you want. Give it to charity. I don't care. Without Chris, the money—"

"Dammit!" he exploded, his fist striking the mantle. "Don't act the part of the grieving widow, Red. It don't suit you."

"I—I beg your pardon?"

"Just how long did you think you could keep the truth from me?" His mouth curled in disgust. "I

29

know where Chris was the day he died. Married only a few hours and he was already having to visit whores for consolation."

The blood drained from Lacey's face. She shakily tried to rise, wanting only to leave this room and Nick's vehemence.

"Oh, no!" He moved suddenly to block her exit, leaning over her as she slumped back in the chair. "You ain't runnin' out on me! I want some answers. Tell me that he wasn't in Frogtown the day he died, Red. Convince me what a perfect little wife you were and how you did your duty by him!"

Lacey swallowed the knot in her throat, her fingers nervously twisting the gold and emerald rings on her left hand. "I—I can't," she admitted in a painful whisper, but added, louder, "You've got to understand, Nick—"

"Oh, I understand, Red, better than you think. You married Chris for his money and his name; something Rachel couldn't get from my father." At the shocked expression on her face, a pain tore through him. He hadn't thought it possible to feel such remorse for Lacey. She'd been such a delightful little girl, but she had matured into an almost despicable woman, and was nothing like her mother as he remembered her.

"I'll give your mother this much," he went on in a disappointed voice. "She never pretended to be something she wasn't. She was happy being Pa's mistress. But you had other ideas, didn't you? You had to go after the wedding ring and all that went with it."

"No!" Lacey cried. "It wasn't like that, Nick."

"Then enlighten me, honey. Tell me how it really was between you and my little brother."

Flooded with the shame and guilt she'd experienced before, Lacey turned her face from Nick's glowering gaze. Tears stung her eyes. It wasn't easy, putting the facts into words so that he could understand. She didn't want his condemnation; she wanted, needed his sympathy. As her tears coursed down her cheeks, she groped inside of her skirt pocket for her handkerchief there.

"Aw, hell!" he groaned, moving away from her. Crying women had always been his downfall, and Lacey was no different. But she'd caused Chris's death and he wasn't going to give in to her tears. "That's the oldest trick in the book, Red. I thought maybe there was an ounce of honesty in you, but I was wrong. You're not a damn thing like your mother." With that, he turned and stormed out of the room.

Lacey quickly wiped her face and started to follow him, but the front door slammed hard, rattling the front windows. If only he'd been more patient, she thought, leaning weakly against the doorjamb. If only he'd given her time to explain. If only he'd waited before accusing her and jumping to his own conclusions, he would have learned the truth of the matter. Well, her side of it, anyway. Chris's side would never be known now. And as it was, Nick had succeeded in increasing her sense of guilt tenfold.

Nick's hands sawed at the double set of reins with angry, jerky movements. The chestnut geldings, more accustomed to gentle handling, responded to

31

his rough treatment as they nervously made their way down the muddy gravel road toward town.

Even with the cold wind blowing in his face and down the front of his opened overcoat, Nick couldn't cool down. Never in his thirty-one years had he ever been this angry at a woman. Angry and disappointed, he amended honestly. She had changed so much from that feisty little girl he remembered. That warm, husky voice of hers that had, at first, sent a jolt of desire surging through his loins, disguised her deceitfulness well. Though she didn't look it, she was probably as frigid as an acre of Alaskan wilderness in February. Because if she wasn't, Chris would never have gone to Frogtown. . . . Not so soon after the wedding, anyway.

All this time, all the trouble he'd taken to get home, and he had been too late. Nobody was left now; nobody but Lacey. His mother was dead; his father and Rachel killed; and now Chris. The friendly faces he'd expected to greet him on his return were all dead and buried.

"Damn weather," he muttered, wiping his eyes and sniffling. The cold always made his nose run.

Tense and brooding, he drove the few miles into Dallas, his thoughts more on the woman he'd left behind than on the road ahead of him. He could see her face, her hair, her eyes. Jesus, he could even smell her soft, flowery scent! Chris should never have married her. Take her to bed, yes! But not marry!

The carriage wheels skidded onto the slippery wooden bridge that crossed White Rock Creek, bringing Nick's attention back to the present. Looking around at the damage wrought by the recent storm, he saw huge tree limbs lying on the ground just the other side of the bridge near pools of murky water. A small farm wagon waited there, since the bridge wasn't wide enough to hold two vehicles at once. The mules, hitched to the farm wagon, splashed their hooves in the water, skittishly moving to one side as Nick and his geldings passed.

Tipping the brim of his hat in a gesture of thanks, he saw that the driver of the farm wagon was an elderly, white-haired woman. A grandmother, he told himself, who had probably earned the love and respect of her family through years of devotion and fidelity. That was something Lacey Gallagher would never achieve because the only thing she was devoted to was her greed.

Nick was still brooding over Lacey when he entered Jake Goldstein's office some time later. But when he found Jake hunched over his cluttered desk, he forgot about his sister-in-law and smiled. If Jake didn't lighten up, Nick thought, he'd work himself into an early grave.

At Nick's entrance, Jake raised his tousled blond head, removing his wire-framed spectacles, and grinned. He leaned back in his squeaky chair, stretching his taut shoulder muscles, and heard his joints protest. "I didn't expect you today. Didn't you say something about having personal business with Lacey?"

"I took care of it already," Nick grumbled, flopping down into the chair in front of Jake's desk. Sitting forward, he rested his elbows on his knees. "Listen, Jake, I want you to draw me up a legal document, one that my sister-in-law can sign. I want it put down in writing that she won't ever try to get her greedy little hands on anything other than what Chris left her. Lord, as manipulatin' as she is, I wouldn't put it past her to try and foist another man's bastard off as Chris's kid, and I won't have that!"

Jake gazed pensively at Nick. "Why don't you just tell her to move out if you dislike her so much?"

"I can't," Nick negated with a firm shake of his head. "She's still underage, so I'm morally beholden to be her guardian. Maybe I can make her halfway decent between now and the time she turns twenty-one, but if she don't change by then, you can bet your bottom dollar I'll be the first one to help her pack."

"What would happen to Lacey if you married and brought home a wife?" Jake queried.

"There ain't no chance of *that* happening." Nick laughed caustically. "I ain't in no hurry to get myself tied down. Can you get me that paper?"

Jake opened his mouth to say that he could, but closed it again, his gaze sliding past Nick as the outer door of his office opened and a lovely face appeared. In wordless wonder he beheld the pixielike vision there. Dark brown hair, topped with a frivolous lilac hat festooned with ribbons, bows, flowers and birds, could not detract from the sparkling hazel eyes that danced merrily beneath the veiled brim. About a bow-shaped mouth played an entrancing pair of dimples. Her lilac velvet suit, clearly the latest thing from Paris, hugged her petite, hourglass figure in all the right places.

"I thought it was you!" The dainty, feminine creature teased Nick accusingly as she stepped inside the office.

34

Nick stood, as did Jake, and looked down at the girl with a half-puzzled, half-amused frown.

"Well, what's the matter, Nicholas?" she giggled. "Cat got your tongue?"

"Am I supposed to know you, miss?"

"Well, I should hope so!" she replied, thoroughly delighted at his disconcertion. "Why, the last time you were at our house, you and Tommy made pigs of yourselves on the pies Momma had hid away in the kitchen. Both of you ended up with bellyaches, as I recall."

Nick's frown deepened. Then a memory flashed through his mind of a pixie-faced urchin who had been more like a shadow to him and his friends than a well-heeled young lady. She had tried desperately to be one of the boys, he recalled, but hadn't succeeded, thank God.

"Darcy?" His uncertainty gave way to outright laughter at her nod, and he enveloped her in a bear hug. "My Lord, Darcy Patterson! You were only ten or eleven when I left Dallas."

Grunting, she shrugged out of his embrace and took a deep breath. "I've aged a bit since then." Then she nodded sagely at his readable look. "Yes, I know what you're thinking; I may have aged, but I haven't grown any."

Nick gave her small, voluptuous figure a thorough perusal. "Maybe not in height," he conceded. "How's Tom? I've been meaning to drop by and see him, but—"

Darcy's smile vanished. "Tommy died in Cuba, Nick, just a little over a year ago. It was about the same time your daddy passed away. You see, Tommy was with Mr. Roosevelt's Rough Riders and

35

developed some kind of fever that the doctors couldn't cure. They lost as many soldiers to that wretched climate as they did to the wretched Spanish."

"I sure am sorry to hear that, Darcy. Tom was a good chum," Nick said sincerely. His eyes suddenly noticed Jake, shifting uncomfortably. "Oh, I haven't introduced y'all yet, have I? Miss Darcy Patterson, this is Jacob Goldstein. If you're ever in need of a good lawyer, Jake's the man to see."

Darcy dimpled, her mantle of sadness lifting. "I'll try and remember that," she remarked, extending a white-gloved hand to Jake and twinkling as he gave it a gentle squeeze. "Mr. Goldstein, it's been a pleasure meeting you. Now, I'll let you two get on with your business. I really must dash. Poppa's waiting in the dress department at Sanger Brothers for me. He's promised me a new gown for the season. Oh, if you haven't gotten your invitations yet, Nicholas, don't give up looking for them. When all the mommas know you're back in town, they'll have your name right at the top of their guest lists."

With a flippant wink and a twitch of her skirt, she was out of Jake's door and gone.

"Now, there's a lady!" Nick declared.

Jake looked at the closed door and nodded. "Yes," he agreed somewhat introspectively.

Standing before her bedroom window, Lacey held her chilled arms beneath her shawl. In the watery gray light of early evening, she could see a flock of geese flying south in a V-formation, a sure sign that winter was not far away. But if the temperature of her soul was an accurate indicator, winter had already arrived. Since her last encounter with Nick, she felt positively frozen inside.

It was impossible to stay in this house any longer, in this home in which she'd lived for so long and had grown to love. Nick had taken all that love away. Now she felt that she had nothing.

Where would she go? she asked herself, turning from the window. Remaining in Dallas was out of the question. The gossip about her and Chris had been bad enough; she wouldn't stay here and watch it grow worse with speculation about her and Nick.

Opening her wardrobe, she began calculating how much would fit into one trunk. No, one trunk wouldn't do; two or three would probably hold all of her things. Then she remembered her mother's possessions, the many gifts and trinkets Max had given to Rachel over the years. There were the many lovely, expensive pieces of jewelry that, by rights, were now hers, as well as the small collection of seventeenth-century snuff boxes that Max had presented to Rachel on their tenth "anniversary."

The knock at her door interrupted her mental inventory and, as Hattiebelle's head appeared, she tried to brighten her expression. But she wasn't quick enough.

"What's the matter with you, baby? You've been mopin' around like this all mornin'."

"I'm . . . going away," Lacey announced softly.

"Where you goin' to?" the black woman retorted instantly. "This is your home, baby; here with me, Willie and Nick."

"Not anymore," Lacey rejoined, closing her wardrobe door. "Nick made it plain that he doesn't like me, so I think it would be better for all of us if I just went away before the situation gets worse."

The housekeeper's lips pressed into a disapproving line. "Mmm-mmm! I knew that boy's temper'd get the best of him one day. Ain't nothin' like his brother at all! Too hotheaded, Nick is, to think 'fore he opens his mouth. But you can't change a man's nature, I guess, no matter how hard you try. Gotta take 'em as they are or not at all."

"Well, I'd rather not *have* to take him, if it's all the same to you!"

"He's just like his pa," Hattiebelle continued. "Lor-dee but Mister Max could raise the roof when he took a notion to shout an' carry on. Caused poor Miss Lillian some terrible heartaches, he did."

From the blurred photographs she'd seen of Lillian Gallagher, Lacey presumed her to be a frail and fragile woman. No wonder she had died so young, living with a blustery, temperamental—and unfaithful?—man like Max. Thank heavens her own mother had had a bit of temper herself, and could return to Max in kind what he so liberally dished out.

"Now, Chris," Hattiebelle was saying, "was more like his momma. Always was a quiet boy, even when he was a baby. Never cried, 'cept when he was hungry or wet. But Nick screamed *all* the time; never was satisfied 'less somebody was holdin' or carryin' him around. An' spoiled? Whoooeee! He was spoiled. But my little Chris was just like a sweet, precious angel from heaven, and . . . aw, baby! I didn't mean to make you cry." She hurried over to

Lacey and pressed her copper-gold head to her ample, apron-covered bosom.

"I don't want to leave, Hattiebelle."

"Then don't, sugar!"

"But I *have* to. Nick's so hard. I shouldn't blame him, though. He doesn't understand about me and Chris."

"You mean, you ain't told him?"

"I tried to, but he wouldn't listen."

"That boy! He needs to be knocked up side the head! His Pa had to get a hold of him more'n once when he was little, and I'd sure like to get a hold of him myself!"

"It wouldn't do any good." Sighing, Lacey moved out of Hattiebelle's comforting embrace. "He's much too obstinate."

The loud banging of the front door caught both their attentions and Hattiebelle's black eyes narrowed. "That's him now! I got a good notion to go give him a piece of my mind."

"No! Don't do that!" Lacey's plaintive insistence was born of good cause. If Nick suspected that she had complained to Hattiebelle, he would be angrier than before. "Please, just forget I ever said anything to you. And send William up with a couple of trunks from the basement. I have to start packing."

"You really mean to go away?"

Lacey nodded solemnly.

"Where you goin' to?"

Lacey said the first thing that came to mind. "Europe." It was as good a place as any. At least over there the people were more open-minded. Maybe they wouldn't frown so on her illegitimacy.

"Hattiebelle!"

The black woman's eyebrows raised at the guttural roar from downstairs. "Oh-oh! Sounds to me like he's been drinkin'."

Nick had been, but he was far from drunk. He was, however, about as frustrated as he'd ever been. Slamming the door behind him, he stalked across the library to his liquor cabinet. He poured himself a stiff measure of bourbon with one hand as the other loosened his collar and tie. He hadn't been this frustrated since he was a boy, having a hard time trying to become a man.

He'd gone to Cora Noble's place after leaving Jake's office, but her girls had only aroused him more, without easing the ache in his loins at all. It was a helluva thing for him to admit, but he was just like any other man . . . fallible in the bedroom.

"Lacey," he growled. It was all her fault. If she hadn't been on his mind, none of this would have happened.

Hattiebelle opened his door and slammed it behind her. "You wanted me?" she demanded, glaring at him.

"Yeah." He glowered at her before tossing down his drink. "When's supper?"

"When it always is!"

"Something got your dander up?" he queried.

"No, sir. Why'd you think that? All you done since you come home is rant and rave. Why would *that* get my dander up?"

"I got problems, Hattiebelle. Don't add to 'em."

"We *all* got problems," she told him. "But just 'cause you think you got more'n your share, it ain't no reason to take out your spite on Miss Lacey. She's had a hard time of it, poor baby, and—"

" 'Poor baby,' hell!" he roared, grabbing the bottle of bourbon and dispensing with his glass. "I don't need you to defend her! She's a connivin', two-faced little—"

"Naw, she ain't!" Hattiebelle countered loudly. "She's one of the sweetest girls I've ever known."

"Ha!" He guzzled the fiery brew straight from the bottle, wiping his mouth with the back of his hand.

"Then it's a good thing she's leavin'," Hattiebelle remarked contemptuously, having heard as much as she could stand. "Wouldn't want her to have to live in the same house with a fool like you. Fact is, I ain't so sure I want to *work* for a fool, so I'm leavin' with her. I quit!"

To say that Nick was astonished was an understatement. "Wait a minute!" he spat. "What do you mean, she's leavin'? Where's she goin'?"

"Europe, she said. But anyplace has gotta be better'n here. Just look atcha! You done been home only a few days and already you're runnin' us off. I hope that makes you happy!" Then she wisely made her exit before he could reply, slamming the door loudly behind her.

Shocked, confused and feeling slightly numb from the alcohol he'd consumed, Nick continued to glower at the door. So Lacey thought she was going to leave, did she? Like hell, she was! She wasn't walking out on him, not until *he* was ready to let her go.

He stalked over to the door, wrenched it open and looked up the curving staircase. *"Lacey!"* he bellowed. *"Mrs. Gallagher!"* Then he stood there, weaving slightly, until her slim, black-clad form appeared at the head of the stairs.

"Yes?" she asked coldly.

"I'll see you in here, if you can spare me the time!" he jeered. Watching her graceful descent, he thought she could certainly move like a lady. She didn't really walk down the stairs; she sort of floated down them. And when she passed him, he caught a lungful of her light, flowery scent and had to restrain his impulse to reach out and touch her.

"Hattiebelle tells me you're thinkin' of goin' to Europe," he challenged, closing the door behind him.

Lacey avoided looking at him. "I thought it would be best, considering how we antagonize one another."

"I antagonize *you?"*

She stiffened with indignation. "You've accused me of a lot since you came home, Nick. I won't stay where I'm not wanted. Only a fool would do that."

"And you're no fool, are you? No sir, Red, you sure ain't that!"

Her narrow nostrils flared. "Don't call me Red! My name is—"

"I know what your name is, *Red,"* he drawled, and began to close the distance between them.

She followed her first instinct and backed away, but a chair suddenly appeared behind her and she fell into it. Nick merely leaned over her, bracing his hands on the chair's arms, his face a mask of contradiction. His voice, no longer angry, purred huskily. "But Red suits you so much better."

Her green eyes were ensnared by his brown ones

as they raked over her coiled, coppery locks. "My—my hair is blond," she countered breathlessly. Why was her pulse racing? And why was her heart pounding so? "St—strawberry blond, if you will. It's not true red like Momma's was."

"In this light," he voiced softly, his gaze falling from her hair down to her emerald eyes and on deliberately to her full breasts, "it's fiery red. A man could get burned runnin' his fingers through it. That's what you do to men, Lace. You burn them with your fire. . . . Or do you freeze them with your coldness?"

She found her breath coming in short, labored gasps. He was mesmerizing her with his sensuality, making her painfully aware of the empty ache within her. In his rugged, unhandsome face, she saw an unexpected gleam appear in the depths of his dark eyes. His mouth, wide and well-chiseled, slowly came closer to hers, causing her heart to beat even faster. Her head tilted back so that her lips parted instinctively, hungrily.

Nick knew only one thing at this point: He wanted her more than he'd ever wanted anything or anyone in his life. "Lace?" he whispered hoarsely, not believing that it was possible for him to feel this way about her.

Their lips met, the skin barely touching, their breaths mingling unevenly, and their eyes began to close.

The library door burst open.

Wrenched apart as if they'd been rudely doused with ice water, Nick could only blink stupidly at William while Lacey hid her eyes behind one hand, groping wildly for some sense of composure.

43

"You want me to get one trunk or two?" the young black man asked innocently, unconcerned with the results of his well-timed interruption.

"She don't want *any*," Nick growled, staggering toward his liquor cabinet. "She ain't goin' anywhere."

"Nick's wrong, William. I *do* want the trunks. Would you take two of them up to my room, please?"

A dangerous, mocking laugh brought her attention back to Nick, and she saw his dark head shake in bitter amusement. "Until you're twenty-one, Red, you're staying right here!"

"What does my age have to do with it?"

"A helluva lot! As your husband's brother, and your only living relation, I am now, unfortunately, your legal guardian."

"That's absurd!" She jumped to her feet.

"Yeah, but it's the truth. Until you're twenty-one, and an adult in the eyes of the law, you will remain here under my watchful eye. And you can't touch a penny of Chris's money, or your mother's either, unless I give my permission first."

"I will not stay under the same roof with you, Nick Gallagher!"

With a bored shrug he leaned against the mantle to sip his bourbon. "You ain't got much choice, Red. If I decide to lock you in your room, I can damn well do it. And if I think you need a paddlin'—"

"You lay one finger on her and you'll answer to me!" William growled suddenly.

Nick jerked around to face the young black man, seeing his lip curl back into a snarl. He'd threatened Lacey only to get his point across; he hadn't really meant what he'd said, but he hadn't anticipated this defense from William. "Look," he reasoned, "just let me handle this."

"I ain't foolin'. You won't hurt her. She's a lady, and you'll treat her like one or answer to me!"

"A lady! *Her?*" Nick laughed harshly. "She's the daughter of a strumpet, William. A strumpet's spawn can't be a lady."

"Strumpet's spawn can't be a gentleman, neither!"

William's rapid-fire retort hit home and Lacey gasped as she saw the instant contortion of Nick's face. He didn't open his mouth, though, to defend Lillian as she expected him to; he just stood there, a dull red flush creeping up his neck.

"Get out," Nick growled at last. "Both of you, just get the hell out of here. And no trunks! She ain't leavin'!"

Lacey quickly left the room and was halfway up the stairs when William caught up with her.

"He didn't harm you, did he?"

"No." She shook her head and laughed bitterly. "He really does hate me, you know."

"It's 'cause you look like a girl he was once sweet on," William confessed quietly.

Lacey blinked stupidly at him, realizing that what he said made sense. It would explain all those looks Nick had given her from time to time, when he thought she wasn't noticing. "Did she have strawberry-blond hair and green eyes?"

William nodded. "He was just about seventeen, his momma had just died and this girl—Jane, her name was—she found out that Miss Lillian wasn't really his momma, but his stepmomma. Some farm girl from down Waco way was his real momma, and Jane was about as hateful to him as a girl could be. Called Nick a lot of bad names 'fore she run off with a man older'n her who had lots of money. Tore Nick up somethin' awful!"

"He hadn't suspected that Lillian wasn't his real mother?"

"Nope. Mister Max tried to tell him about it. Told him that his real momma died givin' birth to him but that Miss Lillian wanted to raise him herself. She was a good woman, Miss Lillian was. Didn't treat Nick no different than she treated Chris."

"How sad," Lacey frowned. "But it still doesn't give him a reason for hating me. I can't help it if I look like that girl."

"You ain't much like her really. Hair's about the same, I guess, and the eyes, but that's all. You're taller'n she was and lots nicer."

Later, in her room, Lacey knew the situation was growing more impossible by the minute. But she had to stay here! Her only hope was in keeping out of Nick's way. Doing that, she wouldn't antagonize him too often. It would be hard, but it could be done. . . . But for how long?

Chapter Three

LACEY'S COPPER-GOLD HEAD WAS BATHED IN A GLOW of early afternoon sunlight. In the middle of planning menus for the upcoming week, she stopped and wondered why she even bothered with the task. Chances were, she would be the only one home at night to eat them.

In frustration, she tossed her pen onto the table just as Hattiebelle appeared in the morning room doorway. "That painter friend of Chris's is here."

"Peter Thorne?" Surprised, Lacey got to her feet. She had forgotten his promise to call on her. "Would you show him in here, please? And if you aren't too busy in the kitchen, would you fix us a pot of tea?"

With a nod, Hattiebelle disappeared, and Peter came in moments later. He greeted her with an affectionate kiss on her upturned cheek.

"You're looking exceptionally well." Obviously pleased with her appearance, he smiled and made himself comfortable in the chair across from the settee where she sat.

"Thank you," she rejoined. "So are you."

"Oh, I've been much too busy to succumb to

illness. I've had two portraits commissioned since I last saw you."

"You have been busy! Were they of anyone I know?"

"Could be." He loosened the bottom button of his gray vest and leaned back. "Misters Little and Michaels from Oak Cliff Township across the river."

Lacey frowned, then shook her head. "No, I've never heard of them. Now that you've painted their portraits, though, I'm sure it won't be long before their names will be on the lips of all the Dallas matrons."

"You give me more credit than I justly deserve," Peter laughed lightly. "But, enough of my paltry accomplishments. How have you been, my dear?"

She held out her hands. "As you can see."

Giving her a dubious look, Peter kept his thoughts to himself as Hattiebelle entered with their tray of tea and cookies. After Lacey had poured the tangy brew into two cups and had served him, he asked, "When are you going to let me paint you?"

"Probably never." She chuckled. "I'm afraid I wouldn't make a very good subject . . . or is that model?"

"Model," he replied. "But I beg to differ with you. I happen to think you would make a very beautiful model. With your hair in a less severe style and dressed in a more complimentary color than black, I can easily visualize a dozen different poses for you. You're quite a remarkable-looking woman, Lacey, but I'm sure you're aware of that."

As his painter's eye examined every angle and plane of her bone structure, as well as the texture and shading of her skin, she reddened and dropped her gaze. Surely he was seeing her as a subject for one of his canvases and not through the eyes of a covetous man. To want his friend's widow so soon after the friend's death was almost too obscene to consider. But then, she knew artists were a different breed of men, set apart from all the others.

Thinking that he might have been joking with her, she looked into his aristocratically handsome face, hoping to see there a sign of hidden humor; but there was none. His wide forehead was unlined in his straightforward perusal of her, and his gray eyes held her green ones with frankness and total candor. It was then that she noticed the streaks of silver hidden in the temples of his thick black hair, and the fine wrinkles surrounding his compelling gray eyes. She had thought him to be in his late twenties, but now realized he was nearer the age of forty.

"I didn't offend you, did I?" he asked. "Wanting you to model for me, I mean."

"No, of course you didn't. I've just never thought of having my portrait painted. Everyone these days has their photograph taken at a studio."

Peter frowned with ill-concealed revulsion. "Those detestable things! They can never capture the spirit or the character of the subject, not when one has to pose as stiff as a corpse! But don't listen to me. If I get started on the subject, I'm likely to go on for hours. For what it's worth, though, Chris wanted me to do a portrait of you. We hadn't gone so far as to arrange a fee or anything, but the subject had been mentioned on more than one occasion. He thought a portrait of you, hanging above the library mantle, would improve the looks of the room. Your picture," he added more softly, "hanging in any room would make it come alive, my dear. You have such color, such life, such vitality!"

Lacey blushed and looked away. "I'm surprised that Chris wanted me painted."

"You shouldn't be. He loved you very much, Lacey."

"I . . . I loved him, too," she admitted painfully. His death had come as a terrible loss. Loving and losing a dear friend was as hard as, or harder than, loving and losing a lover . . . possibly worse.

"I know you did." Peter inhaled deeply and stood up. "Give it some thought, will you?"

"About having my portrait painted?" she queried, standing also. "And how would you pose me? What would I wear?" She lifted her skirt and let it drop again. "You said yourself that black is not my best color."

Peter cocked his head to one side, giving her question some thoughtful speculation. A slow smile stretched his moustache-framed mouth. "If I had my way, my dear, you would be sitting on a rock at the edge of the ocean, the white-capped surf behind you. You would be staring out past the horizon, looking for your lover's ship, and your skin would be completely uncovered and kissed golden by the sun. With your glorious hair tossed about in wild disarray, you would be the enchantress Circe in mortal form."

His words, so eloquently spoken, made her catch her breath. His vision of her seemed much like a poet's song. "Well!" She laughed nervously. "I'm afraid I would *have* to insist on wearing clothes, Mr. Thorne. And where in Dallas would you find a white-capped surf? Perhaps a sea of bluebonnets in late spring, or White Rock Creek in the background when it's past flood stage, but that's as close to your image of an ocean as you'll get here."

Peter laughed. "If I began a portrait of you, dearest Lacey, I'm afraid it would have to be some other place than Dallas at this time of year. Although," he drew out the word, "placing you in a mound of autumn leaves with your magnificent hair unbound and flowing does have its temptations . . . and using a background of bluebonnets is not so unappealing as you might imagine."

Walking with him toward the front door, she waited as he pulled on his topcoat and adjusted his hat and muffler. "If you're really serious . . ."

"I am!" he insisted, detecting her tempted tone.

"Maybe . . . next spring."

"Take all the time you need, my dear," he smiled, patting her hand. "May I call on you again soon? I would love to spend hours sketching you and getting to know you before I put your likeness to canvas."

Though she knew it was nothing more than flattery, she truly needed his flowery compliments now. "Thank you for dropping by," she responded sincerely.

"I wish I could stay longer, but I'm due at the Howard Steeles' soon, to have a look at their daughters. The man wants them forever enshrined on canvas, if you can believe it. God knows why; they'd all be better off hidden away in the attic."

Lacey giggled at that. Howard Steele, she knew, had only recently come into money and he was spending it as fast as he could. His daughters—all six of them—looked just like him, too, even though he was one of the homeliest men in the state.

Joining in her laughter, Peter leaned over and kissed her now-glowing cheek. "Maybe next time we can discuss Chris."

"There's no need," she said, sobering. "I understand the situation better than you think."

"Are you sure?"

"Oh, yes!" came her sincere whisper.

Peter's hand reached for the knob just as the door flew open. Nick came in, looking wild and windblown, and saw Lacey's lovely, gentle smile vanish as a cold mask of haughty disdain slipped into its place. She could thaw out for another man, he thought, but not for a Gallagher.

"You comin' or goin', Thorne?" he asked rudely.

"I was just on my way out," Peter remarked, lifting Lacey's hand to his lips. "Until the next time, my dear."

"Good-bye, Peter."

She stood there, watching the artist climb into his carriage and drive away down the drive, then closed the door. Knowing Nick was watching her, she deliberately kept her back to him as she turned and started for the stairs.

"Not so fast!" His hand stalled her forward progress. "You've been kinda moody lately. You feeling all right?"

"I'm not sick," she remarked levelly, wondering why he should be suddenly concerned with her well-being.

"Then you're . . . not pregnant?"

"No! I most assuredly am not!"

"That's good to hear." Nick relaxed visibly, a half smile appearing on his face. "Then, I don't suppose you'd mind signing this little document I got on me, would you?"

"What document?" She frowned.

He reached into his coat pocket, withdrew a legal-looking paper and opened it up for her inspection. "It's just something that says you won't try and claim any of your future offspring as my brother's kids."

"Let me have a pen," came her instant response. "I'll sign it right now."

Nick reddened with embarrassment. But he produced a pen from his breast pocket and watched uneasily as she signed her name on the designated line with a flourishing scrawl.

"Not that I would do anything so unscrupulous, mind you," she said, returning the pen and paper to him. "But I don't want you to be in any doubt about my integrity. Believe me, Nick, if I *were* expecting Chris's child, I'd call it something other than Gallagher just so it wouldn't have to be associated with you."

"What gives you the right to insult *me* that way?"

A defiant gleam appeared in the depths of her green eyes. "Well, Nick, as one bastard to another, I—"

She gasped as his hand flew up from his side, and she held her breath, fearing that it would strike her. But his trembling fingers slowly curled and he dropped his arm again as a tight expression formed over his features. He would have hit her, and she would have deserved it, because her goading had struck a raw nerve in him.

Stubborn pride caused her to turn her cheek to

him. "Go ahead, Nick. If it will give you pleasure to punish me for what that other girl did to you, you can hit me. Now that I know about her, I feel sorry for you. Your insults and accusations can never hurt me like your physical violence can. And you *will* have to use violence to get me to respond from now on."

A muscle jerked furiously in Nick's jaw as a fleeting look of guilt flashed across his face. He'd never struck a woman before, but then one had never called him a bastard to his face, either. Grudgingly, he was forced to admire her courage in standing there, challenging him. And as much as he hated to admit it, he had to respect her, too.

Turning, she looked squarely at him. "If you're through with me, I'll leave," she said coldly. "I have work to do."

Nick slammed into the library after she walked away. He went directly to the liquor cabinet and poured himself a stiff drink, tossing it down in one swallow. She had hit the bull's-eye with her assumption, God help him. He *had* been comparing her to Jane, though he honestly hadn't been aware of it.

The girl who had humiliated him so long ago was a lot like Lacey in looks, but that's where their similarities ended. Jane had gotten a strange thrill out of dropping him so casually for that older, wealthier man. And if that had been her only crime, he could have forgotten about her ages ago, but she had, with almost perverse viciousness, told him his real mother had not been Lillian Gallagher.

Max had reluctantly confirmed Jane's story, and not without a great deal of embarrassment. He had stressed to Nick that he *had* cared, in his own way, for the older, half-Comanche woman who'd unwittingly conceived Nick.

Nick could still recall each word Max had said to him that day twelve years ago, the scene was so clear in his mind. He could see the expression on the old man's face so vividly, it was as though he had reached out across the span of years and conjured up his father's form.

"I've been damn lucky in my life, son," Max had declared emotionally. "I've come from bein' an abandoned orphan to where I am now. I've made money while others have lost everything they owned. I've got me two fine boys to carry on for me when I go—which, Lord willin', won't be for a good while yet—and I've known me three of the finest women God ever put breath into: your ma, Lillian and Rachel." He had frowned then, shaking his head. "I wish I could do more for Rachel and little Lacey, but when Lillian was buried, I took an oath on her grave that no other woman would take her place. I don't intend to go back on my word, either, even though Rachel deserves better than bein' my doxy. It don't seem to matter to her, though. She's a lady, and don't think she ain't! She's made these last few years without Lillian worth livin' for me. And that precious angel of hers is as close to a daughter as I'm likely to get.

"Just be glad," Max had said earnestly, "that that bitch Jane ain't in your life no more. She never was much good, and I'd be willin' to bet she don't end up good, either. She's got too much of her pa in her. And hell, Marshall Stratton's about as bad a seed as they come."

The memory of his father faded and Nick set

down his empty glass to walk over to the window, where he pushed aside the heavy drapes to look out into the late afternoon sunlight. There were times when he felt pity for Lacey. She hadn't had an easy start in life, not like he'd had. She had known from the beginning all about being a bastard, while he had been insulated from his base birth by seventeen years of pampered living and love from his father and mother.

His mood changed abruptly and anger mounted within him as he recalled the aloof, almost superior attitude Lacey flaunted when around him. It was as if she thought herself better than him, and he didn't like that! He was no better or no worse than the next man, and that included Lacey Anne Douglas Gallagher!

With a groan, he turned from the window. It wouldn't do for him to stand here, trying to second-guess Red. Dammit to hell, though, she had an annoying way of creeping under his skin, especially when he least expected it. She had a strange way of popping into his thoughts, too, when he needed all his concentration for more important matters.

"What you need," he muttered sagely, "is a good lay!" A long night spent in the arms of some loving woman would ease the ache in his loins and put him in a much better mood.

Cora Noble's place may not have been the best-known "house" in Dallas, but it was the most exclusive. She tended to cater to a higher class of clientele, not just the average working man. All of her girls were by far the prettiest, the most talented to be found, and they came from all four corners of the globe. "If you want the extra-special, the unusual," the saying around town went, "you have to go to Cora's to get it."

Standing barely five feet tall, Cora was a feisty little madam . . . literally! She could run circles around most of her girls, and if the price was right, she sometimes did. But her job these days, since reaching the age of forty-five, was to rake in the cash and greet the gentlemen who called at her establishment.

Her drawing room was usually populated with the city's better-known men, ranging from lawyers, to bankers, to merchants, dressed in their evening finery. Cora's ladies, of course, wore extremely tasteful and quite modest dressing gowns of the finest silks, satins and velvets that money could buy. There were no flabby, bare bosoms or chunky, pale thighs on display in Cora's drawing room. Her ladies were not common by any means, and there was no open clawing at crotches or intimate fondling of feminine parts allowed downstairs. One behaved like a lady or a gentleman at all times, or one didn't stay very long at Madam Cora's.

Nick entered Cora's house and handed his hat, coat and gloves to the elegantly clad black butler, then sauntered casually over to Cora, who greeted him with an affectionate kiss.

"You haven't been to see us lately, Nicholas," she accused sweetly.

"I've been tied up with family matters," he replied, patting her slim arm as his gaze drifted down the front of her gown. "You aren't free this evenin', are you, Cora?"

"Not tonight." She laughed. "I have a feeling that

my . . . abilities? aren't exactly what a randy young buck like you is in need of. You're wound up tighter than a clock spring."

"Then don't line me up with a fighter. I ain't in no mood for a boxin' match tonight."

"I take it the family matters are bad."

"You could say so, yes. Who've you got to take my mind off her . . . I mean, them?" He felt his skin flush at his unexpected slip of the tongue.

"Look for yourself," Cora instructed with a sweep of her hand. "Do you fancy a blonde from Norway? A raven-haired lovely from Spain? Or what about an auburn-haired beauty from the emerald green isle of Ireland? She could weave a spell around you that would last for a while."

Surveying Cora's unattached girls, Nick thought the blonde too cold and remote, and the black-haired señorita looked a bit too feisty, but the Irish girl had a fine, come-hither look about her that caused his loins to pulsate with eagerness, and he gave her an easy-to-read smile.

"What's her name?" he asked. "The Irish girl, I mean."

"Sally," Cora informed him, her outstretched hand beckoning to the well-endowed young woman.

Sally rose gracefully from the settee and slipped her smooth ivory hand into Cora's. Her peridot green eyes glittered as she peered up into Nick's rugged face, and her small pink tongue appeared for a moment to lick her rouged lips in anticipation of what his virile looks promised.

"Sally, this is Nicholas," Cora pronounced, linking their arms together. "Why don't you take him up to your room and show him how Irish girls comfort their menfolk after a hard, wearysome day. May I send up a bottle of champagne, Nicholas?"

"I don't think that'll be necessary, Cora," he responded huskily. "We don't want anything takin' the edge off our senses, do we, honey?"

Smiling slyly, Sally shook her head in agreement. She turned and led him toward the stairs at the end of the main hall.

A nameless apprehension fell over Nick as he followed the comely prostitute. He was at a loss to define it. Trying to ignore it as he entered her room, he asked, "Are you really from Ireland?"

"I'm from a place in New York City called Five Points," she admitted honestly as she wandered about her bedroom lighting the lamps. "But my mother and father were from the old country, if it really matters to you. I can effect a brogue so thick even leprechauns would think I was the real thing. Is that what you're wantin'? An Irish lass who'll sing you Gaelic ballads while she soothes the ache in your loins?"

Nick's head moved in a slow negative motion. "I want honesty, Sally. I'm sick to death of the fakes and liars in this world."

She returned to him and began to loosen his clothes, slipping his arms out of his expensive coat before moving to his tie. "Well now, *that* I'm not." She chuckled. "I know what I am and I'm not ashamed of it. I like pleasin' men, Nicholas, and I like them to please me. I won't ask if you're married, and I won't get jealous if you mention your wife; I'll just turn a deaf ear to your ramblings. What you have or do outside Cora's doesn't interest me. It's what we do here and now that matters most."

Her mouth, warm and eager for his first kiss, opened over his. She greedily explored his teeth with her tongue before pressing herself to him, her breasts flattening against his white silk shirt.

It was then that Nick's former apprehension came flooding back. A vision of Lacey flashed through his mind and, groaning, he pulled away from her.

"Lover?" Sally purred quietly.

"I can't do it," he growled with disgust. "Dammit, I just can't do it! Oh, it's not you, Sally—it's me. I guess I'm growin' impotent early in my years."

"You're not impotent, lover," she soothed. "You've just got too much on your mind. Why don't you tell me about it? I might be able to help."

But Nick firmly shook his head. He wasn't about to discuss Lacey, or any other part of his private life, with a common prostitute. It was none of her business.

"It's a woman, isn't it?" Sally challenged. "Now don't look that way. I can tell! I know it's not your conscience, because if it was, you wouldn't have come here in the first place."

"Yes," he finally admitted, slumping into a nearby chair. "It's a woman."

Sally followed his lead and sat down on the end of her bed. "Is she after you to marry her? Is that the problem?"

"No!" came his heated retort.

"Well then, there must be something about her that draws your thoughts to her. Is she comely?"

The vision of Lacey became clear and precise in his thoughts. "Oh, yes! She's beautiful, all right," he acknowledged grimly. "But she's about as deadly as a black widow spider."

"If I were you, lover, I'd exorcise her. But you'll have to be careful. Black widows have a way of killing their mates after loving them."

Sally moved off the bed, drawing Nick's gaze to her. Through the dim lamplight he could see her well-endowed curves beneath the diaphanous fabric of her gown. Her breasts were large and firm, tipped with lovely coral nipples. Her waist was slim and her hips gently rounded, but her legs, oddly enough, were short and slightly bowed. It was then that he noticed the hair at the juncture of her thighs. It was dark brown, contrasting sharply with the bright auburn on her head. Henna, he thought with a rueful grunt, and stood up.

"Maybe you're right, Sally," he remarked, pulling on his coat. "Maybe I will exorcise the bothersome witch."

"You aren't leaving, are you, lover?" Sally queried in surprise.

"I think I should." With his tie back in place, he extracted some money from his coat pocket and handed it to her. "Here, you deserve this for putting up with me. I'll pay Cora later and she won't have to know a thing about this transaction."

"You're a damn fine man, Nicholas," Sally remarked frankly. "I've never met one finer. If you ever want to talk . . . or anything, you come see me. I'll not charge you a penny."

After tonight, he doubted if he would ever be coming back. But giving her a wink of assurance, he linked her arm in his and started to escort her back down to the drawing room.

Just as they reached the head of the stairs, she gasped and abruptly pulled him back to her room.

"I'm not going down there!" she bit out.

"Why?" he asked, closing the door behind them.

"Didn't you see that man? He makes my skin crawl." She shivered. "I never did go in for making love to animals, and that's one who reminds me of a bull."

Nick rested his shoulder against the doorjamb while Sally returned to sit on the side of her bed. "Cora wouldn't force you to entertain him, would she?" he queried.

"No. She's got a man who used to live with them Chinese out west when they were building the railroads. He fights real strange! I don't know how to describe it to you, but he uses his feet and hands, and he kicks and chops at his opponent."

"I know what you're talking about," Nick nodded. "I've seen a couple of them Chinese goin' after one another. Real scrawny little bastards, they are, but they sure can do a lot of damage. I saw one man take on a guy three times his size and flatten him out inside of a minute. I stayed clear of 'em."

"Well, Harold, Cora's man, can tackle a whole mob and come out the winner, so the clients who come in here never bother us if we tell them to keep their distance. I have to say this for Cora; she does take good care of us. When one of us gets sick, we always get the best doctor in town to look after us."

"Uh, this man you want to avoid," Nick urged. "Who is he?"

"Marshall Stratton," Sally shuddered. "There are so many ugly rumors about him. Like he's got his wife locked up in their house and won't let her out! And like his only child—a girl, mind you—is off in some sanitarium, crazier'n a betsy bug. Word is, she had a baby that wasn't her husband's—the daughter, I mean, not his wife—and her husband kicked her and the kid out of his house right after they were married."

"Good God!"

"Yes! Anyway, now you can see why the sight of him gives me the willies."

So Jane had had a baby, Nick mused. But whose baby had it been? Not his, certainly! Fortunately, he had respected Jane in the old days and treated her like a lady.

Straightening his coat and tie, he said, "I think I'll go on down, if you don't mind. I should be getting home."

"You take care of yourself, lover." Sally came to him, stood on her tiptoes and gave him another deep kiss. "If Cora should ask, tell her I'm . . . oh, tidying up, or something."

When Nick reached the lower hall, he casually glanced into the drawing room and saw the round, bull-like body of Marshall Stratton. He had a thick neck and massive arms, longer than his stocky proportions demanded, with a pair of hands that had obviously done heavy labor during his younger days. His legs, short and bowed out at the knees, were encased in expensive fabric, which did nothing to enhance his appearance. For all his body's being slightly grotesque, it was his face that was the most frightening. Deep, purplish pits were in his cheeks, and a long, white scar ran from his hairline to his jaw, puckering his drooping left eye.

Shaking his head, Nick continued toward the vestibule, where the butler waited patiently with his coat and gloves. The girl who ended up with Stratton in her bed tonight would certainly have to put up a convincing act, Nick thought. He doubted seriously if any female in her right mind would enjoy making love to a little beast like him.

Outside the crisp November air whipped through the bare trees, moving the branches about in strange, ghostly formations. Nick pulled his muffler tighter about his throat and hopped agilely into the buggy, unwrapping the reins from the brake handle before sending the gelding into motion. As a horseman, he would have preferred to ride into town rather than drive, but since coming home and being a man of importance, so to speak, he had to keep up appearances, even if it did make him feel like some dandified fool. Few men in his social circle rode horseback these days, if they could ride in a more comfortable manner. One or two of his acquaintances even sported about in the new automobile, a contraption that intrigued him more each day.

The exceptionally bright moon looked like an enormous silver medallion suspended in the blue velvet sky, where a thousand brilliant stars twinkled. It illuminated the route Nick took as he drove away from the more populated area of Dallas. It was hard for him to comprehend how his hometown had grown during the years he'd been away. It hadn't been this big when he left twelve years ago.

Surely it would stop growing soon, he thought. Farms would be destroyed in its productive wake if it grew anymore. And if that happened, major plots of land would dwindle down to nothing more than tiny city lots, but he supposed that was the price one paid for progress. This was no longer the wide-open frontier town it had been fifty or sixty years ago, a haven for outlaws with six-shooters strapped to their hips. Dallas was now a bustling commercial city, ruled by bankers and wheeler-dealers—another type of outlaw, in his opinion, who used paper and pen instead of a revolver for their dirty work.

Turning the buggy eastward, Nick followed the streetcar tracks for a few more miles, letting the metal rails guide his direction in the moonlit darkness. His thoughts were chaotic, to say the least. One thing was certain; changes would have to be made in his life soon. He couldn't go on living as he had been.

Nick relaxed in the badly sprung but well-enclosed buggy seat. The reins hung loosely in his gloved hands and the steady, muffled clip-clopping of the gelding's shod hooves acted as a gentle sedative to his still-tense emotions. The ache in his groin was still with him, but it wasn't as bad as it had been.

The wheels of the buggy ground against loose gravel, telling Nick that he'd left the city proper. The night was relatively quiet and exceptionally lovely in its dark austerity. He could hear a dog barking in one of the farmyards as he drove past, and he heard an owl's plaintive hooting from the tree branches overhead. Off in the distance, behind him, he could hear a wagon, traveling too fast for this time of night.

Moments passed and the sharp sound of a whip cracking penetrated his drowsy stupor, forcing him to sit up and take notice of his immediate surroundings. Just ahead lay the bridge crossing White Rock Creek, a rickety structure that had withstood the stress of the elements and the weight of many

vehicles. If the conveyance that followed him continued to approach him as quickly as he suspected it
would, they would reach the bridge at the same time.
He knew with a certainty that it wouldn't carry both
vehicles, so with the intention of getting there before
the other wagon did, Nick snapped his reins above
the gelding's back and urged the old horse into a
faster gait.

The bridge lay ahead, just beyond the rocky
drop-off into the creek at the curve of the road. It
was an inch or two over six feet wide and approxi-
mately a dozen yards long. Too late, Nick realized he
should have pulled over to the side of the road and
allowed the other vehicle to pass. They would reach
the bridge at the same time now, and only one of
them would make it across. The other would end up
in the deep, very deadly ditch below.

Nick braced himself, seeing the other pair of
horses come into his line of vision. His hand tightened on the reins instinctively. But it came as quite a
shock when he heard the horrible cracking sound as
his buggy turned the curve in the road. The traces
connecting his horse to the buggy were breaking. His
only hope now was to jump and pray that his gelding
could extricate himself from the broken harness
before the weight of the buggy pulled him over into
the ditch.

In a flash, Nick dropped his reins and leaped free
of the seat, hitting the hill with a force that knocked
the wind out of him. He began to roll, uncontrolla-
bly, down the steep embankment and into the
shallow, muddy creek at the bottom of the ravine.
His body was subjected to brutalizing torture as it hit

rocks and rolled over the stiff dry brush protruding sharply from the sloping earth. But all of it ended suddenly as his head came in contact with something solid and his body finally stopped moving. The last thing he saw was a crazily tilted, spinning wheel, outlined against a black, star-bright sky. Then he slipped into peaceful, enveloping unconsciousness.

Chapter Four

LACEY'S LONG, ELEGANT FINGERS MOVED WITH EFFORT-less grace over the grand piano's keys. She was lost in the melody that seemed to drift out into the acoustically perfect music room, her talent a pleas-ant testimony to the fact that she loved to play. It was hearing the haunting notes hang sadly in the air that she loved most when her mood matched its somberness, as it did tonight.

The final note of the sonata sounded, lingering for a moment in the stillness around her. Her hands fell away from the keys and she turned on the bench to smile at Peter Thorne, who sat in silent amazement across the room.

As if coming out of a trance, he began to breathe. "Chopin clearly had you in mind when he composed that, my dear," he remarked, coming to her side.

Lacey's skin became suffused with color under his intense perusal. "I doubt that, Peter. The man never met me. But I thank you for the compliment." Then her green eyes slid past him and widened with alarm.

Nick stood inside the doorway, looking dirty, hurt and mad as hell. "Don't stop on my account," he sneered. A rage built within him at the sight of her and the dandy.

Ignoring his sarcasm, Lacey stood and started toward him. "What happened?" she asked, extending a hand to his wounded face.

"Leave me alone, Red." He jerked away from her touch. "I had an accident. I'll get Hattiebelle to look after me. You go back to lover-boy there."

"Gallagher, I think you have the wrong impression," Peter interposed. "I dropped in this evening, uninvited—"

"Yeah, I bet you did," Nick muttered caustically. Seeing her with another man caused a pain in his gut, a gnawing ache that ate at his reasoning. "Did Chris know this was goin' on while he was alive?"

Lacey gasped, shocked that Nick would ever think such a thing, but she quickly moved in front of Peter when the other man started toward Nick. "No, Peter, don't!"

"He's being insulting, Lacey."

"His insults can't hurt me and he knows it."

Nick ignored the look Peter shot Lacey. He hurt too much to really give a damn what the dandified fool thought.

"Shouldn't you give my offer a bit of serious consideration, my dear?" Peter asked softly.

Nick pushed away from the doorjamb he'd been leaning against and fell into a nearby chair. "What offer's that?"

Lacey hesitated, thinking Peter's earlier proposal had been made in jest. "He asked me to go to Austin with him." She started to add more, but Nick's jibe interrupted her.

"She'd make one God-awful mistress for *you*, Thorne."

"Not a mistress, Gallagher—a *wife*. Like Chris, I'd be honored if Lacey consented to marry me."

Groaning silently, Lacey knew the situation had now gone from bad to horrible. She'd *never* discussed marriage with Peter! Why he was egging Nick on this way was a mystery to her.

In a great deal of jealous pain, Nick threw back his head and roared with laughter, paying the price for his insolence when his ribs began to throb unmercifully. "Good God, Thorne! You've gotta be crazier'n I thought, wantin' *her* for a wife. She'd make your life hell, like she did my brother's. Why, you'd be pickin' up little stableboys in a—"

Nick never finished, nor did he have time to duck. Peter's fist lashed out through the air and firmly, viciously hit his already bleeding mouth.

When the stars cleared from Nick's vision, he found himself lying on the floor, looking up at the angry artist, who was being restrained by a white-faced Lacey.

"I will not let you stay under this brute's roof another night. You're coming with me! We'll leave Dallas in the morning and be married in Austin."

"I can't leave, Peter," she negated with a shake of her head.

"What!" He pulled her aside to safety as Nick slowly got to his feet. "You can't mean you want to stay here with this . . . this scum?"

"That's not what I mean." She had meant that she didn't want to go with Peter. It would certainly add to her already lengthy list of innocent crimes Nick held against her. Why she should continue caring what Nick thought of her, she wasn't sure. But she *did* care and Peter's overprotectiveness wasn't helping matters any.

Rubbing fresh drops of blood from his jaw onto his pants leg, Nick grumbled, "No, what she means is, until she turns twenty-one, she can't do a damn thing without my permission."

It wasn't her reason, but seeing Peter's questioning look, she thought it was good enough. "He's right. Nick is my guardian."

"That's the most ridiculous thing I've ever heard! My God, the idea of *him* being a fit guardian is preposterous!"

What Nick had intended to be a chuckle came out as a coughing groan. He staggered over to the piano bench and dropped onto it, banging the keys sharply with his muddy elbow. "Yeah, well, that's the truth of it, though. When Chris died, she became my responsibility. She's my . . . ward, I think they call it. As much as I hate the notion, I'd hate it ever worse if you got your perverted hands on her."

"That's twice you've insulted me, Gallagher! It had damn well better be the last."

"Or you'll do what? Stomp your little foot and pout?" Suddenly tired of the baiting, Nick inhaled a deep, painful breath and got to his feet. "I'm gonna go to Hattiebelle. It's gettin' late, Thorne. You'd best be runnin' along."

Once Nick had gone, Lacey turned her back to Peter, gripping the edge of the piano to steady herself. Never had she felt so hurt and humiliated, and more than ever now, she despised Nick Gallagher. The man was positively brutal.

Peter's hands fell on her shoulders and turned her

around to face him. He enveloped her in a comforting embrace and held her for a long while. "He's not worth crying over, my dear."

Angrily wiping at the moisture on her cheek, she sobbed raggedly. "I'm not crying over *him*. I'm just so mad I can't do anything else *but* cry. I feel so . . . so useless, so inadequate when I'm with him, Peter."

"So you just stand there and let him insult you."

"Well, I don't have much choice, do I?" she countered with a bitter laugh. "I can only stay out of his way and pray that I don't antagonize him more than I have already. He certainly won't let me leave . . . not yet, anyway."

"Why not? It's obvious that he isn't happy with your presence."

"I don't know. Maybe he's using me as a substitute whipping boy for Jane Something-or-other. She was a girl, you see, he knew, who—"

"I know the story," Peter interrupted softly. "Chris told me about her and Nick when Marshall, Jane's father, tried to commission me to paint his portrait. I couldn't fit him into my schedule, thank God! But it's insane of Nick to punish you for something she did."

"Maybe Chris's death unhinged him," she speculated. "I only know that we can't be in the same room together for more than a few minutes before he starts being abusive."

"You should get away from him," Peter advised, touching her cool, pale cheek. "It's cowardly, I know, but in your case, it would be the wisest thing to do. He could harm you if he got angry enough."

After a momentary pause, Peter remarked, "I think I'd better be going. I shouldn't have dropped in unannounced with Nick away. For that blunder, my dear, I humbly beg your forgiveness."

"You couldn't have known how things were between us, Peter. Don't blame yourself."

"But if harm should come to you, Lacey, I will!"

When they reached the front door, Lacey retrieved his coat and hat from the massive oak hall tree and handed them to Peter. Donning them, he said, "I'll be in Dallas for two more days, then I must leave for Austin. I'll be staying at the Capitol Hotel there, so if you should need me at any time, don't hesitate to come to me."

She nodded, neither accepting nor rejecting his offer. This was her problem and she would deal with it herself. But it was reassuring to know that she had someone to turn to if things got out of hand.

After closing the door behind him, she listened for a moment until she heard his buggy drive down the carriage sweep and out through the front gates. That highly explosive fuse that bound her to Nick was growing shorter by the moment. It was pulling them together and she didn't know how to stop it. Tonight, seeing him with all that blood and mud covering him, she had wanted only to reach out and comfort him.

"Dearest Lord," she prayed softly, slowly extinguishing the few lamps that remained lit in the hall. "What am I to do?"

Ascending the curving staircase with a tired, defeated gait, she realized that in less than a month she would be twenty years old. But she had to be twenty-one before Nick would let her leave. Torn between wanting to leave him and wanting to go to him, she wondered if she could stand it for another year.

"I'll have to," she whispered, entering her darkened bedroom. After lighting a lamp, she slipped out of her dress, petticoats and corset. With only a light wrapper to cover her, she went out into the hall again.

There was no bar of light shining through the crack beneath Nick's bedroom door as she made her way to the bathroom. She cringed at the memory of his injured body. If only she'd been Hattiebelle, she could tend to him and ease his discomfort. Those horrible bruises! she shuddered. How had he had the accident anyway? Knowing how reckless he was, he had probably been driving too fast, and drinking too, most likely. His tolerance for alcohol was positively phenomenal! Although, if he'd been drinking tonight, she hadn't smelled it. The strong odor of perfume, clinging to his clothes, had been more prevalent than any scent of liquor he may have had.

Recalling that heady, cloying scent caused an unbidden pain to shoot through her, but it was quickly replaced with a sense of indignant outrage. Her lip curled into a distasteful sneer as she told herself that any man who consorted with prostitutes and drove under the intoxication of liquor probably deserved to suffer a few bruises. God alone knew what his liver was like—or the rest of his body, for that matter! All sorts of vile things could be festering within it. After all, weren't loose women notorious for carrying dreadful social diseases? But that was Nick's worry, not hers, she concluded with a shake of her head. She wouldn't spend her time worrying about him; she'd end up a blithering idiot if she did.

Momentarily putting him from her thoughts, she turned into the bathroom and closed the door behind her before turning on the bath taps to fill the huge porcelain tub. Once her black stockings were removed, she folded them neatly on the bench nearby and divested herself of her sheer cambric camisole edged in delicate *broderie anglaise*. As she pulled it over her head, she noticed a small rent in one of the seams. Though it was not a very large hole yet, she knew she would have to mend it before she wore the camisole again. This decided, she folded the garment and placed it on top of her stockings, then turned and began to unfasten her drawers.

Her eyes flew up at the sight of Nick, standing half-naked in the doorway, and her arms quickly crossed over her bared breasts. She knew she should protest his presence, but the painfully haunted look in his eyes caused her to remain silent. A mood she could not comprehend fell over her, and she allowed her eyes the freedom to scan his incredible-looking masculine form. Never having seen an almost naked man before, the sight of his body gave her more pleasure than she cared to admit. Her green eyes clung to him as if they were held by a powerful magnet. She raked his body with an inquisitive hunger and felt sensations of delight course through her. His broad, powerful shoulders were balanced above a wide chest, the muscles there bulging beneath the taut, sun-bronzed skin. A dark pelt of hair stretched from one brown nipple to the other before tapering in a V down to his narrow waist and beyond. But seeing the fabric of his trousers stretched over his loins abruptly brought her examination to a halt and her eyes returned to his face, where they were hit with the full, potent impact of his hooded gaze.

Reaching out blindly for something with which to cover herself, her hand encountered a bathsheet. "Y—You shouldn't be here, Nick," she stammered, nervously wrapping it around her.

Nick moved then, shutting the door behind him. "I'm where I ought to be, Lace," he rasped, closing the distance between them. He had been drawn, with the same invisible magnet she'd felt, to this room when he'd seen the light. Knowing she was just a matter of inches away from him, he had been unable to resist the forceful pull of that magnet's energy. "I can't fight it no more, Lace. I haven't got the strength, so I'm givin' in."

He reached out and loosened the sheet she'd just tied with shaking fingers, letting it fall to the floor. "Oh, God, you're beautiful!" he groaned, his eyes dark pools of desire as he beheld her near-perfect form.

Her small breasts were high and firm, tipped with lovely, dusky pink nipples. Her narrow, nipped-in waist was small enough to span with his two hands, which he did now, bringing her soft, womanly hips into electrifying contact with his.

His gaze traveled upward, reexamining her perfection, as one hand slowly pressed against her spine, bringing her nipples toward his crisp, curling pelt of chest hair. When they brushed him, he heard her gasp.

Looking into her enchantingly lovely face, he touched it reverently and whispered, "Oh, God, Lace, I'm so glad I didn't hit you. To mar this pretty face of yours would be a sin."

He brushed his lips against her cheek and he felt her relax and melt into him. Then his mouth moved unerringly toward hers until he could sip the rare sweetness from her lips.

He pulled back after a moment and looked down at her. She had the softest skin he'd ever touched, softer than velvet and smoother than satin. But its texture was nothing compared to its color, which was like peach-hued cream. Even her lips were peach tinted, inviting his fingers to outline the curves and slopes of her wide mouth before tracing a line from her jaw to her neck and on into the silky fire at her nape.

With a heavy moan, he pulled out the pins which confined her hair in a coil. It fell over his arm and down into a cascade of curls to her hips. It was the loveliest thing he'd ever seen and his hand eagerly became entangled in its fiery gold mass. When he could no longer suppress the urge, he pressed it to his face, inhaling its sweet fragrance like a starving man.

Lacey was unable to move. His nearness was like a drug to her willpower, his touch a stimulant to her rapidly beating heart. When he moved his face away from her hair and looked down into her face, she searched for and could not find the will to evade his descending mouth. Her lips parted in anticipation of what was to come, and when she felt his mouth close over hers, an ache began to flower and bloom in the hidden recesses of her body. She nearly cried out as some nameless hunger suddenly assailed her.

Nick tried to hold back the tide of desire that washed over him. He wanted to restrain this moment and make it last. Exorcising this lovely woman from his mind was proving to be a double-edged undertaking; for the longer he held and kissed her, the greater his need for her became. Without wanting to, and without realizing it, he had fallen headlong into this blackwidow's web.

His tongue invaded the soft inner sweetness of her lips as his hand captured the weight of her breast, eliciting a surprised gasp from her. The sweet orb, becoming taut under his questing fingers, beckoned loudly to him and he answered its call. His mouth fell away from hers and descended until he held the pointed tip between his lips. He teased the nipple with his tongue, rolling the base around and flicking the tip until it became a hard, wet button. When her other nipple summoned him, his head moved again, and he paid homage to it as well.

Lacey's head fell back weakly, her lips open as she gasped for ragged breaths of air. Her body cried out for something, but she knew not what. Her fingers dug into his shoulders, holding him to her breasts as her hips arched toward him. The throbbing ache between her legs became an exquisite agony. This pleasure he was inflicting so sweetly was the most wonderful kind she'd ever experienced. She wanted it to go on and on forever and never end.

Nick moved, causing her to cry out as his head left her breasts. But he brought his lips back to hers, silencing her instantly. His tongue plundered her mouth with a gentle viciousness, telling her without words that he hadn't deserted her. The knowledge of this brought her hands up to his head, and she held him while her mouth silently worshiped his.

Progressing with measured slowness, Nick found the fastenings of her drawers and loosened each button before pushing the cotton down and over her hips. When the heel of his hand found and pressed against the mound at the juncture of her thighs, he growled, "Touch me, Lace! Undress me and hold me next to you. I hurt, babe, and only you can make the pain go away. God in heaven, Lacey, please love me!"

With no thought about the consequences of her action, she responded to his earnest plea. Her fingers slowly unbuttoned his trousers before her hands splayed wide beneath the band, pushing the mud-stained clothes off his narrow hips. And when he kicked them aside, her hands returned to him, touching and exploring his bare, male body. Timidly, she marveled at the texture and warmth of his swollen member when her fingers brushed against it for the first time. Then recklessly, she possessed it wholly in her hand, feeling it stiffen and throb.

"Oh, God, babe!" he groaned against the curve of her throat, unbridled longing in his voice. "Let me love you. Please—let me ease my pain inside you."

A warning bell sounded then in the back of her mind, but it came much too late. Nick was lowering her to the thick rug at their feet, his hungry mouth cutting off any objection she might have made. But as his knee parted her legs, fear cried out within her as the memory of her encounter with Chris flashed through her brain. She pushed hard against Nick, trying to stop him when his mouth refused to leave hers so she could verbally explain. He was a determined, hungry man, deaf to her pleas, and could not be forestalled.

Lost in the sensations of her desirable body, Nick was unaware of her pitifully weak blows. He was completely numb to everything but the driving ache that compelled him. His mouth devoured hers relentlessly, closing off the incoherent cries she uttered as his insistent maleness poised itself at her nest. His blessed release from weeks of frustration was at hand and he could no longer stop himself.

In one, swift thrust, he entered her, breaking the hard veil that had protected her virtue. She screamed as the pain ripped through her, but the room remained oddly quiet due to the suddenly still male mouth that had absorbed her cry.

Too late, Nick lifted his head and stared down in astonished horror at her pain-contorted face. Then it registered in his fevered, overwrought brain just what had happened. But all reason quickly fled as the sensations of her body began to overtake him again. All he could feel was the tight, hot velvet wrapped about him and the pulsating tension that built within his loins.

"Oh, God, baby, hang on!" he whispered huskily. "Just hang on . . . please! I . . . can't . . . stop!" Each word was punctuated with a slow, gentle thrust that seemed to quicken in intensity until at last his many weeks of impotency vanished in a blinding, gut-wrenching climax.

Lacey lay still and quiet beneath him as he shuddered atop her. She didn't know what had happened but, curiously, there was no longer any pain. But when she heard his groan, she held him to her, hoping that by doing so, she could ease *his* discomfort.

Finally he moved. He rolled aside and held her close to him as he comfortably settled her head in the crook of his arm. He noted the damp streaks on her lovely face and, wiping them dry, asked, "Why didn't you tell me? Dear God, why didn't you say something before I let this happen?"

"I tried," she breathed raggedly. "But you wouldn't listen."

Nick groaned. He didn't like being reminded of his impatience and stupidity. And he didn't like admitting—especially to himself—that he had faults. It was a helluva thing to know you had deficiencies just like everyone else. Lately, he was beginning to suspect he had more than most.

"What was the matter?" he asked finally. "Why couldn't Chris break it?"

"He tried," she confessed. "But he was so ashamed and embarrassed . . . and mad! He finally just gave up and said he wouldn't hurt me anymore. Oh, Nick, I didn't marry him for his money; you've got to believe me. If he was alive today, I would be the best wife he could ever want. Really, I would!"

"Shh!" he soothed, cradling her head against his. "I believe you." The thought of his brother tore at his heart. If Chris had lived, could he have left Lacey alone? She had tormented him from the first moment he'd seen her again; would he have felt differently, reacted differently toward her, if his brother had been around?

Lacey grew uneasy, realizing that they were lying, as naked as the day they were born, on the bathroom floor. Moving, she tried to get up. "I . . . I need to wash 'myself, Nick," she mumbled.

But Nick refused to let her leave. "If I let you go now, we'll never get this thing settled between us. And dammit, I'm tired of all this anger. I don't like fighting with you anymore'n I 'spect you like fighting with me. Hell, I'm not a brute, no matter what I've said or done."

"I know," she assured him reluctantly. "But you've got to leave me alone for a few minutes . . . please!"

Nick didn't, though. He stood up and helped her to her feet, then swept her up into his arms and deposited her into the big tub of warm water. He knew she expected him to go away, but he knelt down beside the tub and took possession of her scented soap and began gently to cleanse her tender skin.

"I wish this tub was big enough for the two of us," he confessed as his hands roamed her silky flesh. Washing her rosy breasts and soaping her neck, he caught sight of her flushed face and realized just how embarrassed she was. "Oh, hell, Lace! Don't look like that. I know I've got some nerve, expectin' you to be offhand about me doing this, but you're gonna have to get used to me being around. I've been a rotten son of a bitch, I know, but I won't ever be again."

His hand moved over her belly in ever-widening spirals as he went on to explain, "You don't know what it was doing to me, being with you day after day and not being able to touch you. Hell, it was tearing me apart inside, honey. You're the most beautiful woman I've ever seen, yet I couldn't get near you without losing my control . . . so I blew up and made you cry. I'm so sorry, I did that."

She stiffened and gasped loudly when his fingers finally made contact with her sensitive sex. The pain there was a throbbing one, but oddly, not as bad as it had been. And when his fingers tentatively moved over her torn skin between her legs, she bit her lips to hold back the whine that threatened to escape.

"Look at me, babe," he commanded in a soft, earnest voice, turning her face toward his with wet, dripping fingers. With her chin in his grasp, she had no choice but to look directly into his tortured brown eyes. "I'm the sorriest human alive for having caused you so much pain. If I'd known, I . . . hell, who am I fooling? I'd have come after you anyway, even knowin' you were a virgin. But I wouldn't have been so rough. I'd have been more careful and a lot gentler . . . like I will be next time."

Next time! her mind screamed. "No, Nick!" she objected as he began to lift her out of the tub. "Please, not again."

"Hush now," he soothed, holding her close to him as he wrapped her with the dry bathsheet. His moustache brushed against her neck and up her jaw before his mouth finally made contact with hers.

A curious weakness invaded her legs and she leaned weakly against him as he kissed away all her fears and apprehensions.

"I won't hurt you," he whispered after a long moment. "I swear to God I'll *never* hurt you again. But I can't let you go, remembering nothing but the pain and no pleasure. You gotta trust me, Lace," he growled, taking her hand and pressing it to his abdomen, "'cause I want you again."

At the imperceptible nod of her head, he smiled his lopsided, boyish grin and lifted her effortlessly into his strong arms. He held her protectively, cradling her as he might an infant, and she felt all her unvoiced objections flee from her mind.

Before he walked out of the bathroom, he took a bottle of scented oil off the shelf above the clothes-bench and turned off the gas bracket lamp in one economical movement. Then, with his taut, bare buttocks exposed to the frigid hall air, he carried her to her bedroom, crooning to her in his soft, husky voice in between the drugging kisses he placed on the sensitive underside of her ear.

Lacey loved this new tenderness of his. He was being so sweet to her, so gentle, that it surprised her when she found herself nibbling his rough, leathery neck. It wouldn't take much, she thought, for her to grow used to his kisses.

"Lovely, lovely, Lace," he purred, shutting her door behind them with a backward kick of his foot.

He carried her to the bed and removed her damp towel before placing her between the cold, crisp sheets. Then he turned her lamp down, but not off, and crawled into bed beside her, holding her against him so that his body heat would take away her chill. Slowly he caressed her, gentling her and creating a hotter, inner fire.

When at last they were both warm, he found her hands and brought them up to his mouth, kissing both palms before placing them boldly on his body. He wanted her to touch and explore him with those graceful hands. And she did, shyly at first, then with more daring as her curiosity grew stronger.

He was so big, so strong, so powerful, she thought as her hands played a tuneless rhapsody on his flesh. And he was quite smooth-skinned, for all the hair on his chest. She could never have touched Chris like this. She had only seen him undressed once, at a distance for a moment, before he had donned his nightshirt. But in those few moments, she'd seen that Chris wasn't muscular at all and already possessed a thin layer of fat around his middle. There wasn't an ounce of superfluous flesh on Nick; he was all muscle, skin and bone.

Unable to stem the inner flow of tears for her late husband, Lacey mourned the awful hell that had been their few days together. He had tried, more than once on their wedding night, to breach that impenetrable veil that had protected her virginity. Eventually, he had given up, frustrated at his inept attempts. He had stormed out of the bedroom and out of the house . . . and three days later, he had died.

"I went to a doctor at St. Paul's," she explained quietly.

Nick didn't say anything. He lay still next to her, his caressing hands ceasing their movements as her soft words penetrated his thoughts.

"He was a gynecologist—a new kind of doctor who sees only women and tends their ailments. He told me my . . . my maidenhead was far too thick."

Nick nodded, indicating that he understood, and placed a kiss at her temple.

"He told me I wasn't the only one who had that . . . problem. He said a lot of young women suffered from the same disorder, but that I was luckier than most because I had come to him soon enough and he could help me. He did something to me—Oh, it was so embarrassing!—then he told me Chris would be able to consummate our marriage." She paused, taking a deep breath, and continued. "But Chris went to Frogtown the very same day the doctor treated my disorder. While I was making myself . . . perfect for him, he was being run over by that beer wagon. He never even knew what I had done!" she ended on a tremulous sigh.

Beer wagon! Nick frowned into the darkness, repeating her words over again in his head. There had been a beer wagon outside Cora's place tonight as he had started to leave. He hadn't paid much attention to it at the time; he'd just assumed it was there making a delivery. But stores, he realized now, never made deliveries at night—only during the day.

"Lacey?" Gently caressing her back, he drew her closer to him. "Do you know the name of the company that that beer wagon belonged to?"

"I'm not sure." Her curious fingers continued to explore his amazing body without shyness or embarrassment. "Stratton's, I think it was. Oh! Did I say something wrong?" she asked, feeling him stiffen.

"You've said something very right! I'll bet no one ever even questioned it."

"What?" His sudden change of mood had her baffled.

"Never mind," he told her. "I was just thinking out loud. Are you warm now?"

Snuggling against him, she nodded.

"Good!" he chuckled. "Then we'd best be getting

on with the important stuff and stop all this chitchat-ting."

"Nick," she began to object.

"Now you just settle down, Lace. You're gonna like what I got in mind. You ever had a rubdown?" He asked this as he sat up and reached for the bottle of oil, sitting on her night table.

"No," she responded, watching him remove the stopper from the cut-glass bottle.

"Turn over. Let me rub your back."

"My back?"

"Yeah," he nodded. "Go on, turn over. I'm not gonna hurt you."

She complied, reluctantly, and gasped as the cold oil was poured onto her warm skin. Then, feeling the bed move as Nick shifted his weight, she realized he was straddling her.

"Loosen up," he laughed. "It won't be bad. I'm just going to rub you all over until you . . . well, you'll see."

His hands began to work the scented oil into her back. His fingers spread it over her shoulderblades, down her ribs and past her buttocks to her legs. Then, as they began working up her body again, he pressed strategic areas around her hips. She moaned at the sensations it created within her. It *was* nice, she thought, relaxing.

He rubbed her for a long time, soothing her tensed nerves until she was almost asleep.

"Now turn over and I'll get your front."

She issued a protesting groan, disappointed that she would have to move out of her comfortable position.

Nick eyed the two pale globes of flesh that topped her long legs. With a grin, he gently pinched one, receiving a surprised grunt of indigation from her.

"That's mean!" she accused, turning over to face him.

"But it's a helluva lot different from gettin' your butt paddled when you were seven, isn't it?" he observed, pouring more oil onto the palm of his hand. He swirled it over her flat abdomen until his fingers curled around her sharp hipbones. Working the fragrant lubricant into her skin, he slid upward over her ribs and to her breasts. When his thumbs encountered the firm flesh there, he paused for a moment, watching the guarded, almost expectant expression on her face. Slowly his fingers curled over and around the small mounds before sliding his hands erotically off of her turgid pink nipples. He did this again and again, watching her lids grow heavy and close. Her lips parted and he heard her draw in labored gasps as his own blood began to race. When at last her head began to move from side to side on her pillow, and her fists began to clench and dig into the tautened muscles of his thighs, he allowed one hand to move down toward her fiery nest of curls.

Lacey's mind swam from the exquisite sensations. She couldn't believe that something so simple as touching could be so wonderful. But when she felt his fingers encounter that ultrasensitive nub of her sex, she stiffened and cried out, "Nick!" as that nameless hunger began anew within her. "Oh, my God, Nick!"

"Relax," he whispered, his fingers never ceasing

their delightful ministrations. "Just relax and enjoy it, lovely, lovely, Lace."

How had he ever thought her frigid? She was anything but that. There was an untapped source of fire, lying dormant within her just begging to be unleashed. If he was lucky enough to be with her when that fire began to burn out of control, he would be consumed by its glorious blaze. God only knew that that was what he wanted, what he needed, and what he was going to have!

Bending over her, he tasted the sweetness of her nipples. He held one gently with his teeth while his tongue fondled it into life. By the time this night was over, she would know the intense pleasure a man's body could give her. He had cheated her the first time; but this time she would know. She would know the art of lovemaking and be one helluva woman to contend with because of it . . . if she wasn't that already.

A disturbing thought came to him then, and he unconsciously slowed his movements. Once he taught her everything he knew, would he be willing to let her go? To some other man? The question brought an awareness to him that he didn't like facing. He didn't want to think of her, going to someone else; yet he knew he had no hold over her, and would have no choice. She was young and wouldn't want to live the rest of her life as his brother's widow. Naturally, she would one day want to marry again, settle down and raise a family. But the thought of her with another man caused a subtle rage to build within him.

Lacey had reached the point of mindless arousal.

Her loins ached, her nipples throbbed, and yet it was agonizingly pleasurable. She wanted more of it, not less, because there was something, some sweet pinnacle she couldn't put her finger on, just beyond her realm of comprehension. Breathing raggedly, she frantically sought that pinnacle with an arch of her hips. Her hands coursed over Nick's slim, muscular body, pulling him closer and closer to her until she could explore the hot, hard length of his maleness.

With a groan, he moved away from her suddenly, causing her to gaze up at him in disappointment. But she relaxed when she saw him pour a small amount of oil onto his palm before he smoothed it over his distended staff.

"Why?" she queried breathily.

"It'll make it easier. I won't take the chance of hurting you again, because this one's all yours, love. Ready?"

She nodded and watched his hands cover her inner thighs. He pushed against them and she opened for him like a flower. Then those same slick, calloused hands lifted her hips and he moved onto her.

He was right, there was no pain as he filled her, only a resurgence of that nameless, undefinable sweetness. Sparks of pleasure began to radiate throughout her in ever-widening spirals as he withdrew and thrust, withdrew and thrust. She panted for breath as her hips, wanting more of the sensation, undulated in tempo with his. Her hands, needing the feel of him, raked his skin, causing him to gasp for air like she.

Then it started. Tiny explosions began to build and build in intensity until she was crying out in a thin, plaintive voice.

"Lace!" he growled against her fragrant neck as she writhed beneath him. No other woman was like her. She was all sensation, all feeling, all fire, and she was burning him with her heat.

Her hips arched and retreated as did his, causing their mutual blazes to burn out of control. She dug her nails into his broad shoulders and let him carry her, push her, force her into an explosion so cataclysmic that it ripped her world apart and caused her to cry out his name loud in ecstasy.

Nick captured that scream in his trembling mouth just as his own pulsating climax began, sending his frustrations into oblivion and leaving him a totally contented man.

Slowly, inevitably, they drifted down from their high plateau of pleasure. Nick wrapped his arms possessively around her pliant body and held her to him, experiencing such a fierce need for her that it frightened him. Then, rocking gently, he rolled onto his side before covering their sweat-drenched bodies with the satin coverlet. He kissed her tear-dampened eyes, her cheeks, and finally her mouth. With their lips still clinging together, they drifted off into quiet slumber.

Chapter Five

SOMETHING WARM AND FURRY WAS PRESSED AGAINST her back. Becoming aware of this, Lacey opened her eyes just as the dawn light filtered through a slit in the drapes. She tried to turn, but then a throaty moan penetrated the morning stillness and an arm suddenly wrapped around her and dragged her back into place.

It was Nick, she remembered, feeling his hand move. It left her hip and found her breast, cupping it possessively. Then his moustache tickled her neck as he nuzzled the sensitive spot beneath her ear.

A chillng wave of reality washed over her as she recalled their abandonment of last night. She winced, wondering how she was going to face him now, in the light of day. How could she have let it happen so easily anyway? They'd been at each other's throats one minute and in each other's arms the next.

But her niggling imp of a conscience could give her no answer. It merely insisted that it had all been well worth it!

Nick began to fondle and caress the breast he

held. The accuracy of his touch told her he was fully awake, as well as halfway aroused, if the hard, insistent prodding at her buttocks was any proof to go by.

"Nick," she whispered breathily over her shoulder. "If Hattiebelle comes in here now and finds us like this . . ."

"She'll get a shotgun after me and send William for a preacher," he chuckled, turning her over to face him. "Jesus, you're beautiful when you first wake up."

"Well, you're not!" she quipped. He was in bad need of a shave, and his thick, unruly brown hair was falling down into his eyes. But its uneven length couldn't hide the look of desire in their warm brown depths.

"I don't get to sleep all night with a woman very often," he purred. "It's a nice experience I'll want to have again." His warm lips pressed provocative kisses against the base of her pale, ivory throat before they moved on to her dusky rose nipples.

Lacey's lids fluttered and closed, her heart beating an erratic tempo. "Last night, Nick . . . it just happened. It wasn't planned," came her breathy admission.

"They're the best kind," he chuckled, lifting his head from her breast to gaze at her drowsily. "Aw, now don't go getting all prudish on me, Red. You weren't last night. You were all woman for a change."

Heat warmed her face and she averted her eyes from his. "I felt . . . different," she confessed quietly.

Nick kissed the tip of her upturned nose and

hauled her closer to him. "I feel like kicking myself for ever hurting you, Lace."

It was strange, she thought, how his shame made her feel so good inside. But knowing that he felt guilty for what he'd done, she couldn't find it within herself to berate him further for his error. He was human, after all, and considering the loss he had suffered, perhaps he had just cause in being suspicious.

"What happens now, Nick?" she asked. Their lives were irrevocably changed; they couldn't go back to living as they had been.

"I'll be damned if I know, Lace. What do you want?"

It was the answer she'd expected, or wanted. In fact, it was a blatant evasion. But he was probably just as confused as she was. Shrugging one bare shoulder, she murmured, "I'll have to give it some thought, I guess."

Looking at her profile for a long time, Nick examined the soft perfection of her face and felt a twinge of jealousy shoot through him. "You . . . you want to marry that painter?"

"No!" She turned her head sharply to look at him. "His proposal was made in jest. I don't really know why he made it, but I know he wasn't serious."

"Lucky for you," Nick mused dryly. "You'd have a helluva fight with his boyfriends if you did decide to marry him."

"Nick! That's a horrible thing to accuse a man of."

"Look, Red, I'm not gonna get into an argument with you over the likes of Peter Thorne. We got a nice little truce between us now, so what do you say we just drop the subject of him, hmmm?"

A frown appeared on his rugged face as he added, "I gotta go see Jake Goldstein this morning. Want to go into town with me? You could buy yourself something pretty to wear while I take care of business. I, uh, hate to tell you, Red, seeing as how you're so fond of the color and all, but you look like a damn ghost in black."

"I have to wear it until I'm out of mourning," she replied, mustering up her dignity. But even to her, the declaration sounded insincere. After all, lying nude in his arms this way, with his muscular chest brushing the tips of her breasts, she felt anything but dignified.

"Oh, hell! That's a lot of hogwash and you know it. If you looked good in black, it'd be a different story. You need something bright, something that'll make men's heads turn. Lord knows, you're worth a second look."

"You really think so?"

Nick slid a hand down her back and pressed her hips against his, letting her feel his heated arousal. "You know you're a beauty, so stop digging for compliments." Then he growled and lowered his lids, letting her know with a movement of his hips just what he had in mind. "Sweetheart, if you don't let me get out of this bed pretty soon, I won't be responsible for what happens."

"I'm not stopping you,' she purred, kissing his jaw.

He drew back a bit, his beakish nose lifting as he sniffed the air. "Is that coffee I smell?" But before she could answer, he glanced at her lazily and swore, "Oh, to hell with food! Who can think of eating at a time like this?" Then he pressed his lips to hers before easing away their mutual, all-consuming sensual hungers.

Jake Goldstein flexed his shoulders, hoping to relieve some of his tension. Standing at his third-floor office window, he looked down at Commerce Street and saw all the traffic that bustled about there. It was a busy morning. Streetcars were stopped on both sides of the street, picking up and letting off passengers. Delivery wagons from Union Station were carrying luggage to the Grand-Windsor and the new Oriental Hotels just down the street.

Having been to the Oriental when it first opened, Jake had to admit that old Adolphus Busch hadn't skimped on its luxuries. It had just about every modern amenity found, from private baths in the suites to total-electric elevators, and it had been chosen for the prestigious New Century Cotillion, too, which was to be held there at the end of the month on New Year's Eve. He knew because some-one had just sent him an invitatiton. He couldn't be sure, but he sort of suspected that that someone had sleek brown hair and deep hazel eyes.

Sighing, Jake hooked his thumbs in his vest pock-ets and looked up the street toward the Dallas Opera House, across from the Grand-Windsor. A new play was opening there tonight, and though the star wasn't as famous as Lillie Langtry or Sarah Bern-hardt, who had both played there to packed houses in years past, the newspapers said that the young actress appearing in tonight's performance was "up and coming"—whatever that meant. He wondered what his chances of getting Miss Darcy Patterson to go to the play with him would be? But with a groan, he put the notion aside, knowing his chances would be pretty slim. How could he possibly expect a wealthy Baptist deacon's daughter to go to the theater with him, a poor Jew?

He flexed his shoulders once again and started to turn back to his desk, deciding that work was more important at the moment than thinking of Darcy. But he stopped and peered down into the street again as Nick Gallagher's carriage caught his eye. He knew it was Nick's because William Turner was perched atop the driver's seat. Jake watched as it stopped in front of his building, then saw Nick hop agilely out of the coach. But instead of coming directly inside, Nick turned back to the coach's opened door and said something to the unseen person there.

Probably one of his lady friends, Jake surmised with a grin.

A black-veiled head appeared, and Jake watched Nick lift a corner of the concealing silk to place a long, lingering kiss on the unknown woman's lips. But then Jake almost roared with laughter when Nick reached out and audaciously fondled the woman's rounded breast, receiving a slap on his arm for his efforts.

Something clicked then, and Jake stared down at the couple with an insistent, disbelieving frown before he gasped, "My God, that's Lacey!" Had it been just a week ago that Nick was here in this very office, berating the young woman? "He's sure changed his tune!"

Minutes later, after the carriage had driven away, Jake heard the sputter and cough of the elevator at the end of the hall. At a familiar knock on his outer door, he bid his caller to enter, and when Nick came in, Jake was hard pressed not to laugh at the lopsided grin his friend wore.

"You seem mighty chipper this morning," Jake observed, suppressing his mirth. Leaning back in his chair and locking his fingers behind his head, he thought how strange a man behaved when he'd found a new love interest. Almost like a kid with a new toy. "Are, uh, things a little better at home?"

"You know damn well they are," Nick growled sheepishly. "I saw your face pressed against the windowpane, so don't act like you're surprised."

"But I *am*, old buddy, I *am*. And with your sister-in-law, of all people! My, my, my, who'd've thought it?"

Nick shifted his feet uneasily, actually looking contrite. "I ain't usually wrong about folks, Jake, but I sure as hell screwed up good with her!"

"You did what?" Jake asked, blinking innocently.

Reddening at his slip of the tongue, Nick shrugged out of his overcoat. "Never mind!" He'd already put his foot in his mouth once; he wasn't about to make a bigger fool of himself by trying to explain what he meant. "Let's just say it's all right between me and Lacey now and leave it at that."

With an accepting nod, Jake reached out for his cigar box and flipped open the top. "Whatever you say, Nick. Have a cigar, make yourself comfortable and tell me just what brought you up here this morning."

Like Jake, Nick spent a few moments lighting up. When the tip of his slim wand of tobacco finally glowed red, he blew a stream of bluish gray smoke over his head and said, "Somebody tried to run me off the road last night."

Jake stopped puffing and looked at Nick with a stern frown.

"Yeah, they did! They wrecked my buggy, but I got away with only a couple of light cuts and bruises."

"Any ideas as to who it could've been?"

"I didn't see who was driving; it all happened kinda fast. But I got a hunch it was one of Stratton's boys."

He then went on to tell Jake about his trip to Cora's, wisely deleting the part about Sally, who had been in Cora's parlor as he had been about to leave, as well as about the delivery wagon outside in the shadows. "I stopped at the bridge this morning as we were coming into town, and had me a good look-see at the traces on the buggy. The damn things had been sawed half in two."

"That definitely points to sabotage," Jake agreed. "But that's all it points to. You've been in Dallas how long now?"

"'Bout a month."

"Made any enemies?"

Nick's lopsided grin reappeared. "Yeah, but we became, uh, friends . . . *close* friends last night."

Jake let this bit of information pass. "Would anybody from twelve years ago still hold a grudge against you?"

"Marshall Stratton," Nick declared smoothly. "Oh, and Jamieson Crawford. I thought he was my friend, but I got a feeling he was the one who lied to Papa 'bout me dyin' up in the Yukon. God knows," he added, frowning, "I never did a damn thing to him that I can remember."

"It's just a guess, but I'd say Crawford was coerced into lying by someone who held a lot of influence over him."

"Stratton." Nick nodded. "I wouldn't be surprised if he had a hand in Chris's death, too." Seeing the questioning arch of Jake's brow, he added, "The wagon that ran him down was one of Stratton's."

"Yes, I know," Jake admitted with a nod.

"And you didn't bother to tell *me?*"

"What good would it have done? Half the delivery wagons on the streets of Dallas belong to Stratton Storage and Hauling. His delivery company literally keeps this city running. But that's not a good enough reason to believe he's behind every accident his wagons are involved in. You've got to have irrefutable proof of your suspicions, Nick. You can't just hurl out a few accusations and hope that one of them sticks. Look where that got you with Lacey."

Nick slumped in his chair, looking sullen and annoyed. He wanted a quick solution to this mess, one that would be brought out into the open and solved in a short span of time. But now that Dallas was no longer a wide-open frontier town, there was no such thing as instant justice—there was the damn judicial system to wade through.

"Crawford's tied in with Stratton," Jake surmised. "Look what he had to gain if you never showed up again. He had Chris's power of attorney before he died, and he had Lacey's trust and confidence. He had a damn good thing going for him, living off your father's and Chris's investments. But you came back home and fired him. Not the wisest move, but an understandable one."

"If we could get some evidence tying him to Stratton," Nick mused, "I'll bet we could get them both put away for life. Maybe even send 'em on a trip to the gallows."

"What about those claim jumpers who attacked you?" Jake queried. "Could you get them to swear that Crawford or Stratton hired them?"

Nick shook his head. "I killed the bastards. Well, hell, Jake, I didn't have much choice! I mean, it was either them or me. When I found myself lookin' down the barrel of their Springfield rifle, I grabbed up my pickax, coldcocked one of 'em with the handle, then gutted the other one with the business end. I buried 'em both up along the Canadian border."

Jake absorbed the explanation as an idea began to take root in his devious legal mind. After a moment of thoughtful concentration, he murmured, "It might take some time and a lot of *patience,*" he stressed for Nick's benefit, "but we just might be able to get something on those two."

"Take all the time you need," Nick said, leaning forward with interest. "I ain't plannin' on goin' nowhere."

"Well now, I haven't figured out all the details, but if we could get someone . . . someone who isn't connected with either of us . . . if we could get that someone close to Crawford, who's the weaker of the two, we just might have a chance of getting them."

"Get someone close to Crawford?" Nick laughed harshly. "Hell, Jake, he don't even trust his own wife!"

A smile formed about Jake's mouth. "You don't say!"

Lacey held her pale, bare arms out wide as Mrs. Beale pulled the measuring tape taut over her small bosom. "With just the slightest train in back, I think the dress would be quite becoming, Mrs. Gallagher. You know, it's the latest thing in Paris now, and with your coloring, pale peach satin would be beautiful."

"I don't know," Lacey responded, dropping her arms and shivering slightly as a draft swept through the small back room. "Would a bright color be appropriate for me just now?"

"It's just for the one night," Mrs. Beale urged. "Surely you won't be expected to ring in the new century in a gown of dreary black. One of my other customers is wearing *red* and she's been a widow for less than a year, too!"

Lacey stepped past the table piled high with fabric samples and designers' sketches to disappear behind the dressing screen. "Well, I'd like to have a look at the fabric first, but I'm not making any promises."

"We'll never ring in 1900 again, and everybody's planning on making it a big night," the dressmaker stressed, jotting down some figures in her little book. "You are going to the ball at the Oriental, aren't you?"

"It's possible," Lacey replied. Though Nick hadn't said anything to her yet, she knew he had received his invitation. Perhaps that was why he had insisted she buy a new gown today.

She stepped into her black wool skirt and fastened it around her slender, corseted waist. Her breasts were pushed up and flattened out by the stiffness of her stays and when she had slipped on her white georgette blouse and turned to look at her reflection in the mirror, she thought she looked like a black and white pouter pigeon. Her black jacket on, she stepped out from behind the screen and said, "I'm ready to look at those sketches now."

Mrs. Beale hurried toward the nearby table and produced a thick, hardbound folder for Lacey to look through. Flipping the pages, she had to admit that Mrs. Beale knew what she was talking about. The gowns were exceptionally lovely this season.

"Oh, I *do* like the rounded neckline on this one," she said, her eyes falling on one lovely creation. Most of the gowns in the book had the popular low, square-neck bodices, but the rounded line on this gown made it appear softer, more feminine. "But there's entirely too much ruching on the skirt."

"That's no problem. I'll just leave it off." The dressmaker made a notation in her book. "What do you think about the back?"

Lacey scrutinized the drawing, trying to visualize the train of the dress without all the decoration depicted. "Well, with all this pleating and smocking and complicated ruffling removed, it wouldn't be quite as tedious a chore to sit on, and I wouldn't have to fuss with a bustle form, either."

At that moment, the curtain that protected the small back room from the main part of the shop parted and Lacey turned to see Nick's grinning face.

"Got all the embarrassin' stuff taken care of, ladies?" He gave Lacey a rakish look, causing her to blush, when Mrs. Beale turned her back to them.

"Almost," she admitted, waving her hand for him to go away. "Just a few last details and we'll be done."

"One question," Nick persisted. "Are all these boxes out here yours?"

"Yes, and don't you dare look through them! They're Christmas presents."

"Christmas! Lord, I clean forgot. That means a tree and all those decorations, don't it?"

"Just worry about the tree," she instructed. "I'll take care of the decorations and Hattiebelle, as always, will see to the food. Now, go away so we can finish."

With a reluctant nod, Nick turned, letting the curtain fall back over the doorway. He didn't particularly like this place; being surrounded by all these frilly female things made him very uneasy. He fingered a few silky items on a nearby table, then looked up and grinned as he spied a headless dress form with an expensive, but suggestive, gown and negligee draped over it. It reminded him of the pleasure-filled hours he'd spent with Lacey the night before.

His provocative thoughts were suddenly interrupted when the bell tinkled above the shop's front door.

"Nicholas?" a soft, familiar voice called out.

Feeling like a schoolboy caught with his hand in the cookie jar, he turned, red-faced, and saw Darcy. "Well, hi there."

"Whatever are *you* doing in here? Buying something special for a lady friend?"

"Uh, no," he admitted, shuffling his feet nervously. "Lacey's back there, getting fitted for a dress."

"She is!" Darcy's eyes widened as her dimples deepened. "You know, we live in the same city and I haven't seen her in ages—not since her wedding, in fact. She made the *loveliest* bride."

"Yeah, I know. I've seen her photograph." For some reason, he felt angry. Just the thought of his handsome, younger brother crawling into Lacey's bed and fondling her beautiful body set his teeth on edge.

"Nicholas?" Darcy's concerned tone intruded on his thoughts. "What*ever* is the matter? You had the oddest look on your face, like you were contemplating something violent."

Nick shook his head, issuing an uneasy laugh. "Now why would you think a thing like that?"

"Well, your expression . . ." she began to elucidate, but stopped when Lacey stepped through the curtains.

Seeing Nick smile at the other girl caused Lacey's temper to flare unexplainably, and her green eyes glittered.

Nick spied her and his smile widened. "There you are. All finished?"

"Yes," came her polite reply. "I told you I wouldn't be long. How are you, Darcy?"

"Oh, I've never been better," the other girl twittered. "And I can see that you're doing fine. You certainly look well, Lacey."

"Thank you," Lacey smiled, gliding to Nick's side. "Is that a new hat? It's lovely."

Darcy patted her overembellished piece of nonsense with a giggle. "Yes, it's new. Papa nearly hit the ceiling when he saw the bill. Momma and I both bought three new hats last week and two more the week before that." Gasping in mock horror, her dark hazel eyes widened expressively as a gloved hand found its way to her dove gray, velvet-covered bosom. "He was fit to be tied, let me tell you! But I'm just like Momma, positively hopeless when it comes to saying no to a new hat." Dimpling prettily, she emitted a silvery giggle and added, "I tried on one of those Gainsborough hats at Sanger Brothers the other day. It had those magnificent ostrich feathers that trailed down over one shoulder, and it was the *exact* shade of my newest suit, but it positively devoured me. I would give anything to be tall like you, Lacey, instead of short and dumpy. I'd be able to wear just about any kind of hat then. That Gainsborough was *so* scrumptious! You know, *you* ought to go see it!"

Lacey was silent for a moment, feeling guilty for having misjudged Darcy. There wasn't a devious, dishonest bone in the girl's whole body. She was totally guileless; just a sweet, uncomplicated little butterfly who loved life and people. And Nick had every right to talk to her if he wanted . . . to Darcy, or anyone, for that matter. She didn't own him. The one night and one morning they'd spent loving each other did not entitle her to possess him. But knowing this was hard for her to accept.

Determined not to show how she felt, Lacey lifted her chin and smiled sweetly at Darcy. "Maybe I will go see it, if it's as special as you say."

"Oh, do! It would look beautiful on you."

"I doubt that," she demurred, dropping her gaze. It was then that she noticed Nick, or rather his shuffling feet, and asked, "Are you ready to leave?"

"If you are," he admitted almost gratefully.

"Will y'all be coming to the holiday party at our house? It's in a matter of days, you know?" Darcy stressed.

"If nothing happens, we'll be there," Nick assured her.

It took a few minutes for Lacey to load her parcels into Nick's brawny arms so that he could take them out to the waiting carriage, but once they were out of the shop and Darcy's hearing, she heard him expell a loud, *"Whew!"*

"Nick!" she rebuked with a smile. "Darcy's not that bad!"

"It wasn't just her," he confessed, waving at William to drive on. He closed the door and settled himself in the seat beside Lacey, loosening his overcoat so that he could draw her into the circle of his arm. "It was all them naked dummies around the shop. I kept seeing you underneath all that ruffled silk."

A reproof formed on Lacey's lips, but it was never uttered. Nick's mouth swooped down hungrily on hers, his torrid kiss blocking out all objections that came to mind. With a defeated purr, she gave in and felt desire begin to flicker within her.

Fortunately, sanity intruded after a while and she found the stamina to push him away. "Nick!" she gasped. "Not *here,* for heaven's sake. We're in the middle of downtown Dallas!"

Somewhere in that kiss, he had lost his reasoning, but he sat back against the seat and blew out a deep lungful of air. "You do have a way about you, Red."

Lacey angrily tugged off her gloves. "I *wish* you

wouldn't keep calling me that, Nick." Her voice was level, but it held an underlying note of tenseness, and Nick heard it.

"Why not? That's how I think of you. You're all fiery, like there's a red-hot flame blazing away inside you when you're doing your damnedest to be cool and composed. Jesus," he muttered regretfully, "how could I have been so wrong about you?"

Her cheeks burned furiously and she gnawed her bottom lip. Now was the time to tell him he hadn't been totally wrong. "Nick, I—"

But his hand instantly covered her lips. "Shh! I know you don't like me talking about it, but I can't help it. Last night, Lace . . . well, last night was pure magic! God knows if I'll ever feel that way again, but it was . . . magical. From now on, though, we're gonna be extra careful."

Extra careful? she thought, blinking at him. *What does he mean by that?* But Nick didn't explain; he changed the subject.

"Jake and I were discussing some of the land deals Chris and Papa put together," he divulged, peering out the window at the passing scenery. "There's a big plot of land in East Texas that some geological surveyor wants to dig on. I'll need your signature on the lease agreement before we can let the man have it."

"I'll sign whatever you need." She shrugged, recalling the land that was situated a few miles south of Nacogdoches. Max had gone down to look at it shortly before he was killed, and Chris completed the deal afterwards, never questioning his father's reasons for the purchase. It was farmland—that's all she knew—surrounded by towering pines and not really having enough rocks around for a geologist to get excited about.

"Lord knows what he wants to look for," Nick remarked. "He said something about fossil formations in his letter."

It all sounded very confusing to Lacey. Not being used to discussing business with a man, she suspected that the only reason he was mentioning it now was because he needed her signature. And knowing that he was in a receptive mood, she suddenly decided to bring up the subject of her inheritance.

"Uh, I'd like to get rid of some of those utilities Chris invested in," she began, watching for some sign of disapproval in Nick's rugged face. When none appeared, she continued. "I don't know how much they're worth, but I know he wasn't happy with the paltry dividends he'd been receiving."

Nick knew the reason: Crawford had been skimming from the top. But he told Lacey he would see that the stocks were sold. "You might think about investing the profits . . . in land, for instance."

"You approve, then? I mean, you *are* my guardian. I can't sell them without your approval."

Nick peered at her blankly for a moment before dropping his gaze. "I told you I was wrong about that, Lace. Whatever you want to do with your inheritance is your business; I won't put up any barriers in your way."

Taking a deep breath, she decided to go one step further, to find out precisely where she now stood with him. "You mean, if I want to leave Gallagher House, move out on my own, you won't try and stop me?"

"I don't have that right." His face was averted from hers, but she noted the stiffness in his shoulders. "Do you want to leave?" It came out in a tight whisper.

Swallowing back her unnameable joy, she answered, "No."

Relaxing again, Nick turned to her, smiling. "Good! 'Cause I don't want you to leave. I think we ought to spend some time getting to know each other."

It was what she wanted to hear, and she smiled at him in return.

Chapter Six

CHRISTMAS EVE DAWNED BRIGHT AND PLEASANTLY warm. Everyone in the house was busy, seeing to all the last-minute chores that could no longer be postponed. There were gifts to be delivered, baking to be done; and some presents still had to be picked up in town, brought home, wrapped and placed under the big tree in the drawing room.

Hattiebelle was in her kitchen, waving flour-covered hands at her two young helpers, who had been hired to work for the holiday. They weren't polishing the silver to suit her; they hadn't ironed the ivory damask tablecloth and napkins wrinkle-free; and there were still a million and one spots on the crystal. She was being extremely exacting with the girls when Nick peeked in to tell her he wouldn't be home for lunch. He winced as her usually cheerful voice rang out an octave higher when she reprimanded the older of the two helpers, and with a shiver, he quickly ducked out the back door, not wanting to be a recipient of her wrath. He'd already felt the sting of her tongue plenty of times since his return.

He took the flagstone path through the now-barren rose garden to the stable yard and found William on his knees, inside the carriage, polishing the brass lamps there. "Have you seen Lacey this morning?" he asked, getting William's attention.

"She saddled Lady up an hour ago and said somethin' about takin' a basket of goodies out to an old lady she knows."

Pulling on his riding gloves, Nick frowned. "What old lady? She never said nothin' to me 'bout knowin' any old folks."

"Oh, her and Miss Rachel used to go see Miz Sloane quite a bit." William backed out of the carriage and stood on the gravel beside Nick, wiping his hands on the soft rag he'd been using. "Course, she ain't seen much of her since you two . . ." He stopped, giving Nick a slightly embarrassed grin. ". . . er, uh, since y'all made up, that is. The old lady lives alone, out on the old coach road between here and Mr. Buckner's home for orphans."

Feeling uneasy under William's disconcerting gaze, Nick cleared his throat and asked, "Did she say when she'd be back? I got a surprise in town I gotta pick up for her. Don't want to bring it home unwrapped if she's around."

William shrugged. "Naw, she didn't give me no time as when to 'spect her back. She's been comin' and goin' on her own for a long time now."

Knowing that she could come back at any moment, Nick decided to get moving. He saddled his horse, Major, then mounted up and rode out, his mind on the pretty bauble he'd bought for Lacey. Once out the front gate, he turned toward town, cantering Major at a steady pace until he reached the bottom of the hill. He would have headed toward the creek bridge then, if he hadn't spied the small, saddleless, chestnut mare, grazing beneath the huge pecan trees in the opposite direction. His curiosity aroused, he pulled at the reins and headed toward her instead.

Drawing closer, he saw the mare's reins dangling on the ground beneath her hooves. She shied nervously from Major, sidestepping away from the stallion and trodding on one of her reins so that it pulled painfully at her mouthbit.

It was Lady! Nick knew that no other chestnut in the area had her particular white blaze and four white stockings. He dismounted and captured the reins, looking over Lady carefully until he noticed the nasty scratch that marred her underbelly. How had that happened? And where the hell was Lacey? He glanced up the road, but could see no sign of her.

Growing concerned, he remounted Major and returned to the house with Lady in tow, riding into the stableyard at a clipped pace.

William glanced up at his entrance, startled. "Hey! That's Lady, ain't it? Where's Lacey?"

"She must've been thrown off somewhere along the road. I'm goin' out to look for her. If I'm not back in an hour, telephone Jake Goldstein and have him get out here on the double."

William nodded and took Lady's reins from Nick. "You want me to come with you?"

"No!" Nick barked, turning away. But he stopped and looked back at William. "On second thought, go ahead and telephone Jake now. Don't wait!" Jake ought to know right away what had happened.

The old stagecoach road curved and swerved,

bypassing clumps of stark, leafless trees as it wound past the wide meadow adjacent to the Gallagher property. After a few miles it finally settled down to a nice, straight stretch of road. Nick forced himself to take it at a slow, steady pace, his gaze frantically searching for some sign of Lacey. But the only thing he could see in the ditches were tall, dried weeds.

Riding on, his fears increased by the minute. Just as he reached a dairy farm and was about to turn in and ask if anyone there had seen her, he saw a bright patch of green, partially concealed in the tall yellow weeds. He wasn't sure how extensive Lacey's wardrobe was, but he had a hunch that it included a bright green riding habit.

Sure enough, urging Major closer to the far side of the road, he saw that his hunch had been correct. Lying at the bottom of the ditch, looking peaceful and innocent, was Lacey. Her jaunty green riding hat was askew, covering half of her pretty face. Her divided skirt rode high up one leg, giving him an enticing view of her high-button-boot-covered ankle.

Nick was off Major and down the slick embankment in one easy move. He knelt beside Lacey and watched her chest move up and down with steady regularity. Sitting back on his heels, he let out a shaky sigh of relief. Thank God, she wasn't dead! He hated to think how empty his life would be if she had been.

But he didn't have time for morbid notions now. He wasn't a doctor, but he had to find out if she was seriously hurt. As he carefully straightened her bent legs, he felt them and her arms to make sure that she had no broken bones. Then he gingerly put his hand beneath her averted head and lifted it, removing her hat and a few of the pins that secured her copper-gold coil to the crown of her head.

No telltale bumps protruded from the back of her skull. But as her head turned toward him, he grimaced at the sight of the nasty bruise marring her temple. It was swollen, but not bleeding. Her eyelids fluttered and Nick thought he heard a soft moan come from deep in her throat. Her chest expanded as she inhaled deeply, then settled down again to its former tempo.

"Lacey?" he called. "Lacey, can you hear me? It's Nick."

Her lids twitched. A tiny frown appeared for a second between her wide-spaced, sooty-lashed eyes.

"Lacey, my love? Come on, wake up!" His fingers gently struck her pale cheeks, hoping the contact would stimulate her senses.

Her lashes fluttered and her dark, emerald eyes gazed up at him in glassy confusion. "Nick?" she queried weakly.

"Yeah. No! Don't pass out on me again! Goddammit, keep those eyes open!" Her passing out this way worried him to death. And not knowing what else to do, he slapped her cheeks with more firmness than he had the first time.

"Don't hurt me, Nick," she whispered on a sigh.

Nick groaned and enfolded her in his arms. His heart was slowly breaking in two, as his contorted expression revealed. "I'll never hurt you again, my love," he promised in an aching whisper.

"Love you," she sighed before drifting into unconsciousness.

Nick sat there in the ditch, holding her close, as a

jumble of previously unknown emotions flooded his soul. She loved him! But did she mean it? It was hard to tell, when someone had been knocked on the head. Sometimes they just babbled, saying the first things that came into their minds.

After a long while, he realized he had to get help. He picked her up and cradled her lovingly in his arms, brushing his rough cheek against her softer one. Clumsily he ascended the slick embankment and started across the road to the dairy with Major tagging along behind.

Lacey drifted in and out of consciousness, not knowing for certain if she was dreaming of the past or experiencing the present. One moment she felt the warmth and security of strong, protective arms, and the next she was at her seventh birthday. Her mother, young and beautiful, was telling her that they were going to leave their old house and move to a bigger one. Then Max, big and friendly, was holding her in his arms and hugging her.

"You gonna be my daddy?" she asked him and felt his deep rumble of laughter.

"If your momma'll let me. I always wanted a little girl like you, sugar. I got two, roughneck boys who could sure use a sweet little sister to tone 'em down a notch."

Two faces appeared; one pale, topped with shaggy blond hair, and the other chocolate brown. Her new brothers? But behind them appeared another face. He was older and didn't look as friendly as the two younger ones.

Her mind became fuzzy. She was no longer seven. Max no longer held her. She was lying in a strange bed, in an unfamiliar room, and worried-looking faces frowned down at her. She couldn't understand what they were saying. Everything sounded so muffled through the roaring in her ears.

Her lids drooped and she was back in the other time again, at school. Little girls' voices giggled behind her. They whispered ugly things about her and Rachel. She turned and started to tell them to shut up, but a teacher suddenly came from out of nowhere and told her that little ladies didn't raise their voices in anger. And Rachel agreed with the teacher.

"She knows what's best, honey," her mother said, smoothing down her vibrant red hair with one hand as the other nervously fingered the pearls at her ivory throat. "You shouldn't pay attention to what those silly girls say. They're just bein' spiteful. A lady puts up with all kinds of gossip, but if she's worth her salt, she'll act like nothin's been said and keep her mouth shut."

"But Momma! They called you a name . . . a *bad* name!"

"I don't care, precious. I know what I am, and *who* I am. That's all that matters to me. What they say about me can't hurt me."

Rachel's beautiful image faded. Voices called her name and asked her questions. Through a haze, she saw Jake Goldstein talking to Nick in a disapproving manner. Then William's kind, brotherly face hovered over her and he clicked his tongue with concern.

The questions and the people disappeared. Lacey found herself in City Park with Chris while a band played lovely music nearby. Sun glinted off his golden blond hair and love shone in his pale blue eyes. Then his smile vanished and he was earnestly telling her how much he loved her and how badly he wanted her for his wife.

She was standing in the long reception line in the ballroom of the Grand-Windsor Hotel. Her long white dress and veil trailed behind her as an endless line of faces appeared and disappeared in a never-ending succession. The false smiles the women wore and the almost leering looks the men gave her were most prevalent in her mind.

"You should've said something about it!" Chris began to accuse as he paced up and down the carpet in their bedroom, a cigar in his mouth puffing out billows of smoke through his clenched teeth. He looked worried, angry, uncomfortable and more than a little embarrassed.

"How was I to know?" she asked, adjusting the bedcovers over her upraised knees as her wobbly chin rested on them. She sniffled back the tears that wouldn't stop spilling. "I've never done this before . . . with anybody! How *could* I know?"

"You gotta do something! *Soon!* I've waited a long time for this night, Lacey. I wanted it to be extra special, not the disaster it's been. I've even stayed away from Lyla's and Cora's for the past month just so I could be ready for you."

Nick's face became transposed over Chris's, and he sneered at her and called her vile names. "You're a damn cold, greedy woman, Red." Then his sneer changed to an expression filled with desire. "You're magic for me, Lace. Magic!"

Lacey's head ached and her body felt bruised and sore. She twitched convulsively to relieve some of the tiredness in her muscles. Slowly, blessedly, all the unpleasant memories and dreams faded away and, hearing a slight sound, she opened her eyes to find herself in her bed, at home.

"Blessed be!" Hattiebelle cried out joyously. "You're awake! That knock you got on your head must've been a doozie."

With a groan, Lacey pushed the covers aside, wanting to get out of bed. It was the most uncomfortable place she'd ever been in and she couldn't understand how she got here. "I've got a basket of things to take to Mrs. Sloane."

Hattiebell refused to let her get up. "Where you think you're goin'? It's freezin' cold outside, girl."

She stared in confusion at the stern-looking black woman. "But it can't be. The sun was shining when I got up this morning, and it was warm when I saddled Lady." Then, noting her clean, ivory nightgown, she frowned. "How did I get here?"

Clucking like a big, brown hen, Hattiebelle fussed around her, straightening her covers. "You been out for almost two days, Lacey honey."

"Out?"

"You . . . er, uh, you fell off your horse and hit your head. You don't recollect fallin'?" At the negative motion of Lacey's head, Hattiebelle added, "Well, Nick and that nice Mr. Goldstein brought you back home here long 'bout midafternoon, Christmas Eve. *Ooooeee!* Nick was in a state you would not believe! Had the doctor a runnin' around here like you was the queen of England, or somethin'. And you—well, you looked like death warmed over, sugar. Your pretty little face didn't have a drop o' color to it, an' I thought there for a while you was a goner for sure! The doctor, though, he said

119

somethin' 'bout a con-cussion—I believe that's what he called it. Told us to leave you be and let you sleep it off, that your head would have to heal itself 'cause he couldn't. You oughta be thankful you didn't break your fool neck, fallin' off that horse, missy! How come you fell off anyway?"

Lacey rubbed her temple, a slight throbbing beginning there. "I don't' remember. Did Mrs. Sloane get her basket of food?"

"I 'spect so. Willie couldn't find no sign of the basket, so you must've been comin' home when you took that nasty spill."

"I've been sleeping for two days?" It was inconceivable to her that she'd lost that much time.

"That's right."

"I missed Christmas, didn't I?"

"You didn't miss nothin'." Hattiebelle chuckled. "We been savin' it for you. Nick said all them packages under the tree would wait for you even if you was out a month. Nothin's been touched, not even my pies."

The housekeeper started to leave the room, but at the door she looked back just as Lacey closed her eyes and covered her face with her forearm. "You feel like eatin'? Won't take me no time to fix somethin' and stick it in the dumbwaiter."

The thought of food revolted Lacey. "No, thank you, but I would like a glass of water."

The door closed silently behind Hattiebelle and Lacey turned over, resting on her side for a change. She had been unconscious for two days! How was that possible?

The last thing she could remember was laughing.

Yes! laughing at something Mrs. Sloane had said. "I must've been on my way home," she whispered into her pillow, frowning as she tried to recall what had happened next.

She'd been laughing, cantering Lady down the road, just enjoying life and the day in general. She remembered she'd heard something—a wagon?—coming up behind her. She turned to look over her shoulder as she moved to the side of the road so the conveyance could pass her. It had been going faster, as if it was in a hurry, then it had caught up with her and . . . what? What had happened after that? But she couldn't remember; her mind was a total blank.

"It must've hit me and driven on," she mused quietly.

"What hit you?" a deep voice asked from her doorway.

Turning, Lacey tried to focus on the blurred image. "Nick?"

"I brought you a drink of water," he said, sitting beside her on the bed. "Can you sit up?"

After adjusting her pillows so that she could sit upright, he held the crystal goblet to her lips. "Not too much now," he warned. "You haven't had anything in you for a while and it might upset your stomach. That bump on your head won't help you, either."

The liquid inside her dry mouth was a welcomed relief, but the spinning of her head caused her to feel dizzy and she fell back weakly on her pillows, looking into Nick's rugged, unhandsome face. "It's made my eyesight fuzzy," she confessed. "The knot on my head, I mean."

"You were saying somethin' when I came in," he remarked evenly, setting the glass on her nightstand. "Something about it hitting you. What was *it?*"

"I don't know. A wagon, I think. But I'm not really sure. I can't remember the last thing that happened." She tried to tell Nick what had gone through her befuddled mind moments earlier, but it wasn't easy.

Nick sat there beside her, though, patiently nodding as if he understood what she was saying.

"Oh, I know I'm not making much sense," she frowned. "I mean, how could a whole wagon hit me and nothing but my head get hurt? Wouldn't the rest of my body be injured too?"

"Who can say?" He shrugged. "Don't let it worry you. You're gonna be all right now, and I'll make damn sure you're never out alone again."

"Lady!" she gasped suddenly. "Is she all right?"

Nick grinned lopsidedly. "She's fine. Fact is, she came home without you. I found her down by the creek and brought her up myself." Not for anything would he tell her about the deep scratch on Lady's side. He still couldn't figure out how the little mare had gotten that. There were no low-hanging branches along the road, so if no tree had caused the gash, that left only one alternative: Somebody must have used a knife to cut the saddle loose after Lacey had been knocked off Lady's back.

"Hattiebelle said you held up Christmas on my account." Lacey's voice intruded on his musing. "Why did you do that?"

Nick's face softened. Finding her hand, he held it tightly in his. "Because Christmas is for families, and you're all the family I got. If I couldn't share it

122

with you, Lace . . . well, I just thought it'd be better to wait so you could enjoy it with me."

She could see in his eyes that he was leaving something unsaid. But what? His hatred, indifference and disgust, she could detect in a moment, as well as his look of desire; though for some time now, she hadn't seen that look on his face. He'd said they were going to be careful, and indeed they had been, for he hadn't touched her since their first and only encounter. But this new expression he wore was by far stranger than all the others. It was most vulnerable.

"I'd like to go downstairs tonight," she requested politely.

"Nope. Doc said you should have a week of bed rest and—"

"That's nonsense! I feel all right. I'll sit on the sofa and won't move about. I'll be just fine. Really, I will!"

Nick tried to talk her out of it, but she won. When she started to change for dinner, he insisted on helping her rather than ring for Hattiebelle, who was busy in the kitchen. He helped her out of her plain ivory nightgown, suppressing a groan as her lovely contours were revealed, and barely succeeded in checking his urges while she pulled on her fancier gown of peach silk, trimmed in beige lace. But when she went to her dressing table to brush out her long, tangled copper-gold hair, he took the brush from her curiously weak fingers and brushed it himself, enjoying the silky texture that slipped through his hand. From the top of her head, he gently pulled the brush down, watching the lamplight play on the many different colors in each strand. Pale, silvery hairs glimmered like newly minted coins, and honey-blond hairs glowed with a healthy, coppery sheen, while the vibrant red locks highlighted both the silver and gold, making up Lacey's unusual strawberry blond shade. He'd never done this before; played lady's maid. He was amazed at how sensual and provocative such a simple chore could be.

Finished at last, he placed the brush on the dressing table and lifted her carefully in his arms, treating her with the care he would bestow on a piece of fragile porcelain, just as he'd done the night they made love. This time, however, he behaved the gentleman and carried her toward the door, rather than her bed. She was in no condition to be seduced, but feeling her under him certainly would ease a lot of his frustrations, frustrations he'd hoped never to feel again.

"I thought we'd have dinner in the dining room before we opened our presents," he remarked, descending the stairs. "If you're up to it, that is."

Her head nodded against his shoulder. "You don't have to carry me, you know. I can walk."

"But why walk when I can carry you? Anyway, I like it better this way. You know, for a big girl, you're as light as a feather."

"I'm not big, Nick. I'm tall. There's a difference."

"Big . . . tall . . . it's all the same to me. I never thought I'd . . ." His sentence left incomplete, he reddened beneath his leathery skin. She wouldn't want to know that he used to prefer small, petite women. Lord, she wouldn't want to hear that at all! "We're almost the same height, you know, when you wear those high-heeled shoes. It's a little different for me, bein' able to look you straight in the eye."

Smiling, she countered, "You'd rather I went barefoot, so you could feel superior?"

"Not just bare feet, bare everything." He grinned, arriving at the bottom of the stairs.

"That would be very impractical at this time of year."

"Dangerous, too! With your body, Lace, running around bare-as . . . uh, naked would definitely affect my sanity." What little he had left, that is. He placed her on the settee and pulled a soft, woolen blanket over her. "You'd find yourself swollen with a baby in no time."

A strange and quite wondrous sensation swept over her. Warmth flowed through her veins at the thought of Nick's child growing inside her. "Would that be so terrible?"

His dark eyes flew to hers and he frowned at the warmth in her emerald gaze. "You tryin' to tell me somethin'?"

She blinked until her eyes became cool chips of green. Her head remained motionless for a moment, then it slowly moved, negatively. "I simply asked a question, Nick. I wasn't making any embarrassing announcement." Her voice was heavy with disappointment. "I like children. I hope to have a couple one of these days. Don't you like children?"

His mumbled reply was slightly vague. "They're all right, I guess." He moved across the room and poked the fire in the grate until it began to blaze. When he turned around again, he replied, "Liking kids ain't enough, Lace. You gotta want 'em before you have 'em. Hell, maybe I don't have what it takes, 'cause I don't think I'm ready to become a daddy just yet."

"How do you know? Have you ever been a father?" As trite as her question was, once it was phrased, she knew what the answer would be. With the kind of life he'd led, it was quite probable that any number of his offspring were wandering about.

Nick sat down beside her, resting his elbows on his knees as he studied the turkey red carpet beneath his booted feet. "There was a girl in Canada," he began hesitantly. "It was about four or five years back. She kept house for me while I fur-trapped with my partner. I wasn't in love with her, or anything like that, but I liked her." He paused, took a labored breath, then admitted, "She died, having a baby . . . *my* baby, I think."

Lacey's heart ached for him. She could sense the remorse he felt and knew he'd been hurt by the tragedy.

"The trouble is," he continued, "I didn't mind it when the kid didn't live; the baby, I mean. I was a little sad, of course, 'cause a child had died, but that's all I felt. I didn't mourn it 'cause it could've been mine. Maybe if I had loved Giselle, or maybe if the kid had been a boy, I might have felt different—I don't know.

"That's one of the reasons I haven't slept with you lately. I'm afraid you'll get pregnant. I couldn't stand it if that happened, Lacey. A whore—a prostitute," he amended carefully, "knows how to take precautions. She knows who to go to if her precautions don't work. But I don't guess a properly brought-up young lady like yourself ever got *that* kind of training in school . . . did you?"

"No. Cooking, sewing, household management

and deportment were on my school's curriculum," she replied. "Not birth control." It was very hard for her to accept being denied by him. They'd had only one night and one morning. He had opened a door for her, allowed her to experience a world of fantastic pleasure, then he'd closed the door in her face before she'd had her fill.

"See there?" he nodded, wisely leaving *I told you so* unsaid, then stood and started to walk away.

Lacey quickly countered, "Don't you *ever* want children? You're thirty years old, Nick. You're not getting any younger. Wouldn't you like to have a son to carry on after you're gone?"

"I ain't all that interested in immortality, Lace," he declared evenly. "I'm here through no fault of mine and that's the way it is. If I have a child, I'll have it because *I* want it, not because I need it to continue the great Gallagher line. I wouldn't want to shackle a kid with that kind of responsibility. God knows, I don't need an heir for my kingdom." His sarcastic quip was issued dryly. "My father had me when he didn't need me, and he had Chris because he had no choice—Lillian wanted him. Oh, he loved us—in his own way, but he would've been just as happy if we'd never been born. Children and little babies are for women, Lace, not for men."

By the time dinner was over, Lacey was thoroughly exhausted.

"I don't understand it," she muttered weakly against Nick's chest as he carried her up to her room. "How can I be so tired? I've only been out of bed a couple of hours."

"Now that you've got something solid in your belly, you'll get to feeling better. All that bouncing around you did the other day made you weak."

"But I wanted us to have Christmas together," she complained as he entered her bedroom.

"We can have it tomorrow night."

By putting her to bed and tucking her in, he wordlessly told her she would be sleeping alone again. But she didn't want him to leave her; she wanted to feel his presence for a while longer. "It's only four more days until the New Century Cotillion," she reminded him. "I need to get my ballgown from Mrs. Beale."

"You're in no condition to do any celebratin', Lace. We oughta just forget about goin' out New Year's Eve."

"But I'll never get to welcome in a new century again," she protested adamantly. "If I have to be carried down to the Oriental Hotel in an ambulance wagon, I'm going! And if *you* won't pick up my ballgown for me, I'll telephone Mrs. Beale *and* Jake and work out something between them!"

Nick was amused at her determination. "All right," he grinned. "If that's what you want, I'll go get the damn dress for you tomorrow. Ain't no need to get Jake involved."

"It's the strangest thing," she frowned. "While I was unconscious, or semiconscious, I thought I saw Jake with you. And there was another man, too . . . I think."

Nick felt decidedly uncomfortable. "Uh, Jake did come out to the dairy with William after I found you. He was worried just like the rest of us." Sensibly, he didn't inform her that the other man had been Jake's friend—a Pinkerton's detective. "Do you remember anything else?"

"No, not a lot. I had the craziest dreams though, all about the past—my childhood and all that, you know—and then the present would interfere with it and I would almost wake up. But Jake really was out there at the dairy with you?"

"Oh, yeah. He was there all right!" Nick could still hear the anger in Jake's voice as he chewed him out for allowing Lacey to leave the house alone, when they both suspected the danger she might possibly encounter.

"And did you ask me questions? I distinctly remember someone asking me a lot of questions."

"Look, Red, if I were you, I'd forget all about it. It's over and done with now. Remembering it ain't gonna change nothing."

Hearing him call her Red, she knew he was beginning to grow vexed. And as proof, he began to walk toward her door.

"Nick!" she called out, wanting to stop him.

"No, Lace. No more questions tonight. You gotta get some rest. We'll talk in the morning."

Lacey found herself staring at the back of her door, then heard Nick's footsteps loping easily down the stairs. It became very quiet for a moment until the sound of carriage wheels crunched in the gravel drive below her window.

Had Nick been expecting visitors? she wondered, starting to get out of bed. Was that why he'd left her so abruptly? But she stopped and lay down again when Nick's voice called out to Hattiebelle just before the front door opened and closed.

"He's probably going to Frogtown," she mumbled

sadly, a twinge of pain tearing at her heart. Prostitutes knew how to take the right precautions, while she didn't. For the first time in her life, she wished she was less respectable than she really was. Maybe then Nick would have stayed home . . . with her.

It was the last conscious thought she had before she turned over and fell into a deep, dreamless sleep.

Chapter Seven

THOUSANDS OF TINY STARS GLITTERED AGAINST LA-cey's ivory, swanlike throat. The magnificent diamond choker necklace covered the bare expanse of her bosom in scalloped tiers, made up in an open grillwork of gold and diamonds, with the largest pear-shaped stone hanging directly in the cleft of her small, firm breasts.

It was Nick's Christmas present to her, and it was the most fabulous thing she'd ever seen.

"Lillian Russell would be envious of you, babe," he said softly, coming up behind her as she gazed, mesmerized, into her mirror. His hands fell onto her pale shoulders as he bent down to plant a kiss on her nape, sending shivers up her spine when his lips made contact with her cool skin. "Jim Brady would be bowled over by the size of that rock."

It was Nick's mention of the famous lady, who was reported to be Diamond Jim Brady's mistress, that caused Lacey's unexpected wave of nausea. She knew she shouldn't let it bother her; after all, she had chosen her present position willingly. Guarding her expression, she stated, "It's quite beautiful, Nick. But I couldn't possibly wear it tonight." Everyone who looked at her would surely come to the conclusion that she was his mistress.

"Why not?" he countered. "They go with your dress, don't they? Your mother's pearls wouldn't look nearly as nice as the diamonds do."

She turned toward him on her tiny, velvet boudoir chair, her eyes downcast. "Nick, they'll know I'm . . . they'll know *we*—"

"I don't give a damn!" Lifting her chin with one finger, he kissed her sweet lips. "I don't give two hoots in hell what the matrons and founding fathers of Dallas think, Lace. It's none of their damn business what you and I are. Anyway, I wouldn't be a bit surprised if the old biddies get jealous of you. They'll be stunned speechless for the first couple of hours, then when they finally do get their tongues, their husbands'll have been so taken with you, they'll make sure the old crows keep their traps shut. If they were giving out prizes for the most beautiful woman tonight, you'd win hands down."

Dressed in black, Nick was pretty dashing himself, she thought. His unruly dark hair had been tamed somewhat, and his moustache had been trimmed. Down the front of his white silk shirt were rows of ruffles and in the center of his silk tie was a gold-and-diamond stickpin, her Christmas present to him. His black satin vest, worn beneath his Edwardian-cut coat, was embroidered in silver and gold. And the tangy aroma of bay rum that exuded from his swarthy skin caused the blood to race just that much faster in her veins.

"They'd be awfully hard-up not to qualify you for

the most handsome man . . . darling." She blushed and lowered her eyes, but not before she saw the smile that tilted one corner of his full, well-chiseled lips. It was the first time she'd called him that endearment, and it embarrassed her.

"Does this have a coat to go with it?" he asked, assisting her to her feet.

Her peach satin gown fell in a straight line to her white-kid slippered feet and on to a flowing train behind her. The simple cut was eye-catching, to say the least. "Yes, I'll get it before we leave," she replied, steadying herself against the dressing table as her ankle wobbled precariously.

"Listen, are you sure you feel up to this?"

"Yes! If I have to sit like a wallflower all evening, I will. But I intend to drink champagne at the stroke of midnight."

"We could have champagne here," he grumbled, running a finger inside his stiff, celluloid collar. "But I suppose it wouldn't be the same, would it?"

She shook her head. "This is an occasion to share with others, Nick. Why, even Hattiebelle and William are going out. Their church is having a midnight service to welcome in the new century."

"Well, I suppose if his momma's around to keep an eye on him, William ought to be sober enough to drive us home afterwards, but—"

"William's not like that!" she burst out.

"William *is* like that. But, like I started to say, I bet he don't make it to church. Hattiebelle will, but William won't. I heard that there's a big shindig down in Deep Ellum tonight. It ought to be livelier than the ball at the Oriental. Sure wish I could go with William."

Ignoring his teasing banter, Lacey pulled her peach satin, fur-lined cape out of the armoire and gave her form-fitting, opera-length kid gloves a final tug. Her only other adornments, besides the impressive necklace, were a pair of modest diamond earrings and two small plumes artfully entwined in her complicated coiffure.

She gave Nick a shy smile when he reached the bedroom door, but had to laugh when he bowed dramatically and allowed her to exit first. He seemed to be in a rare good mood tonight. She hoped he remained in one, too!

From the street, the Oriental Hotel looked much like any other building. Simple, unpatterned brickwork and unadorned windows graced the hotel from the second floor to the sixth, while the first floor gave way to the usual number of windows and entrances that every hotel required. Its only oriental feature, perched atop the corner of its flat roof, was a squatty, Arabian dome. The building as a whole was singularly unimpressive from the outside. Inside, though, was an altogether different story. What Mr. Thomas Field, the original planner of the Oriental, had begun, Mr. Adolphus Busch and Mr. Otto Herold had completed, making the hotel one of the most luxurious west of the Mississippi.

Imported Italian marble covered the floors and made up the graceful pillars which supported the ceiling. Mahogany woodwork gleamed warmly beneath the handsome electric light fixtures, which illuminated the paneled walls and expansive front desk. And that same warm wood, carved into slender newel posts, curved upward in an elegant banister along the sweeping staircase from the lobby to the mezzanine balcony, where many of the guests now stood just outside the grand ballroom.

At one end of the wide balcony, the cagelike electric elevator whirred to a halt and its gilt-painted iron gate was pushed aside. The very formidable Mrs. Everett Lange, matriarch of Dallas's high society and the principal planner of this evening's gala, stepped out. Aiding her stately progress was a silver-headed cane in one hand and her grandson's arm in the other. She was an imposing woman in her late sixties who bore a headful of iron gray hair, tonight bedecked with ostrich plumes. Her well-endowed figure had been tightly constricted in a corset, then stuffed into a gown of plum velvet designed especially for tonight's event. Around the fleshy folds of her throat were the pearls her husband, Everett the first, had bought her on their first trip to Europe twenty years earlier.

Being somewhat farsighted, she had to draw back her head and strain through narrowed lids to see those persons nearest her. She did this now with the young man at her side. Everett the third, she had to admit, was nothing like his grandfather, her late husband. Come to think of it, the boy wasn't even a good facsimile of his daddy, her son. Fact was, he was about the biggest dimwit she'd ever met. He took after his mother's side of the family, not his daddy's.

"Mrs. Lange!"

Henrietta turned to see the gangly hotel manager advancing storklike toward her, his long-fingered hands outstretched in welcome. Taking her gloved hand in his, he bent over and kissed it in a foppish,

European manner, one that she'd always hated. The way she figured it, if a man was going to kiss a woman, there were plenty of other places more suitable than the knuckles of your hand. After all, wasn't that why God made mouths?

"Good evenin', Hallwood." She calmly withdrew her fingers from his. "Have all my instructions been followed?"

"To the letter, Mrs. Lange, to the letter!" His thin cheeks wrinkled as he grinned, and his prominent Adam's apple bobbled effusively above his collar. "We have the champagne icing down right this moment so that by midnight it should be chilled to perfection. And the buffet, if I may say so, is superb! Emil, our chef, has outdone himself tonight. He has driven his minions mercilessly all day, and they've produced a fare that is fit for a king! It's all arranged on tables in the anteroom, adjacent to the ball-room."

"And the orchestra?" she inquired, dragging her eyes away from his undulating throat.

"They're ready and waiting for your permission to begin, madam. The program our conductor has chosen for tonight is extremely appropriate, I think. A great number of waltzes, of course, with just enough polkas thrown in for your livelier guests, and I think there's even a two-step or two for spice."

Henrietta nodded. Of course, the twit didn't know that these Texans would be doing more than waltzing and two-stepping. Get enough liquor down them and there was no telling what they'd end up doing.

In the reception line, Henrietta greeted the three hundred or so guests with a cool smile and conde-scending nod. It gave her an enormous amount of pleasure to see some of the snobbier women stutter and quake as they drew near her. It didn't matter how important they thought they were, they weren't anybody until she invited them to her house for tea—the supreme endorsement into Dallas society!

Henrietta noticed Nick and Lacey near the end of the line, waiting to greet her, smiling at one another and seemingly immune to the presence of others around them. Henrietta's old gray eyes widened as she took in the elegant grace Lacey possessed before she turned to whisper in her grandson's ear. "Now, there's the girl for you, my boy. Nothin' namby-pamby about her."

"Which one, Grandmother?" Everett inquired boredly.

"The redhead, standing next to young Gallagher."

Everett looked down the line, then back at his esteemed grandparent with a skeptical gleam in his eye. "She's not exactly the most respectable girl in town, Grandmother. Haven't you heard the tales that've been told about her?"

Henrietta postponed answering him until she'd greeted another couple, but as soon as they had passed, she replied, "Probably a lot of malicious lies."

"I think not, Grandmother. Her young husband, you'll recall—"

"Was an idiot," she interjected bluntly. "Take a good look at the girl, Everett. Would you forsake a beauty like her for some Boggy Bayou trollop?"

"It was Frogtown, I believe, Grandmother," he corrected gently.

"Frogtown . . . Boggy Bayou . . . what's the difference?" she scoffed with a wave of her hand. "The fact remains: That girl is something special and her idiot of a husband left her for a woman as common as dirt. If you'll use your head, boy, you'll not dismiss her so lightly. And for what *my* opinion is worth, I wouldn't mind having a girl like her for a granddaughter-in-law."

Everett glanced down the line at the couple and noted the look of intimacy between them. Lacey's face was bathed in a glow of happiness, while Nick's stern, unhandsome features were etched with proprietary self-assurance. They were practically oblivious to the others around them.

"Lacey, my child," Henrietta gushed loudly, kissing the young woman's soft cheeks. "How are you?"

A hush seemed to fall over the entire room as many heads turned to stare at them. Lacey managed to keep her voice relatively calm and her head high as she answered, "I—I'm quite well, Mrs. Lange." She certainly hadn't expected this! Perhaps a cool, indifferently polite greeting, but never one *this* friendly.

"Oh, I *do* so like your gown, my child," Henrietta gushed on. "The color is magnificent on you. I never did go in for all that mourning-black nonsense myself. Such a stupid tradition; started by some man, most likely. If one is young and full of life like you, one shouldn't be forced into a life of seclusion and drudgery just for the sole purpose of convention. And speaking of convention—are you on any of my charity committees for the upcoming year?"

"Uh . . . no! No, I'm not, Mrs. Lange," Lacey replied, flustered and breathless.

"Then we must rectify that as soon as possible. You must plan to have lunch with me soon so we can talk about it. A pretty girl like you could get us ten times our usual donations." Her smile fading slightly, Henrietta turned and acknowledged Nick. "You're Max's boy, aren't you?"

"Yes, ma'am!" Nick's crooked grin appeared as he took the old woman's gloved hand. What an old faker she was. Hard as cast-iron on the outside, but soft as melted butter on the inside. There wasn't a damn thing formidable about the old sweetheart from where he stood.

"Quite a man, your daddy was. My husband Everett, rest his soul, was very impressed with Max when he first came to Dallas forty years ago. Nothin' but a youngster he was then, but he had the promise of becomin' somethin'. Everett always said he had the intestinal fortitude of a leader, that he didn't mind takin' a chance if he thought the gamble would pay off. Tell me, are you anything like him, boy?"

Nick lowered his head, his grin broadening. "Well, ma'am, I like to think I am."

Henrietta glanced sidelong at her bored grandson, then shook her iron gray head with disappointment. "Yes, well, *thinkin'* in itself never accomplished a whole lot. *Actin'*, though—"

"Uh . . ." Nick tactfully interrupted, sensing her mood, "I think we'd best be moving on, Mrs. Lange. We're holding up the line."

"You come see me soon, you hear?" Henrietta reminded Lacey. "You won't forget?"

"Oh, *no,* Mrs. Lange. I won't!"

Heads turned and people stared as they made their way to the far end of the ballroom. He was tall and rugged, while she was willowy and stunning; yet they were unaware of their well-matched appeal.

Many males, uncomfortable at having been forced to attend tonight's function with their socially conscious wives, stared in open admiration of Lacey's graceful beauty, while the women, still shocked at Mrs. Lange's affectionate reception of Lacey, looked on with quiet caution.

"I told you we'd make heads turn, didn't I?" Nick whispered.

Heat burned Lacey's cheeks. "I wish they'd just ignore us."

"I don't think that's likely to happen," he chuckled. "You've caused quite a stir, Red."

"I didn't intend to! If I'd known *this* would happen—"

Nick placed one hand on her waist and twirled her onto the dance floor, abruptly cutting off Lacey's statement. She barely had time to pick up her trailing gown's hem with her left hand and place her right one in his palm before her slippered feet began gliding in unison with his across the polished boards in time to the music.

It was a thoroughly enchanting evening for Lacey. She smiled and laughed more than she'd ever done in her nineteen years, openly flirting with Nick whenever it was possible. She enjoyed watching his face darken and his beakish nostrils flare when she phrased a well-aimed pun that only he could understand. It gave her an immense feeling of power, seeing him embarrassed and slightly aroused and not able to do anything about it. She was behaving shamelessly and she knew it, but it was wonderful!

For the most part, she spent the evening partnered with other young men, and occasionally an older gentleman or two. Once or twice, she caught sight of

Nick and suspected that he wasn't pleased she chose to dance with other men, but until he said something to put a stop to it, she wouldn't turn down the other men's civil requests to dance. As far as everyone else in the great room was concerned, she and Nick were only in-laws, and she hoped to preserve that lie as long as possible.

Deciding to give his feet a rest, Nick wandered into the anteroom and surveyed the inviting array of food that graced the long buffet table. Someone must have planned on feeding half the city, he thought with a chuckle, making his way down to the end where he found plates and forks. He served himself from the hot and cold delicacies, filling his plate, then made his way to a smaller table where the massive punch bowl was placed. He ladled himself a cup of the fruity brew and added a dash of liquor to it from the silver flask hidden inside his breast pocket.

Cup and plate in hand, he sauntered back to the archway and looked into the ballroom just as Lacey twirled by in the arms of some young boy. She was smiling at him—not the kind of half-lidded, sensual smile she'd given Nick all evening, and that seemed to ease the jealousy gnawing within him somewhat.

Taking a bite of his thick sandwich, he thought how strange it was that he'd never felt jealous before . . . not even when he'd been so besotted with Jane Stratton. His feelings for Lacey were altogether different from those he'd had for Jane; they made him awfully vulnerable in some respects.

He watched her twirl by again, this time nodding to her when she smiled and waved to him.

"I hope they don't plan on feeding us again at

midnight, but I've heard that black-eyed peas and cornbread are supposed to be on the menu then."

Nick jerked around to blink stupidly at his lawyer friend, who was now taking the same route up the food-laden table as he'd followed earlier. "How'd you get in here?"

Jake chuckled, heaping his plate high. "I walked right past you and even said hello, but you were so busy keeping an eye on that pretty girl in there, you didn't hear a word I said."

"Pretty girl?" Nick frowned. "Oh! That's just Lacey," he mumbled and took a deep swig of his punch.

"'Just Lacey'?" Jake's brows arched. "With the looks you've been giving her, 'just' is a little ambiguous, don't you think?"

Nick reddened sheepishly. "I don't know what you're talkin' about."

A moment passed as Jake examined his friend's expression. "Have you told her yet that—"

"Hell, no!" Too late, Nick realized his voice had been a shade louder than he'd intended, and he looked around to see if anyone else had heard. "Just drop it, will you? God knows what would happen if we were overheard."

Jake dropped the serving fork he'd been holding with a clatter. "I'm a little disappointed in you, old buddy. I thought, surely, a man as worldly as you wouldn't be afraid of anything . . . especially a woman."

"You don't understand, Jake. It goes a helluva lot farther than me just being afraid. It's the first time I've ever had the responsibility of another person besides myself."

"Yes, well, Lacey's involved and she has a right to know what's going on. You've *got* to tell her about Christmas Eve."

"I can't do that."

Taking in Nick's tight-lipped expression, Jake said clearly, "Then send her away!"

Nick's rigidity seemed to crumble. "I can't do that either."

"Use your head, man! She might get into a fix that neither one of us can get her out of. Look what happened when she just went out for a ride. She almost ended up a damn corpse! We don't know what Stratton's going to do next, so send her away until this thing blows over."

"Oh, hell, Jake! You don't understand," Nick rasped, jerking his silver flask out and filling his cup.

"I understand better than you think. But loving her and not letting her know what's going on is the most cowardly thing a man could do."

Nick issued a mirthless chuckle, unoffended at his friend's gentle rebuke. "I can't let her know how I feel—I'm afraid to! After the way I've treated her, I can't just up and tell her that I love her. Hell, the notion's unbelievable even to me!"

Jake could only nod in sympathetic agreement.

"You ever been in love, Jake? Aw, I don't mean horny for some woman, but really, deep-down in love. Have you ever wanted a woman so bad your whole damn body ached just to be near her? Then, when you finally do get close to her, close enough to smell the scent of her skin and hair, you feel like a tongue-tied idiot? Have you ever felt that way?"

Looking just beyond Nick's broad shoulders into the crowded ballroom, Jake experienced a painful ache as he spied someone across the room. "Oh, yes! I've been in that hell for a while now," he whispered solemnly.

"If things were different," Nick went on, not having heard his friend's declaration, "if Chris hadn't died so short a time ago and if the situation wasn't as bad as it is now . . . maybe she could accept me. But I'm not stupid enough to think that I can barge right in on the grieving she must be doing for my brother."

"You've barged in already," Jake pointed out, dragging his attention back to Nick. "I mean, Lacey didn't get that lovely glow just because you're no longer angry with her."

Nick shifted uneasily. "You're too damned observant, Jake. Hell, if I didn't know better, I'd swear you could read minds."

"It doesn't take a mindreader to see what's plainly written on your face and hers each time you're together. Don't let Chris stand in your way. Oh, yes, I know; he was your brother, Lacey's husband, a likeable boy and an all-around good egg, but all the procrastinating and all the mourning in the world won't bring him back."

"Won't bring who back?" came a bright little voice behind them.

Nick jerked around, a smile instantly finding its way to his face as he spied the petite brunette waving a frilly fan before her flushed face. "You still listenin' at keyholes, Darcy? I'd have thought you'd be cured of that habit by now."

She dimpled prettily and giggled, her hazel eyes twinkling. "I've never listened at keyholes in my life, Nicholas Gallagher, and you're a cad for even implying it. Mr. Goldstein, you don't believe this old bully, do you? Do I, in your honest opinion, look like the kind of girl who'd stoop to listening to others' conversations?"

"You wouldn't have to stoop," Nick inserted glibly, eyeing her. "Your ear's already at keyhole level."

Darcy's smiling mouth opened in mock indignation and she swatted at Nick playfully with her folded fan. "You *are* a cad, you silly fool! Mr. Goldstein, don't listen to a word he says. It's nothing but lies."

Laughing at their friendly playfulness, Jake sobered long enough to say, "I wouldn't dream of it, Miss Patterson. You are, far and away, the most honest-looking woman in this assemblage tonight . . . and one of the loveliest, if I may be allowed to add."

"Oh!" she glowed, coming to stand beside him. "You have my permission, yes! Now, you see, Nicholas? This is a true gentleman. He doesn't resort to accusing a girl of indecent things, or give the wrong impression of her to others."

But Nick wasn't listening. He was watching Lacey across the room with Peter Thorne. Sensing, however, that he should say something, he mumbled, "I've done you an unpardonable disservice, Darcy. But then, I've done that a lot lately. Excuse me, will you?" Then he turned through the archway and was gone.

Lacey was looking up at Peter, shaking her head with laughter. He'd just repeated some harmless bit of gossip to her about an eccentric person he'd met on his trip to Austin, just the thing to put her at ease.

He was, she decided, a thoroughly entertaining man.

"Of course," he continued dryly, *"you* wouldn't have had that problem if you were to pose for me."

"I should hope not!" she retorted lightly.

It was then that Nick joined them. Aware of her mood, Peter noticed how her smile softened as she turned to look at Nick. And he caught the belligerent glint in Nick's eye.

"How are you, Thorne?"

"Very well, thank you," Peter commented. "I was just telling Lacey that my offer to paint her portrait still stands. She would make an outstanding study, especially with those magnificent diamonds."

Lacey's hand flew to her throat. "Peter, to tell you the truth—"

"I think it's a good idea," Nick interrupted her. "I'd like to see a portrait of Lacey in my house."

My house, he'd said; not *our* house. A cold ache pierced her heart, causing her smile to fade.

"That's wonderful!" Peter beamed. "It will have to be in the next four months, I'm afraid. I'm preparing to go to New York, and perhaps Europe, in June or July, and I want all of my commitments to be out of the way before I leave."

"If you're too busy . . ." Lacey hedged, wanting to forget about the whole idea. She didn't like the thought of sitting for a painting anyway; it sounded like the epitome of conceit to her.

"Not too busy for you, my dear," Peter assured her. "And the idea you had of using bluebonnets as a background grows more intriguing by the hour. Perhaps by the time they're in full flower, I'll have cleared up my schedule and can devote the proper amount of time to you."

The orchestra cut off any retort Lacey might have made. Nick captured her hand in his, saying, "We'll be seeing you, Thorne," before he whisked her out onto the floor.

Later she would blame her sudden dizziness on the rapidness of the polka, but as she bounced and twirled in Nick's arms, an ache began to throb cruelly in her temple. Before she could say anything to Nick, her cheeks drained of all their color and giddiness overtook her. She tripped over the hem of her gown and almost fell to the floor, but Nick's quick foresightedness didn't allow that to happen. He pulled her into a secluded window alcove where a cool evening breeze was blowing in.

"What happened?" He frowned in concern.

"My head," she whispered, holding her temples with her fingers. "All that spinning around made me dizzy."

"Damn it! Look, stand here for a minute; I'll be right back with some chairs."

Leaning against a pillar, Lacey gulped in the cold drafts of air. Why did this have to happen, and now of all times? There had been moments in the last few days when she'd come very close to fainting. A sudden dizziness would assail her and the room would start to spin wildly. But she'd been at home then, and whenever it had happened, she'd sat down and rested until the giddiness subsided. Nick hadn't known about those spells, but now that he did, he would probably want to end their evening. Well, it had been fun while it lasted.

He came hurrying back to her, carrying two fragile chairs. "Here," he growled, shoving one behind her skirts. "Sit on this and hold your head between your knees."

Lacey had to laugh. The idea of her holding her head between her knees made a very comical picture indeed. "I'm not going to faint, Nick," she said, sobering. "I'm just not as strong as I thought."

"Well," he began, noting the color already returning to her cheeks, "I think I'll send for William anyway, so we can get you home."

"No!" she protested. "It's only a couple of hours to midnight. I won't leave here until I've tasted champagne and sung in the new century with a chorus of 'Auld Lange Syne.'"

Nick placed the other chair beside her and dropped into it, swearing beneath his breath. "You're the stubbornest one woman I've ever known."

"Not stubborn, Nick—determined! And as long as *I* think I feel all right, I see no reason why we should leave."

His scowl was long and tight-lipped, but he reluctantly accepted her decision. "All right, dammit! We'll stay . . . against my better judgment. But we stay right *here* for the rest of the night, and no more dancing!"

Through her thick, sooty lashes, she gazed at him innocently. "Not even at midnight?"

"Well . . . maybe. I'll have to think about it."

So they sat there, secluded in the cool alcove, watching the stiff-shirted, somber, pious businessmen of Dallas shed their traces of sophisticated respectability to become a rowdy, vulgar bunch as coarse and down-to-earth as their redneck forefathers, who'd founded this great state, had been. Ties were discarded. Celluloid collars and starched shirt fronts were dispensed with. Coats were tossed aside and shirt sleeves were rolled up.

The crowning moment came when Mr. Herbert Murdock—deacon of the First Baptist Church, president of the Dallas Merchants' Association and husband of the acid-tongued Norma—took over the orchestra. He and his band of untrained musicians, who were also well intoxicated, thrust gold coins into the regular musicians' hands, pushed them from the orchestra platform and laid claim to the well-loved instruments.

All hell literally broke loose as the crowd's true, somewhat primitive natures surfaced. There was a lot of foot stomping, handclapping and a great deal of whooping and hollering as the drunken group broke down and began enjoying the kind of music they most preferred. Banjo strings twanged, violins were sawed as fiddles, and somebody even produced a harmonica.

Mr. Hallwood, the hotel manager, rushed up to Henrietta Lange, a worried frown marring his face. "What's going on here?"

"Don't worry." The elderly matron smiled indulgently, patting Hallwood's hollow cheeks. "They're simply startin' to have a good time. You'd best have your cleanin' people stand by, though, in case the floor gets slippery. Wouldn't want anyone breakin' a neck while they're doin' a jig."

Mr. Hallwood looked utterly flabbergasted at Henrietta, who sat quite happily in her chair, smiling as her foot tapped in time to the music.

"Well, go on, boy!" she ordered him with a wave of her hand. "Let 'em have their fun! Lord knows, they deserve it."

The tempo of the evening increased as the hour grew late. Precisely at the stroke of midnight, though, a sudden hush fell over the crowd. Someone began singing the old Scottish ballad, "Auld Lange Syne," in a voice that was loud and considerably off key.

Hidden by the potted palms in their alcove, Nick took Lacey in his arms and kissed her. As if his hands had suddenly developed a mind of their own, they moved from her tiny waist, sliding upward to capture her firm breast. But holding her and caressing her wasn't good enough for him. In an aching whisper, he growled against her long, pale neck, "Lace, I want to make love to you! Tonight . . . now!"

Breathless from his highly infectious passion, she gazed up at him, drowsy-eyed. "Yes, oh yes!"

"I know a back way out of here," he replied, helping her to her feet. "We'll get a cab and not even bother waitin' for William."

"My cape," she protested as they made their way through the singing crowd.

"You won't need it." He smiled. "I'll keep you warm."

They went through the anteroom and out a door that connected it to the downstairs kitchen, then took a side hall to the rear delivery entrance. Nick hailed a passing horsedrawn cab and gave the driver instructions and some money before he jumped in inside with Lacey.

Holding her chilled and shivering body against his, Nick's arms warmed her as they traveled silently through the deserted city streets on their homeward journey. His mouth nuzzled her temple, then her cheek, then finally moved to the sweet hollow behind her ears. She relaxed in his arms as his mouth descended further to place tiny, emboldened kisses on her throat and pale, exposed bosom. But her many layers of clothes, separating her beautiful body from his touch, caused him more frustration than pleasure.

The trip seemed interminable. Nick had to yell out to the driver on more than one occasion to hurry it up. "I should've taken a room at the hotel," he growled hoarsely when he felt her lips nibble his jaw. "My God, Lace! What are you doing?"

"I love the taste of your skin," she purred. Her small tongue flicked out and traced the cavity of his ear.

"Mmm! If you don't stop that, I won't be responsible for my actions."

"Nick, I've wanted you *so* badly." This painful admission was muttered as she moved her head to rest it against the breadth of his warm chest, inhaling sharply as his cool hand slipped inside the neck of her gown to caress and fondle her hardened nipple. "I don't want to sleep alone tonight . . . or ever!"

His fingers captured her chin and he tilted it so that he could look down into her lovely face. "You realize what you're sayin'?"

"Yes! I know exactly what I'm saying." She was being brazen, but she was past the point of caring. In the end, she might regret her decision, but right now she didn't give a damn. These past weeks—when he hadn't come to her, when she knew he was seeing other women—her heart had ached with a pain she'd never experienced before. Even knowing of Chris's defection hadn't been as painful as knowing of Nick's.

"I want to be your mistress . . . your *only* mistress," she stressed, pulling his head down to hers. "Tell me the precautions to take, and I'll take them. I'll do anything, Nick, if you'll just love me as I love you."

"Babe, I *do* love you," he muttered before grinding his mouth against hers.

The cab finally reached the house. Nick tossed the driver a generous tip and wished him a happy New Year as Lacey quickly preceded him into the house. Following her, he slammed the door behind him and threw home the bolt, then took the stairs two at a time until he reached the top.

He was already loosening his tie and shedding his coat as he entered her room. Locking her door, he saw, to his relief, that she was undressing as quickly as he was. She really meant what she'd said in the cab—she wanted to be his mistress, and he was damned well going to let her, precautions or no precautions.

In a matter of moments, she stood before him unashamedly nude. Her only covering now was the diamond necklace that encircled her creamy throat.

"Now, you undress me," he growled huskily.

"Nick, I—"

"It's part of being my mistress, babe."

She stepped toward him hesitantly to slowly unfasten the studs in his shirt. She pushed the ruffled garment off his arms, then moved on to his trousers. Her fingers worked the buttons free from their holes at his fly, accidentally brushing his hard erection. Kneeling before him, she pulled his trousers down over his lean hips and muscular thighs, discovering much to her surprise that he wasn't wearing drawers. The sight of his swollen manhood almost took her breath away.

When he stepped out of the confining pants, she tossed them across the room, uncaring where they landed. Her fingers shyly touched the stiff, wiry hairs on his thighs, her nails raking nearer and nearer his aroused staff, tracing patterns on the inside of his taut flesh.

Nick inhaled raggedly as her soft fingers gently closed over him. His eyelids fluttered and closed as she worked her special magic on him, but they flew open quickly again when he felt her lips touch him. Looking down the length of his body, he saw the top of her head, shining like a newly polished copper bowl, resting against his loins. Her fingers and mouth did incredibly delicious things to him, sending electric sensations throughout his entire body.

Unable to stand her unique tormenting any longer, he hauled her up in a weightless effort and carried her to their bed, laying her down as carefully as a fragile doll. Her breasts, swollen and hard, brushed against his furry chest when he pulled her against him. Beckoned by their insistent prodding, his head descended and he captured one of the coral peaks in his questing mouth. He tasted the point, teased and excited it before tasting, teasing and exciting its mate. Then his lips moved down, over her stomach, and planted a kiss on her inner thighs. His hands smoothed down the silkiness of her back to cup the rounded flesh of her buttocks, then his tongue took possession of her pleasure kernel, hidden in her nest of curls.

Lacey ground her hips against his head, gasping with a pleasure she'd never known before. She cried out as tiny sparks began to shoot through her.

Nick moved then, finding her mouth with his as he twisted and turned them until she was on top and he beneath. Their lips clinging, he held her hips and manipulated her until she was impaled her onto his hot, upright staff. A throaty laugh erupted from his broad chest at her sudden gasp, and he buried his tongue inside her mouth, thrusting it with a fierceness that was equaled only by his thrusting hips.

Like the melding of two ores, their fusion was hot and molten. In a matter of seconds, she stiffened and cried out, feeling the shattering explosion of her climax. Her head fell weakly to his shoulder.

"Nick, I—" she began, but stopped when she felt him within her, still as hard as he'd been before. "Nick?"

"You want to be my mistress," he rasped. "And you will be. This is all part of the post. Enjoy it, my love. Enjoy it!"

Without hesitation, he thrust into her again, creating anew the throbbing spirals. Her head rolled from side to side as she whimpered, telling him without words that she was on her way to that special pinnacle again.

This time, though, she did not make the trip

alone. He thrust once, twice, three times into her, and with the fourth and final thrust, shot them both to the summit of ecstasy. Even he could not contain the cry that escaped from him as his own inner world of pleasure exploded.

"Lacey! God, I love you!"

Chapter Eight

Nick's lids opened slowly. Grimacing at the dim light in the room, he wondered what had awakened him. A quick glance over Lacey's long, bare back, then up at the narrow slit in the drapes, told him that dawn had broken some time ago. It was still too early, though, for him to be awake on his own, and he was certain it wasn't because he needed to relieve his lust. Hell, after what Lacey had put him through last night, he wouldn't have that problem again for a long while.

She'd been damn near insatiable. He'd loved her fully once, then she'd fallen asleep. Just about to drop off himself, she'd reawakened and got him going again. They stayed at it through half the night, alternately making love and napping, until they were both drained and exhausted.

Reaching out, he smoothed down the fiery curls that tumbled across her lovely face. He shook his head unbelievingly and wondered how anyone who looked so angelic asleep could be such a wildcat when awake. Hard as it was for him to comprehend, she was! He'd never known a woman to behave with such natural abandon before, and he'd been with quite a few in his time.

After last night, though, there wouldn't be any other women for him; no one but his Lace. And he would be damned if he'd deny himself the pleasure her sweet body afforded him. Having discovered her hidden passions, he knew he couldn't. She was like a drug, an opiate that had to be taken regularly now, even though she was as dangerous as that other, lethal kind.

The telephone rang downstairs and Nick knew that it had been the culprit that had rudely wrenched him from his cozy cocoon. Groaning, he gently disengaged his arm from beneath Lacey's slight weight, hoping not to awaken her. He was going to come back to bed as soon as he'd answered that stupid contraption, and he was going to take up with her where they'd left off last night.

Getting out of bed, he shivered involuntarily when the chill in the room assaulted his bare, sleep-warmed skin. Then, with all the grace of an ungainly stork, he hopped down the hall to his room, where he found his dressing robe on the back of his door.

The phone gave another, persistent ring and he quickly tied the robe's sash before racing down the stairs to the rear hallway where the phone box was hung.

"*Yeah?*" he barked into the mouthpiece on the wall, jamming the cone-line receiver against his ear. Damned contraptions! he cursed, hearing the loud sputter and crackle over the line. Why had this thing ever been invented anyway? Face-to-face conversations were better than bodiless voices.

Hearing something muffled come through his earpiece, he raised his voice and shouted, "Look, you gotta speak up! I can't hear a damn thing you're saying."

"I'm sorry," said the suddenly clear voice on the other end. "There's some confusion here."

"Jake? What the hell do you want this time of the mornin'?"

The pause that followed his query caused Nick to wonder if he'd lost the connection again. But Jake's voice finally came through again, sounding reluctant and worried. "Uh, Nick, I'm at Mercy Hospital. There's been another accident."

"Accident! Who?"

"Your housekeeper, Mrs. Turner, and her son," Jake explained.

"What the hell . . . !"

"Nick, watch your language. There's a profanity rule with the telephone company."

"I don't give a damn . . . *durn* about any rule. What about Hattiebelle?"

"They were both found in your carriage this morning, just before daybreak. They were at the bottom of the hill, near the bridge where you went off a couple of weeks ago."

A weakness invaded Nick's legs, and he leaned, trembling, against the wall. "Go on. Tell me the rest of it."

"William's all right," Jake assured him. "He got hit on the head and was out for a while, and he's a little bruised and shook up. Other than that, he'll be okay."

"And Hattiebelle? How's she?"

Jake didn't answer immediately, and during the long, silent pause, Nick felt his heart sink to the level of his bare feet. His eyes closed as a painful knot formed in his throat. She was dead. God help them all, that dear old lady was dead!

"Uh, it's a little hard to say, Nick. All I know is, she isn't good," came Jake's admission at last.

Allowing his hopes to soar, Nick asked, "Just how bad is she?"

"To be honest, I think you'd better get down here and look the situation over for yourself. The doctor I spoke to doesn't expect her to last the day, but I'm unwilling to accept his diagnosis. Anyway, William needs somebody, and since you—"

"I'll be there as soon as I can throw some clothes on."

"Nick?" Jake called out before he could hang up.

"Yeah?"

"What are you going to tell Lacey?"

"Oh, shit!" he groaned. For a moment, he'd forgotten about her.

"You have to tell her something . . . the truth, I hope."

"I'll bring her with me," was all Nick could promise. Now wasn't the time to go into all that again. "She's close to Hattiebelle; I know she'll want to be there with her."

"Nick, you've got to do something. This situation can't be allowed to go on much longer."

"Look, we'll talk about it when I get there!" he bit out before jamming the receiver back onto the hook.

Nick and Lacey hurried through the cold, dark, narrow halls of Mercy Hospital. An uncomfortable atmosphere of death and decay hovered over the place and they both sensed it.

Turning a corner, they left the newer section of the hospital and entered the older part now allocated for the blacks, Mexicans and poor whites. They spied Jake—and William, who looked very shaken and tired and worried.

"Where is she?" Lacey asked, wringing her hands.

"In there." William indicated with a cock of his bandaged head toward the doors in the wall. "That's the women's ward. No! You can't go in right now; the doc's in with her."

"What have they done to her?" Nick asked both men, leading Lacey to a bench that ran the length of one wall.

"That's why I told you to hurry down here," Jake mumbled tersely. "They haven't done a helluva lot, and even *that* was done under duress." He shook his head and tried unsuccessfully to rub the tiredness from his eyes. His lack of sleep was evident in the lines about his face. "I threatened them with a murder charge if they didn't look after her."

"A what?" Nick all but shouted, his anger mounting.

"That's all beside the point now," Jake declared with an impatient frown. "They've looked at her and seem to think there's some internal damage. She's lost an awful lot of blood and she's still unconscious. But anymore than that, they can't tell for sure." He gave a brittle laugh, then confessed, "At first, when the sheriff came and rousted me out of bed and told me that somebody had been run off the road near your place, I thought it was the two of you."

"That's ridiculous!" Lacey scoffed. "Who'd want to hurt Nick or me?"

The look Jake shot Nick mirrored his disappointment. But Nick returned it instantly with a narrow-lipped warning glare. Just then the doors of the women's ward opened and a middle-aged man sauntered out, looking slovenly in his soiled smock as he wiped his hands on a filthy, stained towel.

Nick's stomach churned as the man's foul odor wafted across his beaklike nostrils. He didn't try to repress the look of disgust on his face as he curtly asked, "Are you the doctor attending Hattiebelle Turner?"

"Yeah," the man responded. "You Nick Gallagher? Her boss?"

Nick's nod affirmed that he was. "How is she?"

The doctor's shoulders lifted in an uncaring shrug as he tossed the towel to the floor. "She ain't gonna make it. You might want to go ahead and line yourself up another maid to do her work and let 'em know out at the nigger cemetery that they'll be plantin' another one pretty soon."

William's bruised and battered frame stiffened. Sensing the young man's outrage, Jake quickly pulled him to one side, behind the doctor's line of vision, to stop him from creating trouble when they didn't need it.

But it was Nick that Jake should have worried about. A muscle twitched angrily in his jaw and his swarthy face darkened with suppressed rage. "Has another doctor looked at Mrs. Turner," he grated, "or are you the only one?"

A deep, disgusting kind of laugh erupted from the doctor's chest. "I done told you, Gallagher, that old nigger ain't gonna see the light of day again. Why should we bother, wastin' all our time on her when we know she ain't gonna make it? Hell, man, we gotta use all our chloroform on the patients that need it most."

One moment the doctor was chuckling, and the next he was staring up at Nick's tall form from floor level. His soiled fingers grabbed his throbbing jaw and he tasted the blood that seeped into his mouth from his split lip.

"That . . . 'old nigger' . . . as you put it," Nick growled, "happens to be a sweet, dearly loved, *lady!* Now you get your slimy ass back in that room and tell your nurses to treat her with care, because I'm bringing in the best surgeon Dallas has got. Then I'm gonna go find your superior and demand your dismissal. I'm gonna make it so rough on you, you son of a bitch, you'll never be able to even *look* at another sick person, much less doctor one."

With that, Nick turned angrily and slammed down the hall toward the chief of staff's office, dragging William along and with Jake following in close pursuit.

Lacey eyed the horizontally prone doctor with undisguised disgust before she turned and entered the ward. Being near the man made her flesh crawl.

If the rest of the hospital had been bad, the women's ward was considerably worse, she decided the moment she stepped inside the swinging doors. Her nose wrinkled at the horrible odor of neglected patients. It was apparent to her that the bedpans hadn't been changed in some time . . . if, indeed, they'd been used at all. As she passed one bed, she was shocked to see that one body, now quite dead, was still in the room with the other women. The staff obviously hadn't thought the corpse important enough to move to the morgue.

At the end of the long row of rusting metal beds, Lacey found Hattiebelle. Separated from the others by a tattered and dirty folding screen, the housekeeper was blessedly unaware of her horrible surroundings. She was unconscious.

She looked awful, lying there so still, Lacey thought. The sound of her breathing was much louder due to the echo in the corner where she lay. Her bandages, which were wrapped around her slow-moving chest, were almost clean; a very minor concession when Lacey remembered how long she'd been here.

Without bothering to look for a chair, Lacey was content to stand quietly beside the bed. Gazing down into the still, composed face, she lifted one of Hattiebelle's hands, instantly feeling the clamminess of the work-calloused palm. This hand, as well as its mate, had given Lacey so much comfort, so many, many times in the past. It had held her with love, maternally so; it had scolded her with gentle patience when necessary; it had taught her things that Rachel, her mother, could not. There was a special bond linking her to Hattiebelle, a bond that transcended meager blood ties.

Tears of anxiety fell down her pale cheeks as Lacey leaned over and kissed Hattiebelle's fevered brow. "We won't let you die," she whispered. "We love you too much to let that happen."

For an unmeasured length of time, she stood there, holding her beloved friend's hand and praying in earnest silence. It was only when Nick burst into the ward, followed by two burly orderlies and another man, that she finally relinquished her hold.

With a few monosyllabic grunts, the orderlies

lifted Hattiebelle onto a stretcher and carried her out of the ward. Lacey, at Nick's side, followed, as did the other man.

"This is not advisable, Mr. Gallagher," the other man said nervously.

"If I want her to live, it damn sure is!" Nick growled. "She'd die in this hellhole and nobody'd ever know it!" He shot a pointed look at the sheet-covered body as they passed it.

"We give our patients the *best* of care!" the other man declared.

"That's a lot of bullshit, Stinson, and you know it! Try and convince that stiff there that she got the best of care. Oh, hell, I ain't got time to argue with you." He pushed Lacey ahead of him, through the doors and down the hall.

Passing through the front entrance, moments later, Nick assisted Lacey down the steps and across the gravel drive to the waiting horse-drawn ambulance. He looked around, through the layers of fog that shrouded the view, and gave his head a quick shake, trying to dislodge the horror of the place they'd just left.

"Do you want to ride with her?" he asked finally.

Lacey blinked back the tears threatening to spill again. "No, William should go with her. He's her son, after all. Do you know where they're taking her?"

"St. Paul's, where she should've gone in the first place! Jake's cousin is a surgeon there. He's gone on ahead now to make sure everything's ready for Hattiebelle when she gets there. These bastards would've let her die without lifting a finger. And they call this a house of mercy—God damn them!"

Nick helped Lacey onto Lady before he mounted Major. He'd never been much for praying—he'd never had anything important to pray for—until now! But while he and Lacey rode to St. Paul's Hospital, and while they waited throughout the long, arduous operation that followed, he and God carried on a long, one-sided conversation.

It was toward the end of April before Hattiebelle finally came home. Her injuries had been extensive, but Jake's cousin had coped and had brought her through the long surgery with no complications. Just as she was getting better, though, a virus swept through the hospital, killing quite a number of the more seriously ill patients. It rendered the still-weak Hattiebelle totally helpless and she developed double pneumonia. But with love, prayer and modern medical technology, she finally pulled through the ordeal and lived.

The last three weeks had been spent in peaceful recuperation at St. Paul's . . . for Hattiebelle; not for the doctors. She had pestered them daily to send her home, where she swore she would rest and not lift a finger until they had given her the go-ahead. Not knowing what else to do, and being tired of her insistent badgering, the doctors relented and let her have her way.

It was evident to Hattiebelle that Nick and Lacey's fragile relationship was strained. She lay in her bed, watching Lacey put away the last of her things in her bureau drawers and closet. Nothing had been said, but she could tell something was wrong.

"Is he bein' mean to you again, baby?" Hattiebelle asked.

165

Lacey darted a quick, embarrassed look in the black woman's direction, feeling a blush slowly stain her cheeks. "It all depends on what you mean by 'mean.'"

"You gotta understand, honey, that boy is stubborn! His head's as thick as granite rock."

"Oh, I understand *that* all right. Better than you think."

Hattiebelle peered at Lacey through narrow, probing eyes, then gave her head a shake, clicking her tongue reprovingly. "Mmm-*mmm!* You done got it bad, ain't you?"

"I don't know what you're talking about." Lacey moved away to examine and rearrange a vase of flowers that graced a tabletop across the room. They'd been cut by Manuel that morning, then brought in and arranged just before Hattiebelle's arrival.

Watching the girl's nervous movement, Hattiebelle laughed at her obvious evasiveness. "You two! You're more alike than you admit to bein'. He said just about the same thing to me."

"Oh, you mean he denied being love-struck?" she countered, turning. "Well, you can take it from me, he isn't!"

"How can you tell? You're too close to see what's so plain to everybody else."

"You're wrong. If Nick Gallagher feels anything for me at all, it's pure and simple lust." Lacey's admission mirrored the pain in her heart. "God knows, I've no room to talk. I feel the same for him, because I can't help myself when I'm near him. *Me*, Hattiebelle; me, who always wanted to be the most respectable woman in Dallas. I act like . . . like some gutter bitch in heat if he so much as looks at me tenderly. You know that we've been lovers since last December, don't you?"

Hattiebelle nodded her head slowly. "I found the stains on the bathroom rug the mornin' after it happened, baby. I felt like takin' a razor strop to that boy when I saw 'im, but I didn't. Wouldn't have done any good."

Tears of self-pity welled up in Lacey's green eyes. She flew across the room and into Hattiebelle's outstretched arms. "Why does he do it to me?" she sobbed. "I know we're no good for each other, but I lose all control when I'm near him."

Smoothing down the errant strands of copper-gold hair, the housekeeper crooned, "Baby girl, that's somethin' only you can answer. Just be thankful you ain't got caught yet."

"Caught?" Lifting her head, Lacey wiped the tears from her cheeks with the backs of her fingers. "Oh, you mean pregnant. Well, I don't have to worry about that; Nick takes care of that chore."

"Hhumph! That boy might get himself some gumption if you *did* get with child."

"He does it for my benefit," Lacey defended feebly. "He . . . he doesn't want children."

"He told you that?"

Lacey nodded.

"And you? Don't you want babies?"

"No. I mean, yes! Oh, I don't know, Hattiebelle. I do and I don't. But there's little chance of that happening as long as I stay with Nick."

"Don't think that!" Hattiebelle warned. "There sure *is* a way of it happenin'. Them little pieces of rubber ain't no surefire guarantee. Now don't go lookin' at me that way. I ain't so old that I don't know what's goin' on these days. Lawdy mercy, they been a usin' them things for ages; ain't nothin' new! But if you really don't want to get caught with a baby in your belly, you'd best tell that randy young buck to walk a chalk line from now on."

Lacey issued a bitter laugh. "If I could, I would, but he doesn't listen to me. He's hardly been home these past few weeks."

"Where's he been?"

Lacey frowned and painfully admitted, "Cora Noble's, I think."

Nick hadn't said anything to her, but then he hadn't had to. She knew the "scent" his paid paramour wore as well as she knew her own. It clung to his clothes almost constantly of late.

Hattiebelle was outraged at the notion. "Why, if I was you . . . and Nick was *my* man, I'd load me up a shotgun so fast it'd make his head swim . . . that is, if he *had* a head by the time I was through with him!"

"That's just it—he isn't my man. He never has been. Nick belongs to no one but himself."

However, at that precise moment, Nick was far from feeling the master of his own destiny. From the looks of things, if Jake had his way, Nick wouldn't be his own master for quite a while, either.

"I mean it," Jake stressed. "If Lacey doesn't get away from here *soon*, she's going to get hurt! They've tried once to get to you through her . . . I wouldn't put it past them to try again."

Slumped in his chair, Nick groaned in defeat. Dammit! He didn't like being trapped in this kind of situation. But Jake did have a point—and a very valid one at that. People had a nasty habit of lashing out when they were backed into a corner, and Stratton was very close to that point now.

"Ain't it a little drastic, though? Making her leave town, I mean."

"For God's sake, Nick, the woman's not stupid! Lacey's got a brain in that beautiful head of hers. Once she's gone and has a chance to analyze the situation, she'll see that you did the right thing in making her leave."

The plan, as Nick knew it, was to get Lacey out of town for an indefinite period of time until she was no longer in danger. But knowing her as he did, she might refuse to go away if he told her the outright truth. Women didn't think the same way men did, unfortunately, so he was going to have to come up with a good, believable lie to get her to leave. God alone knew what that lie would be . . . because he sure didn't.

"I don't know, Jake," he mumbled at last. "She can be awfully stubborn at times."

"Then your only other choice is to explain the situation to her. Tell her you've been going to Cora's and meeting with Sally to get information from her."

"I think she already knows I've been going to Cora's," he admitted grudgingly. He'd seen her nose wrinkle up when he'd come home directly from the brothel. But she hadn't said anything to him, and until she did . . .

"Do you want to risk putting the final decision in her hands?" Jake challenged. "Because we both know she'll want to stay here with you if you do that. She can't be put into that kind of position, Nick. It's not fair . . . and it sure as hell isn't safe!"

For the umpteenth time since he and Jake had started this thing, Nick wondered if he could be blatantly dishonest with the woman he loved. And even if she did suspect he was up to something with another woman, *he* knew in his heart that he hadn't been. He hadn't been intimate with another woman since Lacey had entered his life last winter.

He peered up at Jake and saw the patient, expectant look his friend wore, and he knew that it was all his responsibility now. If he refused to go along with Jake's idea, they might possibly lose Stratton and Crawford. It all boiled down to one thing: choosing between Lacey, and Stratton and Crawford. If he chose Lacey, how many more victims would fall into the hands of those heinous villains?

"All right." He sighed heavily at last. "I'll get her out of town."

Jake nodded, looking relieved. "I suggest sometime next week."

"So soon?"

"The sooner, the better, Nick. She's almost through sitting for that picture Peter Thorne's painting of her, isn't she?"

Nick laughed bitterly and rubbed the back of his neck. "Yeah, she's almost finished. I never dreamed when I asked that dandy to paint her that the picture would be all I'd have left of her."

"You're not going to be without her forever," Jake stressed.

But Nick wasn't so sure. A doubt niggled in the back of his mind. But, he told himself, he'd been plagued with doubts before and had come out all right, so maybe Jake was right.

"While it's on my mind, you might want to give

Sally some money; just in case *she* needs to make a quick getaway," Jake proposed.

Nick agreed with that. Sally had truly been a godsend. She had been their fragile connection into the seedy, less-than-respectable world where Stratton and Crawford often wandered. In the past months, since Hattiebelle's accident, Sally had given them tips and clues that had allowed them to compile the information concerning the nefarious duo's dealings.

"What do you want to bet she won't take it?" Nick speculated, rising to his feet. "Sally does have her own brand of pride, you know. She just might throw the money back in my face."

"You can only try, old buddy. Five thousand dollars ought to be a tidy enough sum for her to get started on again, don't you think?"

Nick buttoned the last button on his coat and nodded. "If she does accept it, it'll be five thousand she's earned! You know something? She hasn't ever asked me for payment for all that she's done."

"I may add five thousand of my own to yours," Jake remarked with a decisive shake of his blond head. "With a girl like Sally, she might want to get a fresh start in another town *before* this thing comes to a head."

"But won't we be needing her testimony at the trial?"

"No, a sworn and witnessed deposition should be sufficient. I can just imagine the furor she would raise by presenting her evidence before a jury. Stratton and Crawford could ruin her credibility with little effort at all. It'll be much safer for all of us if Sally leaves town, too."

"It may take me a day or two to get the cash together," Nick said, ambling toward the door, "but I *will* get it to her before the week is out."

"And Lacey?" Jake asked cautiously.

Nick sighed heavily. "She'll be gone by the beginning of next week . . . I swear it!"

Chapter Nine

THE MORNING WAS TRULY MAGNIFICENT. FLEECY WHITE clouds floated high above in an indescribable cerulean-shaded sky. Trees and shrubs were bursting forth with new life, and Lacey vowed that the roses had never been more fragrant or as lovely as they were now. Sitting, as she was, in Henrietta Lange's phaeton and passing the stately homes in the older woman's neighborhood, she had a bird's-eye view of the world around her.

Henrietta smiled at Lacey with grandmotherly indulgence. "When I was your age, my dear, I didn't have to worry about the sun affecting my complexion, either. Now look at it. I've got more wrinkles than a snapping turtle."

Tilting her green parasol, Lacey tried to shield her face from the warm rays of the bright sun, but Henrietta scoffed, "Oh, don't worry about it, honey," and patted Lacey's gloved hand. "You've got a ways to go before you have to worry about wrinkles."

"Mrs. Lange," Lacey began, "I do want to thank

you for asking me to join your charity committee. I'm just so sorry I won't be here for the picnic you've planned."

"How long are you going to be gone?"

"Nick . . . uh, I mean, my brother-in-law didn't say, but I gather that the business meeting in Beaumont is important enough for both of us to travel there. It has something to do with leasing the land we own jointly."

"It all came about rather suddenly, didn't it?"

"Suddenly for me, yes, but evidently not for my brother-in-law," she responded with a bewildered lift of her shoulders. "Apparently, it's been on his mind for quite some time to go to Beaumont. He just never bothered to mention it to me. Our lawyer, Jacob Goldstein, advised us to see to the matter personally." At least, that's what Nick had told her. Strange that he should suddenly think it urgent now, when he'd known about it for some time.

"Well." Henrietta sighed, interrupting Lacey's musings. "I'm just sorry you won't be here for the picnic. We're still planning the hospital benefit out at the fairgrounds. Nothing draws the men in this town like our annual horse race. They all think their own nag is the best of the lot, but that's all right because they tend to open their wallets a little wider, and *that* is what we're really interested in. If we want that new surgical wing built, we're going to have to get the money from someplace. And, from what I've been told and overheard, we're going to have some pretty spirited stock at the race this year."

Horse racing had never interested Lacey, but she smiled and nodded as Henrietta went on to explain about her own horse that she was hoping to enter.

The open phaeton was leaving the exclusive residential area of Dallas and was entering the district where all the shops and offices were located. Lacey had only one errand this morning, to pick up her diamond necklace from the jeweler's shop. The clasp had been loose the night Nick gave it to her, and she thought it wise to have it tightened before packing it with the rest of her things. Why Nick thought she would need so many clothes for such a short trip, she didn't know, but she'd followed his instructions and had two trunks brought up from the basement and had started packing just this morning. From the looks of her room when she'd left it, this short trip of theirs was going to be longer than Nick had led her to believe.

Lacey smoothed out an invisible wrinkle in her pale green skirt as the phaeton made its way around a corner. The carriage tilted precariously as it swayed over the streetcar tracks embedded in the pavement. She had to hold her wide-brimmed hat when it threatened to fly off with an errant breeze.

"Those blasted things are a nuisance!" Henrietta clucked as she righted herself in the seat. "One of these days there's going to be a bad accident, and it'll be because of those confounded tracks. If the city can't keep them repaired, they ought to remove them!"

"But the streetcars are vital to the city," Lacey said. "A lot of people depend on them for transportation." She was speaking from experience, for until recently, when Nick had bought two new carriages to replace their wrecked ones, they'd been dependent on the public conveyances themselves. Riding a horse into Dallas's busy traffic was a dangerous thing to do, especially if one had to leave the animal tethered to a hitching post for any length of time.

"Yes, I know they do, but the transportation people ought to keep their tracks embedded deeper in the macadam and not let them stick up the way they do now. It's nothin' but carelessness on their part to let them get this bad. One day there's going to be an accident, just mark my words."

Less than an hour later, Henrietta's prediction became fact. There was an accident. But, fortunately, not a bad one.

They were leaving the business district of the city and were going back to Henrietta's for lunch, taking their original route in reverse, when their way became blocked by an overturned wagon. It had been loaded down with produce and crates of live chickens but now the vegetables littered the road and the chickens, having escaped from their broken crates, trotted about, raising quite a ruckus with their squawking. Across the street from the overturned wagon was a horseless carriage. Its front tires had run up into a once-neat yard, flattening the white picket fence there, and now rested in a flower bed in full bloom.

"See there! I knew it. What did I tell you?" Henrietta's iron gray head nodded in pleased affirmation.

Lacey was forced to agree that her elderly companion had been right. The wagon's front wheel, it appeared, had been caught in a deep rut running alongside the streetcar track. It had broken loose from its axle, overturning the heavily laden wagon and dumping its load into the street. The horseless carriage must have dodged the wagon and had landed in the front yard. Now traffic was backed up for a considerable distance and everyone was having to turn around and take an alternate route.

"Sam!" Henrietta barked at her driver. "Take a right at the next corner."

The uniformed driver stiffened at the order and turned on his seat to look at his elderly employer. "Uh, Miz Lange, you sure you don't want me to turn *left?*"

"We'd be going out of our way if we went that way. Turn right, like I told you to."

"But, Miz Lange, ma'am, that ain't a real good part o' town for you ladies to be seen in."

Something flashed in Henrietta's faded gray eyes and an impish grin appeared about her mouth. "I dare anyone to question *my* reasons for drivin' through a red-light district. Turn right, Sam!" Then, giving Lacey a broader grin, she added, "I've always wanted to go to a bordello and see for myself just what all the fascination's about, haven't you?"

"No! I haven't!" Lacey giggled, her cheeks flushing a becoming shade of pink.

"Oh, *I* have. All my life I've wanted to know just what it is those women have that we don't. Well," she sighed, "I'll probably go to my grave still wondering. But I suspect the main difference between them and us is nothing more than an open mind."

Lacey stared at the elderly matriarch. She had never expected to hear *that* kind of admission from this much-respected lady. Wanting to visit a whorehouse, of all things!

Nick hopped off Major's back and tied his reins to the brass-and-wood hitching post. Pink and red rose bushes, in full flower, ran the length of the wide front porch. There was little movement about Cora's place this time of day, leading Nick to assume that most—if not all—of the ladies were still sleeping in.

A young black girl, garbed in a pale blue maid's frock, opened the front door at Nick's knock. She gave him a broad, welcoming smile. "You comin' mighty early today, Mr. Nicholas. Miss Cora's done already up, though. She's in her office back of the stairs."

"Thank you, Lucy." He swept off his new Stetson and stepped into the wide foyer, having a thorough look at the rooms he'd never seen in the bright light of day. They were just as clean as his own at home were, and though the carpet was a bit worn in the drawing room, there was nothing seedy or disreputable-looking about the house that he could see. It looked more like a family home than it did a brothel.

"You want a pot of coffee and some sweet rolls?" Lucy queried politely.

"No, thank you. I really came to see Miss Sally, not Miss Cora."

"Oh, but Miss Sally's still sleepin'."

"Yeah, I sorta thought she might be, but it's important that I see her. She won't mind if I wake her up."

The girl gave him a slightly dubious look, but shrugged her slim shoulders and wandered off down the hall, leaving Nick to ascend the stairs on his own.

Only after he reached Sally's bedroom door did he pause to wonder if she was alone inside. But he decided that she would have to be. It was after eleven o'clock and most of her clients would have been long gone by now. So he tapped lightly on the door, and when he heard no sound come from inside, he turned the crystal knob and entered the dark, quiet room.

Like the drawing room, Sally's bedroom looked quite ordinary. There was one double bed, one bureau, one washstand with a china bowl and pitcher on it, and beneath the bedside table was a china chamber pot, painted with violets to match the washbowl and pitcher. An altogether innocent-looking room, he thought.

Sally, though, was another matter. She didn't look innocent at all. Lying sprawled in the center of her bed, alone, she was stark naked from the waist up. The white sheet was tangled about her hips and legs, but her full, heavy breasts lay exposed on her creamy chest. Her hennaed hair fanned out over two pillows with one errant lock sweeping across her forehead and eyes.

She was a lovely woman, Nick thought as he crossed the room to her bed, and friendly as well. He sat down and, with a smile, reached out and touched one of her tinted locks. How had he ever thought her anything like Lacey? Sally couldn't hold a candle to the woman he loved.

Sally's lids fluttered open slowly. For a moment she stared stupidly at Nick before a lazy, sensual smile spread across her face. One long-fingered hand inched up his muscled thigh as she purred, "What are you doin' here so early, lover?"

"I didn't come for *that*," he admitted, her endearment making him uncomfortable. "I have something for you." Extracting the thick envelope from his breast pocket with one hand, he lifted her questing fingers with the other and pressed the packet into her palm. "I wanted to give this to you now while I could. Things may get too sticky in the future for me to have the opportunity."

"What is it?"

"Open it and see. It's Jake's and my way of saying thanks."

Slowly she opened the flap and spread the envelope apart. Her eyes blinked uncomprehendingly at first, then widened. In an instant she jerked upright, the sheet falling lower on her hips, and her fingers busily removed the crisp one-hundred-dollar notes inside.

"There's a fortune here!"

"Not quite," Nick laughed. "Just ten thousand dollars. Me and Jake thought that cash would be better than a bank account in your name. This way, there's no written record of how much you've got, and you'll always have it with you. If I were you, I'd put it in Cora's safe and take it out only as you need it. But don't flash it around in front of the other girls! They'll start askin' questions that you won't want to answer."

Sally had removed the bills and was fanning them out, holding them in both hands. "I—I don't know what to say, lover. I *know* I don't deserve all this."

"You've earned every penny for all the help you've given us."

"But all I did was *sleep* with Crawford," she protested with wide-eyed innocence. "And while he's not the most exciting partner I've come across, he's certainly not the most boring. Not ten thousand dollars' worth anyway."

"You did a lot more than sleep with him, Sally. All

the information you got from him told us just what we needed to know."

"I still don't think I understand," Sally frowned, adding unneeded lines to her face.

"Well, I'm not gonna go into it with you now; I don't have time. You take the money and, if you have to get away in a hurry, use it to make a fresh start someplace else."

"Why would I want to leave? I like it here in Dallas."

"No more questions. Just take it and use it if you have to."

Nick started to get up, but Sally placed a hand on his muscled thigh and stopped him. "Oh, don't go, lover." A lazy, provocative smile appeared on her lips as a drowsy look crept into her eyes. "Wouldn't you like to stay and keep me company?"

"At eleven in the morning?" Nick chuckled.

"Oh, lover," she purred, "I could take you *any*-time of the day." Her fingers sought and found the sleeping bulge at his groin. "That one night you came to me . . . didn't you like it?"

"Sally," Nick began indulgently, "you got more out of that night than I did."

"If I didn't know better, I'd swear you were smitten on somebody, lover," she pouted.

"Mmm." He nodded. "You could say that."

"Is she better than me?"

"Ah, now Sally, there's no need to get jealous."

Nick looked down in his lap and covered her caressing fingers with his hand, intending to move her appendage to a safer distance. After what he and Lacey had shared last night, when he'd told her truthfully that she was the only woman in his life, he definitely had no interest in Sally, or any other woman for that matter.

Looking down as he was, he didn't see Sally's head turn to look past him, nor did he notice the surprised expression that appeared on her face. But when he did look up, he saw her eyes widen and her mouth fall open slowly in alarm.

Frowning, he started to turn the upper half of his body to see what had caused her sudden change of mood. But from out of the blue, he felt the ceiling fall in on his head. Tiny fragments of china splintered about his shoulders as a dark, damp stain spread over his arms and down into his lap. A pain began to throb at the top of his head where the ceiling had hit him and the room began to tilt and spin crazily. His body fell forward and his face landed on Sally's exposed breasts, pushing her back against her pillows.

"You—you bastard!" he heard Lacey's voice cry out.

Lacey!

In an instant, the room stopped spinning and he turned to see her standing above him with the handle of the water pitcher still tightly clutched in her fist. "Lacey? I, uh—"

"No!" The pitcher handle dropped out of her hand as it came up, halting his flow of words. "No more lies, Nick! After last night . . . after all those things you said . . . I couldn't believe it when I saw you coming into this place. You told me there were no other women in your life, just me! I've got to be the world's biggest fool for believing you." Her voice was thin, tinged heavily with disappointment.

Her skin, pale before from the shock of seeing him, was now taking on a flushed, angry hue.

Oh, God! What have I done now? he wondered silently.

He started to tell her how wrong she was, but her sudden movement stopped him. She reached down into the depths of her purse and he thought for a fleeting instant that, perhaps, she might be carrying a Derringer. After all, she had aimed a gun at him before, and it wasn't as if she didn't have provocation this time. But when the string of shiny stones appeared in her fist instead of a small weapon, he sat back, relieved.

Lacey tossed the elaborate diamond necklace to Sally. "You deserve these now more than I do," she jeered disgustedly. "He's very generous with his mistresses, but he's not at all faithful. Don't build your hopes on him like I did."

Sally just sat there, openmouthed, as Lacey turned and marched out of the room. "Well, I never . . ."

"Jesus Christ!" Nick swore, pushing himself away from Sally. He swayed unsteadily on his feet for a moment until his head cleared, then he brushed the pieces of china from his hair, mumbling, "I gotta go explain to her."

"Lover, that woman's not in the mood to listen."

But Nick was already storming out of her room and sprinting down the stairs in hot pursuit of the quickly departing Lacey. Catching up with her on the front porch, he was much too preoccupied with stopping her to see all of the detoured carriages and coaches that were passing by, watching them.

"You've got to let me explain," he insisted, clamping a hand down on her arm and spinning her around to face him.

But if Lacey had been angry at him before, she was in a fiery rage now. Her green eyes were almost black with fury as she glared up at him through narrowed slits. "Get your hands off me you . . . you nameless cur!"

"Lacey, listen to me!"

"No! Let me go!"

"Not till I've explained. It's not like it looked."

She pulled ineffectually at her arm, her strength no match against his. "I won't listen, Nick Gallagher. I've listened to you long enough, and look where it's gotten me! Take a good look around you. Half the city of Dallas is watching us right now. What little reputation I had is now shot to hell, and it's all your fault!"

"Be still, Red!" His free hand came up, grasping her arm that held the frilly parasol.

"I've told you never to call me that," she growled through clenched teeth. "I hate being called 'Red.' Now if you don't let me go, you'll be sorry!"

Nick just laughed, beginning to feel smug and superior at her feminine impotency. "You're not big enough to do me any damage . . . Red."

But she was.

Her knee came up with such a swiftness, Nick had only enough time to twist his hips against the offending blow. The sharp pain he felt only caused him to tighten his hold on her even more as his body doubled over from the shock.

"Get him again, honey!" cheered Henrietta

Lange, standing in her phaeton as she shook an upraised fist. She'd been perplexed, then surprised, when Lacey had curtly told the driver to stop on this infamous street. But now she, as well as the other passers-by, gazed in utter astonishment at the scene being played out on the bordello's front porch.

The other people in their carriages, men and women alike, looked on as the young couple continued to skirmish. Women gazed in unconcealed fascination, but when they saw and heard Henrietta shout her support, they too. picked up on the older woman's encouraging cheer and loudly began to support Lacey's efforts in extracting herself from Nick's tight clutches. The men, however, sided with Nick. They lent their verbal support to him . . . from a safe distance.

Lacey's chest heaved as she gulped in angry breaths. "LET ME GO!"

Nick's refusal came out in a ragged, pain-ridden whisper. "Not on your life." The agony in his groin was almost bearable now, but he still refused to turn her loose.

"You want more of the same you . . . you son of a bitch?"

From his doubled-over stance, he gave her a strained look. "Where's the refined lady now, Red? Ladies don't talk like that."

"Well, I've changed, Nick. *You* changed me. Now, *dammit,* let me go!" And with that she pulled hard and gained the freedom of her right arm. Clutched in the hand of that arm was her frilly, decorative parasol; a dangerous weapon indeed, if Nick had but realized it.

She took immediate action, striking Nick across his broad shoulders and collar bone. A loud roar erupted from the women each time her parasol came in contact with his body. Of course, the initial impact broke the central spine of the flimsy feminine accessory, but that didn't deter Lacey. She raised it again and again and let Nick have it with all her might across his side, hitting his ribs, then lower on to strike his hips and legs. Then she lifted the hem of her skirt and kicked out at him with a force that almost knocked her off balance, striking his shins and bringing him successfully to his knees.

Without a backward glance at the wounded Nick, she descended the front steps of the brothel, her chin raised high, and marched determinedly across the street to Henrietta's waiting phaeton. With the feminine cheers and applause in the background, she ordered the driver to take her home.

Nick caught only a glimpse of her as she disappeared down the street and around the corner out of sight. Then the front door opened, blocking his already limited view, and Cora's butler came out, quickly followed by Sally, who was now almost presentably dressed. With each of them helping him, they led Nick back inside the house and into Cora's parlor.

"I gotta go after her," Nick groaned, limping unsteadily.

"You ain't goin' no place just yet, Mr. Nicholas." Even with Sally's help, Nick's considerable weight was a burden to the elderly butler. "'At there is one mad woman!"

"She's hurt," Nick defended weakly. *"I* hurt

her . . . again, dammit. I gotta go to her before she does somethin' she'll be sorry for later."

As Nick fell onto Cora's settee, holding onto his aching shin, Sally swished over to him, pouring him a glass of brandy as she came.

"Here, drink this, lover. It'll take away some of that pain in your poor old crotch. Lord, I hope she didn't do you no permanent damage."

Nick shook his head slowly before downing the contents of the glass in one long gulp. Then he handed the glass back to Sally and grabbed the brandy bottle out of her other hand. "Her aim was off . . . thank God."

"That's good to hear!" the girl proclaimed.

"I'll go get Lucy to clean up the mess in your room, Miss Sally," said the butler before leaving them alone.

"I'll be all right," Nick mumbled, feeling the effects of the brandy course through his pain-befuddled brain. "Just let me rest here a minute, then I'll be on my way."

"Good Lord, lover! You really must think a lot of that woman to want to run after her, especially after what she's just done to you."

"She had good reason, Sally. Lacey doesn't usually fly off the handle like that."

"Ah!" Sally exclaimed, a look of comprehension registering on her face. "*She's* the one, isn't she? And I bet you didn't tell her about our little arrangement, did you? Shame on you, lover."

Nick emitted a painful groan when he tried to move. "Lemme up from here!" He wasn't going to stay here any longer, drinking the minutes away, when Lacey was out there doing God knows what. His groin still throbbed, but it wasn't going to hamper him in any way. The pain in his shin, though, was abominable, and as he walked toward the door, there was a noticeable limp to his gait.

"You'd best take care, lover," Sally cautioned with an enticing smile. "That lady of yours might decide to do you some real serious damage if she's given the chance."

Ignoring her, Nick slammed out of the house and descended the steps, weaving intoxicatedly. The brandy he'd so quickly consumed was making its effect known. As potent as it was, though, it did nothing to stop his ire at his own stupidity and at Lacey's outrage from growing steadily by the second.

He mounted Major and turned away from Cora's. Lacey was going to listen to him even if he had to hog-tie and gag her! Where she ever got the notion that he cared for a prostitute was a mystery to him. Men didn't fall for whores—they went to them for physical solace. And he hadn't needed *that* since he'd made Lacey his mistress. But just tossing that diamond necklace around like it was some cheap trinket . . . well, he'd straighten her out on that score, too!

Riding out of town at a clipped pace, he sat gingerly in the saddle, not wanting to injure his already abused masculinity more. And by the time he reached Gallagher House and handed Major over to a solemn-faced William, his irritation had increased tenfold.

William said something as he dismounted, but

Nick didn't reply. His brandy-soaked brain was deaf to everything but his own determined thoughts. He wasn't even aware of Hattiebelle, who moved about the first floor, gathering up things. Instead, he rushed past her and dashed up the stairs two at a time before sprinting with a limp down the hall to Lacey's room.

Without knocking, he burst in, and froze at what he saw. Trunks sat open on the floor before her wardrobe and bureau. She stood in front of them, folding and placing things inside their yawning cavities.

At his entrance, her bright copper-gold head jerked around and a grim line appeared on her full mouth. "You're drunk! Get out of my room, Nick!"

"Not till we've had this out." He closed the door behind him, clumsily twisting the key in the lock, not the least bit deterred by her venomous look. "You're gonna listen to me!"

"I might listen, but I won't believe your lies. You may as well save your breath." With an upward tilt to her chin, she continued to fold another garment with jerky movements before dropping it carelessly on top of the other things in her trunk.

"Goddammit, Red!" He stalked over to her and spun her around to face him. "Sally don't mean nothing to me!"

A mirthless laugh bubbled out of her throat. "Well, I *do* believe that." And she wrinkled her nose at the smell of alcohol on his breath.

"Good!" Already she was listening to reason.

"You don't care a thing about *any*body! Why I ever thought I . . ."

When her words faltered, Nick jumped in as fast as he could, urging, "Go on and finish it. What did you think?"

She shook her head. "I was a fool. A dumb, stupid, gullible fool! Now get out of here and let me finish packing."

He relaxed his hold on her arms, but he didn't turn her loose completely. Instead, he pulled her closer. "Say it, Lace. Spit it out. What did you think?"

Angry tears swam in her eyes when she looked up at him, her bottom lip quivering. "I thought I loved you. But I was wrong! I don't love you. I'll *never* love you because I despise you too much!"

Nick winced. "Oh, babe. I'm so sorry all this happened. Would it make you feel better if I said I loved you?"

"Not now." Her answer was instantaneous and void of any emotion. "I'll never believe your lies."

"But I do love you, Lace! God knows, it's taken me long enough to admit it, but I *do* love you."

Lacey inhaled slowly, her look cold and disbelieving. It was then that an idea came to Nick; he would show her that he loved her, like he'd done last night.

He pulled her rigid, unyielding body to his and began kissing the sweet-smelling hair that curled at her temple. "You're the only woman I've ever said that to, Lace. I mean it. I love you! I *have* loved you from the first moment I saw you again. I've just been too damn stupid to admit it. God, babe, what you do to me!"

Pressing his hard body against hers, he cupped her shapely bottom with his hands and ground his hips into hers, letting her feel the extent of his arousal. She was like fuel to his fire. His desire soon raged out of control, taking with it his last shreds of rational thought. All he could do now was love her, with his body.

Sliding his hands up her back, he began to loosen the fastenings of her gown. In a few moments it fell to the floor in a pale green pool. All the while his lips nuzzled the sensitive cord behind her ear. He whispered words of endearment and passion as he pushed her gently back to the bed, oblivious to the fact that she was resisting him, trying to get away. He wanted, *needed* her so much, he was deaf, dumb and blind to everything but his own desire. He ached with his love for her, an ache that was more like an exquisite pain. When he gained the lovely, bared breast he sought, he lay across her body, nibbling the pink-crested nipple while his one free hand loosened the buttons on his trousers.

When his hardness was at last free, he knelt between her parted thighs, his mouth stifling the sharp cry she uttered as he thrust into her dry, unprepared nest. With each undulating movement, he lost more and more of his self-control. He was showing her in the only way he knew just how much she meant to him, just how much he loved her. The blood rushed through his veins at a phenomenal rate until his sanity was questionable. Then, in one cataclysmic spasm, he felt the explosion that sent jets of his fertile seed into her womb, and he cried out her name in joy.

His heartbeat slowed. His breathing returned to normal. His dark head, tousled and unruly from his recent exertion, rested in the sweet, moist hollow of Lacey's neck until he felt himself once again able to move.

When he lifted his eyes at last, a tender smile etched upon his lips, he cringed at the chilling look of hatred that was carved on her marblelike features.

"Are you *through?*"

Her icy words penetrated straight to his soul with the precision of a well-aimed kick. He had done it all wrong . . . again!

Sweet Jesus Christ in Heaven! he prayed. *What do I do now?*

Chapter Ten

WITH THE PINK GRANITE CAPITOL DOME GLINTING GOLD-en in the distance, the street lined with tall syca-mores and live oaks was quiet and subdued this spring morning. One of Austin's better neighbor-hoods, it was not so much exclusive and elite as it was comfortable and friendly. A perfect family-type neighborhood.

Running alongside the unpaved street was a long, red-brick walk. It wound unevenly past one well-kept house and another until at the end of the street it climbed a gentle slope to a modest, two-story, white frame house. Bordering the walk were beds of yellow and orange marigolds, white daisies and blue petunias, dividing it neatly from the grassy front lawn.

The short-stemmed flowers grew in abundance the entire length of the walk, then stopped abruptly at the edge of the wide front porch. There honeysuckle and climbing roses of pink and bright red caught the eye as they spiraled up and around white wood trellises to the porch's roof and on further to the second floor.

A stray breeze blew the heady scent from all those springtime blossoms through the opened bedroom window. Lacey, sitting in a rocking chair there, inhaled deeply of the special blended fragrance. Smiling to herself, she released a long, contented sigh. Austin was not so different from Dallas in some respects, yet in others it wasn't like Dallas at all. Where Dallas's climate was dry and hot, the temperatures here were of a lower degree, but the air was more humid, as her moist skin and curling hair could attest.

The social climate here wasn't as strained or reserved as Dallas's, either. The citizens of Austin seemed more at ease, not quite as conscious or worried about what others were thinking all the time. But maybe it wasn't everybody else, she reconsidered thoughtfully; maybe it was she who was different. After all, she had changed quite a lot within the past year.

Musical chimes from the mantle clock in the drawing room penetrated her languorous thoughts. They reminded her that she would have to hurry if she was going to be ready when Peter Thorne arrived. The painting he was doing of her now was almost complete, and as close as she and Peter had become since they'd left Dallas, they were still only good friends. But, heavens, if he could see her now . . .

The baby in Lacey's arm sighed complacently and let her tiny dark head fall away from her mother's now-empty breast. At three months of age, Nicole Rochelle Gallagher was the joy of her mother's life and the ruling empress of this all-female household.

Such a precious bundle of love, Lacey thought, to

have been conceived in such anger and bitterness. Though, to be honest, if she were given the chance to rectify the past, knowing what the outcome would be, she would resubmit to Nick's lusts without a qualm. He had all but taken her against her will that day a year ago, but she owed him a debt of gratitude that he would never know about. Her whole life was centered around her child now, and it had been even before Nicole was born. For the first time in her life, Lacey felt as if she now had a purpose and a reason for living.

Placing the baby in her narrow bed, Lacey kissed her before covering her with a light, crocheted blanket. The breeze flowing into the room wasn't cold—at this time of year it couldn't be—but she wasn't going to take chances with her daughter's health. That had been the reason, if not the deciding factor, behind her and Peter's return to Texas. New York City had been wonderfully exciting for a while, but with motherhood impending, she had decided that home was the best place to be.

Assured that Nicole was sound asleep, Lacey buttoned the bodice of her yellow cotton dress and quietly left the room, shutting the door softly behind her. Her yound maid, Daisy Edwards, would be coming up soon, as she usually did when Lacey was busy sitting for Peter. If the baby should cry out, and Lacey didn't hear, Daisy would be there to take care of things.

As she descended the stairs to the first floor, Lacey recalled the other, more regal sweep of stairs in Gallagher House and mentally compared it to the simple, narrow flight she now tred. Heavens, there was no comparison! Chuckling, she thought that the only two things the houses could possibly have in common were indoor plumbing and telephone service. Everything else was as different as night was to day. This house was vastly different from the other, so much so in fact it was strange to think that she'd once lived surrounded by opulence and luxury, where now she lived in understated simplicity. But she didn't mind; she was happy and secure here, and that was all that really mattered.

Reaching the bottom of the stairs, her eyes scanned the dark, polished oak floors. There had been no Persian carpets to cover their bareness in the cold winter months. Simple braided rugs had protected them all from the chill. And there were no expensive paintings hanging on her modestly papered walls, either; merely inexpensive pictures from unknown artists who had sold her their work in order to eat. But it was home, she acknowledged proudly; hers, bought and paid for with her inheritance.

A low-hanging branch from the graceful old sycamore tree in front brushed against one of the drawing room windows as she entered the room. For a moment she imagined that it had been a person, tapping against the pane, but seeing the leafy limb outside, she knew that was nonsense. Only yesterday, her neighbor, Professor Fellowes, had mentioned that tapping on windows was the latest rage at the nearby university, where he taught history. Students, he'd told her, in trouble with their housemothers, preferred to enter and exit by way of the windows to avoid their curfew restrictions. Not only did it save a lot of explanations, it made sneaking girls into their rooms possible as well. He'd shaken with silent laughter then and had said good-bye to Lacey when his wife, Mrs. Fellowes, had called to him.

Smiling at the recollection, Lacey turned to see Daisy, her maid, enter with a tray of coffee and freshly baked cookies.

"Is Mr. Thorne coming again this morning?" the girl asked as she placed the tray on the table.

"He's supposed to." Lacey nodded. "Mmm, the cookies smell delicious!"

"Momma's got another batch in the oven. She knows how Mr. Thorne likes to nibble as he paints. She's got a fresh pot of coffee brewing on the stove, too."

"Oh, good! Peter *does* like his coffee."

"Is the baby already asleep?"

"Yes. She dropped off a moment ago, so there's no need for you to rush up to her now. She's the sweetest baby." Daisy smiled.

"I like to think so," Lacey agreed. "But then, I'm just her mother, so I'm sort of prejudiced."

"I always wanted a baby sister . . . or brother. It didn't matter to me, but Momma never could have any more kids after she had me." The girl sighed heavily after this admission. "Well, if you should need anything, just holler."

"I will," Lacey promised and watched Daisy leave the room.

She moved toward the table where the coffee tray sat and poured herself a cup of the strong, hot brew, adding a dash of cream and a heaping spoonful of sugar to it to cut down the bitterness. Mrs. Edwards, her cook and Daisy's mother, could make coffee only one way, with the bitter chicory root as her mother from Louisiana had taught her. But Mrs. Edwards's coffee was the only thing Lacey could find lacking in perfection. The woman's ability in the kitchen almost surpassed that of Hattiebelle's. She had been fortunate indeed, Lacey admitted to herself, in obtaining the woman's services so soon after arriving in Austin.

That had been a turbulent time in her life, one that she didn't often like to think about. Feeling raw from the pain of parting with Nick, she had been uncertain as to what she was going to do with the rest of her life. But Peter, God bless him, had taken her in tow and had all but told her what she would do. So far, his guidance had been helpful, and only once or twice had she ever had doubts about listening to him.

Stirring her coffee until it cooled, she moved to the window and looked out at the side lawn. It was a lovely May morning. Her roses were in the last stages of full bloom and her wisteria vines were weeping heavily with the clusters of lavender blossoms attached to them. All in all, she had to admit that her garden was one of the most colorful along the street . . . but it still couldn't compare with the gardens at Gallagher House this time of year.

"Stop it!" she scolded herself. "Stop thinking about the blasted past!"

All right, so her house wasn't as grand as Gallagher House. What of it? It was hers! Every inch of it. There was nothing under her roof to remind her of Max or his first wife, Lillian, or her mother's shame. Everything in this house had either been bought with her inheritance, or had belonged to Rachel.

She lived comfortably and securely now, so why was she recalling that more painful time in Dallas? It was a waste, really. Her life was running smoothly, predictably, with very few upsetting occurrences, yet a part of her still longed for that other time, that other life . . . and Nick.

There were times when a vision of him would flash through her mind and she would be overcome with weakness. Her legs would shake, her breasts would tingle and an ache would slowly flower in her thighs. She would recall how his hands had touched her, how his lips had claimed hers, how his erotic, arousing words had been whispered as he thrust against her body with his.

Longing for Nick and what they'd had was bad; she knew it and sadly shook the thought of him aside. Her only link with him now lay asleep in the crib upstairs: her daughter, Nicole. But Nicole was Nick's child as well, and she would never forget that. Maybe that was why she loved her so much.

A loud knock sounded at the front door and Lacey blessed its well-timed interruption. Before she even opened the door, she knew who stood on the other side. But she managed to smile, not wanting Peter to grow concerned about her—he had enough gray hair as it was.

Looking freshly shaven and dapper, Peter hugged and kissed her warmly. "Good morning, my dear. And how is my most favorite model today?"

"Oh, as always, Peter," she smiled, leading him into the drawing room. "Daisy just brought the coffee in a moment ago, so it's still hot. Would you like a cup?"

"Don't I always?" He chuckled.

As she fixed his cup the way he liked it—black with one sugar—he asked, "Have you had a chance to read this week's Dallas paper?"

"No, I haven't got my copy yet. Is there anything in it worth reading about?" Living so far away from her hometown, the weekly newspaper was all she had to keep her abreast of the happenings there. It had been strange at first, reading about occurrences that were days old rather than hours old, but that was the price one had to pay when one lived far away.

Peter pulled the folded newssheet out of his coat pocket and placed it on the table beside the coffee tray. "There's the usual gossip and boring advertisements," he admitted, taking the cup she held out for him. "But the feature story is most intriguing! It seems that one, quite notorious Marshall Stratton has been tried and convicted of murdering a Frogtown prostitute. You, uh, might have heard of her. Miss Sally O'Donnell?"

"Sally O'Donn . . ." She stopped suddenly, her green eyes growing round with astonishment. "She . . . she was Nick's—"

"Yes, she's the one, all right."

"And she's *dead?* Marshall Stratton *murdered* her?"

"Well, according to the newspaper report, he hired someone to do the actual killing. From what I know of Stratton—and that's not a lot, thank God—he wouldn't stoop to doing the killing himself."

"But how? I—I mean, my goodness, why would he want to murder a prostitute?"

"To keep her from talking, I imagine. From all the accounts I've read, it seems as though everyone had assumed she left town. But a few weeks ago, they discovered her partially decomposed body in Jamieson Crawford's barn."

"Jamieson Crawford?"

"Yes! He's implicated in this whole thing, too . . . or was." He tossed the paper onto her lap, adding, "You might want to read all the gory details for yourself. Your lawyer friend, Jake Goldstein, is mentioned once or twice . . . on the front page and in the announcements column."

Frowning, Lacey opened the paper with trembling fingers. Anything Jake had done, she thought, couldn't be half as shocking as what Marshall Stratton and Jamieson Crawford had done. She let her eye linger for a moment on the major headline concerning Stratton, then turned to the middle of the paper, where all of the announcements were printed. She scanned the list of recent engagements until she encountered Jake's name.

"Jake and *Darcy* are getting married?" She laughed, pleased as well as surprised. "I can't believe it! I didn't know they were interested in one another that way. What am I saying? I didn't even know they *knew* one another!"

"You won't believe who played Dan Cupid, my dear," Peter remarked over the rim of his cup.

"Who?" Then it hit her and she gasped. *"Nick?"* Peter nodded and took a sip of his coffee.

"I don't believe it," she retorted.

"I didn't either, at first, but it's true. Some of my former clients in Dallas, with whom I still have contact, told me of the affair . . . if that term can be used. Though, personally, I doubt that Miss Patterson's ever—"

"What about *Nick?*" she asked him impatiently.

"Oh! Well, it seems that Miss Patterson's father wasn't at all thrilled with the idea of having a Jew for a son-in-law. Goldstein might be one of the brightest young lawyers in Dallas with prospects galore in his future, but he's a Jew nevertheless. I also believe that *his* family weren't that pleased with having a Baptist for a relative, either. But your illustrious brother-in-law stepped in, smoothed out all the wrinkles between the two families and now I understand that they're all as thick as thieves."

Feeling a surge of unexplainable heat course through her, Lacey stood and walked toward the opened window, her teeth tightly clenched. "I can't see Nick as a diplomat," she mocked quietly. "He's much more adept at breaking things up, not putting them together . . . especially where people are concerned."

She stood there, letting the breeze cool her heated skin, and heard the clink and clatter of Peter's coffee cup being placed on the table.

"Are you still troubled over him, my dear?" he asked.

"Under the circumstances, Peter, it's a little difficult not to be."

"Oh, Lacey." He sighed, then clicked his tongue. "You really should have returned to Dallas instead of coming here."

"No!" Pivoting on her heel, she faced him, her skin flushing crimson. "I couldn't go back there, and you know it."

"You're still afraid of what the gossips would have said? Yes, just as I thought. You, my dear, are much too conventional."

"Not conventional, Peter. Proud! I couldn't go back there and let my daughter suffer the anguish I had to endure as a child."

"Times have changed," he declared.

"Not *that* much. It's still a terrible handicap to be born illegitimate."

"Your daughter didn't have to be illegitimate!" He stood then and walked toward her. "I've asked you to marry me . . . more than once, if you'll bother to recall."

"I know you have, Peter, and I'm very flattered at your proposal, but it wouldn't be right for us. You know *why* it wouldn't be right, too. I love you . . . but only as a friend, not as a lover. I loved Chris, too," she added, thinking of the special friendship they'd had that had been destroyed with their marriage, "and look what happened to him."

"Christopher Gallagher did not die because you married him, Lacey. He died because some stupid animal ran over him! Now the sooner you accept that, the sooner you can get on with the business of living."

Lacey turned away from him and stared blindly out the window. She was a coward for not setting Peter straight on the matter of her marriage to Chris, but she felt too much guilt for it even to try. And she cursed her inability to obliterate Nick from her thoughts, too. Would she never be able to forget him?

It had been easy to move away from him, to establish roots in another city and create a new life for herself, but it was next to impossible to lose the memory of the man she so desperately loved. Even now, without trying very hard, she could recall each minute detail about him—the thick unruliness of his dark brown hair, the indentations in his cheeks when he smiled lopsidedly, the crook of his beakish nose.

Two weighty hands descended onto her shoulders just before she felt the brush of Peter's beard against her temple. "Look," he murmured softly, "let's forget all about the past. We've got too much to do this morning to waste time on that." He paused, kneading her slender shoulders with his fingertips, then added on a somewhat lighter note, "I've heard from one of my political clients that Governor Sayers has seen one or two of my portraits. From what I gathered, he was quite impressed with my work. Wouldn't it be something for an original Thorne to get hung in the capitol rotunda?"

"Peter!" She turned and smiled up at him in amazement. "Do you mean that the governor has actually commissioned you to do a portrait of him?"

"Oh, no! He hasn't commissioned me yet. But there's a lot of room for hope."

"Why, that's wonderful! Just think, if he does commission you, you can start working on his portrait almost immediately. Your calendar is almost clear, isn't it? I mean, there isn't that much left to do to the Muses, is there?"

"That all depends," he said, and moved back toward the coffee tray. He poured himself another cup, adding sugar and stirring it. "You see, even though you're through with your part, I still have the backgrounds to finish on this painting and the other eight as well. That shouldn't take long, though, not more than a week or two. After that's done, and the paintings have cured, I'll have to take them to be framed. Then there will be the chore of finding a location suitable for the unveiling."

"I didn't know about all that," she admitted. Struck with a sudden thought, she smiled and said, "You know, you could have been finished with all nine paintings months ago if Nicole's arrival hadn't interrupted you."

"Merely a minor inconvenience, I assure you. Where is she, by the way? I haven't heard her since I've been here."

"She's upstairs. She dropped off for her morning nap just before you arrived."

"Ah!" He nodded. "Well then, we'd better get busy if we're going to get finished with the Muse Erato before Nicole awakens and wants you."

As Peter stood to remove his coat, Lacey gathered up his empty cup and saucer and placed them on the tray with hers. But something printed in the corner of the paper lying next to the tray caught her eye, and she gasped, dropping the delicate china pieces with a clatter.

"Peter!" Grasping the paper in her hands, she stared in utter disbelief at what was printed there. "My God, did you see this?"

"What, my dear?" He came to stand behind her, peering over her shoulder as he rolled up his shirt sleeves.

"Gallagher House," she intoned incredulously, "it's—it's been destroyed!"

"Oh, yes, I know." Peter shook his head lamentably. "Sad, it was such a beautifully designed house, too. I intended to say something about it to you, but it completely slipped my mind."

"But how?" she demanded. Surely no ordinary fire had destroyed it. One couldn't have! It had been built of rock and brick.

"I imagine it was the gas," Peter speculated. "It makes a beautiful light, but it's awfully unstable, you know—quite explosive."

"I can't believe it!" She dropped into the chair behind her, her legs suddenly incapable of supporting her. "My Lord, I cannot believe that it's really gone."

"Come now, Lacey," he chided gently. "It was only a house."

It had been much, much more than *that,* but how could she make him see it? After all, he hadn't lived there as she had. He didn't have all the memories tied up in its existence that she had, either.

"There was only one death resulting from the fire," he went on, seeing her head jerk around to stare up at him. "Don't worry, it wasn't Nick, your old housekeeper or her son."

"How do you know?" Suddenly she experienced an inner shame that caused her heart to pound rapidly. She had remembered the house well enough, but she hadn't thought of the people who lived there; not until Peter had reminded her of them.

"They weren't listed in the obituary column," he retorted with amused logic. "Look, I'm going to get to work. I'll be in the studio when you're ready, but try not to be too long."

He left the room, but she remained seated, the

paper absorbing her complete attention. Guided by concern, she thumbed through the newsprint until she came to the last page, where the obituaries were listed. When she could find neither Nick's, Hattiebelle's nor William's names there, she sat back, sighing with relief. Peter hadn't lied, thank God.

Scanning the listings once again, her eyes came across one name she did recognize. Gasping, she sat up straight and read the short paragraph which followed the man's name.

"Jamieson Crawford, noted Dallas attorney and businessman, died the night of May 3, following a lengthy manhunt by local Dallas authorities. It is believed that Mr. Crawford may have inadvertently caused the explosion and fire which subsequently leveled Gallagher House, a noted landmark in this city. Mr. Crawford, a recent defendant in the jury trial involving Mr. Marshall Stratton, was acquitted of all charges brought against him. He is survived by—"

Lacey stopped reading at this point. "What in God's name happened up there after I left?" she whispered, allowing the paper to drop from her fingers.

Sally O'Donnell's murder . . . Marshall Stratton's arrest and conviction . . . the destruction of her childhood home . . . Jamieson Crawford's suicide/ death. . . . They all seemed to be related in some way. Or were they?

Curious to know if she was just imagining things, she bent over and retrieved the paper from the floor where it had fallen. But Daisy's entrance interrupted her search.

"Miz Gallagher?" the girl began hesitantly, seeing

Lacey's distracted look. "Mr. Thorne said for me to tell you that he's waiting."

"Thank you, Daisy. I'll be there in a moment."

"Is—is something bothering you, ma'am?"

Emitting a mirthless chuckle, Lacey shook her head. "No, Daisy. My mind just seems to be elsewhere this morning, that's all."

Daisy seemed to accept this with a slight angling of her head as she moved toward the coffee tray. "Uh, you want me to get a fresh pot of coffee for you and Mr. Thorne now, ma'am?"

"Yes, please," Lacey responded. "And do save this paper for me."

"All right, ma'am." Daisy nodded.

With a preoccupied frown, Lacey moved out of the room and mounted the stairs, determined not to dwell on her perplexing discovery. But it continued to haunt her, even as she changed into her modestly cut Grecian modeling costume. Half-forgotten conversations she'd overheard between Nick and Jake Goldstein came back to her—conversations which hadn't meant anything then, but which puzzled her now. Had they perhaps been in cahoots together? And had the target of their machinations been Marshall Stratton and Jamieson Crawford?

A niggling voice in the back of her confused mind told her that her vague suspicions were not altogether groundless. She wasn't merely imagining all of this—there *was* a connection somewhere.

In the drawing room of Jake Goldstein's Dallas home later that same morning, three people met to celebrate a well-earned victory. Jake worked diligently to open the champagne bottle, and the cork finally popped out with a loud bang, shooting across the room. Bubbles foamed over the lip and down the neck into one of the fluted glasses Darcy held.

"Don't let any of it go to waste, Jacob!" she giggled, thrusting a second glass under the dripping bottle. She shifted, standing back, so that the alcohol would not spill down the front of her cream silk dress. "It's hard to find this particular vintage in Texas, you know."

Jake filled the glass and then another before handing one to Nick, who stood beneath a slightly scorched portrait of Lacey. "Come on, old buddy," he urged. "Loosen up a little. It isn't everyday we send a bastard like Stratton to prison."

With a heavy, regret-filled sigh, Nick tore his gaze away from the painting, only to frown down into the bubbles in his glass. "Lacey ought to be here, celebrating with us," he grumbled. "It ain't much of an occasion without her."

In fact, life was hardly worth living without her. But in the twelve months since she'd left him, he had thought of little else but her. How could he not when her likeness stared down at him all the time?

Sitting prettily amid a field of bluebonnets, Lacey looked like a copper-haired, Victorian wood nymph. Her long, gauzy yellow gown was arranged so that one bare ankle and foot peeped out from beneath the ruffled flounces of her white lace petticoat. Her bright, unbound hair fell freely about her bared shoulders, while a slightly impish smile played about her lovely face.

Peter Thorne had captured Lacey's vitality and inner essence on that canvas. There were times when Nick could stand beneath it, as he did now, and almost hear her husky voice and silky laughter, the painting was so lifelike. At other times, though, when he recalled their final parting at Union Station, he could hear the condemnation in her voice and see the cold look of disdain in her eyes.

That particular day had been a living hell for him. He had wanted to pull her off that train and into his arms, so that he could explain to her how wrong she was in assuming what she did about Sally. . . . But he hadn't. He'd kept his mouth shut, his heart quiet, and had watched her disappear into the darkness of her private car. He hadn't moved until the train slowly pulled out of the station, taking her out of his life.

With each passing day, his life had seemed emptier and more meaningless . . . with the one exception of his victory over that syphilitic fiend, Marshall Stratton. It had been the single most important factor in keeping him sane and motivated; getting *that* sick son of a bitch behind bars where he should have been put long ago.

In the end, it had been Sally's death that had been Stratton's ruin. The long hours of work, the endless weeks of searching for witnesses and victims alike, and the few clues that Sally had passed along to him and Jake had gone for naught. It had been Stratton's hired killer who had turned against him finally and confessed all that he knew. Stratton's connection with Max's and Rachel's deaths could never be established in a court of law now, because there were no survivors to bring forth as witnesses, and the hired killer had said nothing about it.

Again, Nick turned his pain-filled gaze up to the

painting and felt anguish tear through his gut. He almost lost Lacey's picture the night Crawford went berserk and blew Gallagher House off the face of the earth. Of course, the fact that Crawford had gone up with the house didn't mean much to him; his only interest was in Lacey, or her picture, that is. Jake had called him a damn fool—among other things— for risking his life for the canvas, but he had wanted it too badly just to stand by and let it burn with the rest of the house. And as it was, his singed hair and sometimes aching lungs were proof that Jake had had just cause in chastising him.

". . . and soon!" Nick heard Darcy whisper to Jake. "I don't want to be caught ringless like Lacey."

"Shh! Keep your voice down," Jake ordered tersely. "You can't be sure it was her."

"Sure enough!" Darcy countered, then noticed that Nick was watching them and listening. She burned bright crimson.

Nick closed the distance between them in two long strides. "You know something about Lacey, don't you? What is it? What's happened to her?"

"Nothing! Nothing's happened to her," Darcy assured him. "Well, nothing *bad* that is."

She turned pleading eyes toward Jake, but he merely shrugged. "You opened your mouth, sweetheart; you may as well tell him the rest of it."

"Tell me what, dammit!" Nick demanded.

Darcy took a deep breath, then began, reluctantly, "I overheard a conversation between two people when Momma and I went down to help the Galveston hurricane victims. We were in Houston at the hotel there, and I was just outside my room when these two men stopped just around the corner from me. They didn't see me, but I heard every word they said."

"Yes, and?" Nick prodded.

"Well, they were talking about a painting they'd seen in a gallery near the hotel. One said that he thought Lillie Langtry was prettier, and the other said that . . . that he thought Mrs. Gallagher was, because she had a certain innocence about her that Langtry lacked. Then the first man laughed and said, 'Innocent? She's *pregnant;* she can't be innocent!'"

Jake quickly intervened at this point, noting the shocked look on Nick's face. "Now, don't go jumping to conclusions. We don't know for certain that they were referring to Lacey. There's probably a hundred or more Gallaghers in this area."

"But they couldn't *all* have been painted by Peter Thorne," came Darcy's soft response.

Nick groaned as another pang of regret shot through him. He glanced up at the portrait. "Peter Thorne, huh?" Well, he should have known that she wouldn't be alone—but he hadn't thought she would be with *that* dandified fool.

"Yes," Darcy nodded. "You see, I went to the gallery the men spoke of—without Momma!—and found a small painting of Peter's there. It wasn't of Lacey. But I asked the clerk if he'd had any others by the same artist and he said that he had, but that a wealthy politician from Austin had bought them. And when I inquired about the subjects of the other paintings, he told me that the model was a young woman with strawberry-blond hair and dark green eyes . . . in the early stages of pregnancy. He said that one of the paintings was the most beautiful, madonnalike portrait he'd seen in years, and evidently the politician from Austin had thought so, too, because he asked about the painter and the model."

Nick slumped onto the settee behind him and cradled his head in his hands. "My God! What have I done to her?" In all this time, it had never once occurred to him that his misguided behavior that fateful day would have produced a child.

"It's still nothing more than hearsay and conjecture, Nick," Jake professed coldly, his legal mind asserting itself. "You can't know for sure that the woman was Lacey."

"Dammit, Jake, it had to have been her!"

"But if it was, are you sure the baby's yours? After all, she's been away from you a year and—"

"It's mine!" Nick stated firmly. "Lacey . . . well, she wouldn't go to another man after what I did to her. Darcy honey, I'm sorry you have to hear all this."

"That's all right, Nick, don't worry about me," she remarked with a worried smile.

Looking back at Jake, Nick said, "You see, the last time we were together, I failed to take precautions. And when you add that to what Darcy just told us, I know, without a doubt, that it's *my* son she had." Leaning forward, he rested his elbows on his parted knees and hung his head at a dejected angle. "I guess I ought to be thankful she didn't get rid of him, huh?"

"Lacey wouldn't do a horrible thing like that!" Darcy lashed out fiercely. "She loved you, Nick."

"Maybe at one time, she did, but now I'm not so sure."

Sinking onto the settee beside him, Darcy placed a hand on his shoulder and explained, "I know she doesn't hate you, Nick, I just know it! Whatever happened between the two of you that made her leave is none of my business, but I imagine that her pride had a hand in her decision rather than anything else you might have done. She's dealt with quite a lot in her life—more than we've ever dealt with—and she's only had her pride to fall back on when things got too tough for her to handle."

Maybe it was her pride, Nick thought, continuing to gaze with unseeing eyes at the carpet. But could he overcome it? Hell, he would *have* to, if he ever intended to get her back. With no more danger to keep her away from here now, he would go down on his hands and knees and beg her to come back if it would do any good, because he wanted her! More than that, he wanted to spend the rest of his life making up to her for all of the pain he had caused her.

Nick finally lifted his gaze, moments later, and stared at Jake unwaveringly. "If you'll take a word of advice, old buddy, you'll dispense with any long engagement you might've planned to have and marry your lady here quick! She's too good to lose."

"Believe me, a wedding is on the agenda," Jake promised, pulling Darcy to his side.

Nick stood then and gave Darcy a brotherly kiss before clapping a hand onto Jake's shoulder. "It couldn't happen to a nicer couple, either. If you didn't already have a daddy to give you away at the wedding, Darcy honey, I'd offer to do it, but I'm afraid I won't be here. I've decided to go bring Lacey and my son back home."

"Why do you men always think of a son first?" Darcy queried with an impatient shake of her head.

"You'll need to tie up a few loose ends before you go," Jake inserted, drawing Nick's attention to him.

"That shouldn't take too long, should it? I want to leave Dallas by the end of the week if I can. I'll give you my power of attorney so you can handle things while I'm away."

"You're not afraid I'll suddenly develop sticky fingers like Crawford did?" Jake questioned glibly.

Nick emitted a rumble of dry laughter. "If I know Darcy, she'll keep your fingers so busy you won't have time to think of bein' dishonest."

The lady in question gave Jake a sensually smoldering look and purred, "You can be *sure* of that!"

"Well, that does it!" Peter announced, tossing down his brush.

"You're all finished?" Lowering her feet to the floor, Lacey wasn't sure if she was happy or sad that her long hours of posing had finally come to an end. She stretched her cramped back and leg muscles and asked, "What now?"

"Well, the background is first."

"Oh, yes. You told me that already." She stood, straightening the long, classic gown before wrapping a shawl about her bared shoulders. "Where are you going to get the frames?"

"San Antonio," he stated easily.

"San Antonio! Why there?"

"The best wood carver in the state lives there, that's why. Just any old frames won't do for these canvases. I want the very best! And Raphael is the only artisan in the area that I know of who will make

215

the frames in the Greek fashion, the way I want them."

Coming toward her, he removed his paint-stained smock and tossed it over the chaise lounge where she had been reclining. "They're truly masterpieces, you know. If I didn't need the money and the recognition that selling them will bring, I'd keep all nine for myself."

"Well, if they're *that* good," she stated, moving toward the tall easel, "maybe I'll buy one."

"No!" Peter's hands dropped firmly onto her shoulders, halting her progress. "You can't see it!"

"Why not?"

"Uh . . . it's—it's bad luck!"

"Bad luck?" Lacey issued a disbelieving laugh. "I've never heard of that superstition before."

"Yes, well, uh, I didn't let you see your other portrait before it was completed, did I?"

"I don't recall ever asking to see it."

A faint flush stained Peter's tanned skin as he pleaded, "Just trust me, Lacey. All right? They're beautiful, all nine of them. But I don't want you to see them until the night of the unveiling when they will be ready to be viewed."

Lacey held her shawl about her bare shoulders and stared dubiously into his handsome face. She had the oddest notion that he was withholding something from her. He wasn't being cagey with her for no minor reason.

But, with a shake of her head, she relented and turned her gaze away from him. In doing so, she did not see the relieved look that crossed his face. He quickly picked up his coat and thrust his arms into the sleeves, saying, "I'd like you to see me off at the depot when I leave for San Antonio . . . if it's convenient, that is."

"All right," she agreed with a nod.

"It may take a while to get all the arrangements made after I return, so I may not be able to see you as often as I have been."

His hand came up to caress her smooth cheek, and though she wanted to pull away from him, she remained motionless. Only she knew how cold his touch left her. No man's touch, least of all Peter's, could move her the way Nick's had. Maybe someday, a long time from now it would, when the memory of Nick's had dulled, but not now.

His lips, soft and warm, brushed hers, then he pulled away and straightened his tie. "I'll telephone you and let you know when I get ready to leave."

"Take care, Peter. I'll miss you." *If I can,* she added silently to herself.

Chapter Eleven

Austin's busy depot was a beehive of activity the morning Peter left for San Antonio. Passengers were boarding one train while others were disembarking from another that had moments ago pulled into the station. Confusion abounded as huge carts piled high with trunks and valises rumbled down the wooden platform through the throng of passengers. Lacey had to step back out of the way in order to avoid being struck by the lumbering conveyances.

When the way was at last clear again, she joined Peter at the ticket window, her nose twitching as she sniffed the acrid fumes which pervaded the air about the monstrous locomotives. The odor of burning oil and coal was what she disliked the most about the trains. Oh, they were exciting enough to travel on, but they smelled terrible.

With his ticket finally paid for, Peter picked up his valise in one hand and grasped her arm with the other before propelling her down the platform away from the noise and confusion. "My, my, but they're busy this morning, aren't they? One would almost think that the legislature was in session by the number of people here."

Reaching an area of the platform that was neither too noisy nor too crowded, Peter stopped and brushed off a bench with his handkerchief before allowing Lacey to sit down. She adjusted her wide-brimmed hat and waved a folded paper fan before her flushed face, asking, "How long do you think you'll be gone?"

"As long as it takes, my dear." His gaze slid past her to the cart that held his large crate of canvases. "Good Lord!" he cried. "I'd better go with it and make sure those fools handle it with care. The last thing I need now is for my crate to be dropped and broken open. Wait here!" And then he was gone.

Sitting quietly amid the throng of passengers, Lacey felt an odd sense of liberation rather than one of loneliness. Peter was a fine and very gentle man, but he had a very disturbing habit of smothering her at times when he was near. It was probably just his nature to be overprotective, she surmised with a sigh, but it bothered her nevertheless.

A loud banging sound, like the retort of a revolver, caused her to gasp and turn sharply on the bench. Behind her, in the depot's unloading area, she saw a new automobile being driven out of the baggage car. It was not much larger than a horse-drawn buggy, but it clearly lacked the four-legged hayburner. Behind the single, leather-upholstered seat was a black box, and the man who had driven the automobile out of the baggage car was now lifting the lid of that box and was reaching into it, doing something to the engine. The loud banging sound occurred once more, causing Lacey to flinch nervously, then the rattle in the motor died down to a pleasant rumble.

"Hideous things, aren't they?" Peter asked, drawing her attention around to him.

"I find them a little frightening," she admitted, "but not hideous."

"The craze won't last," he predicted with a knowing shake of his head. "Like those silly hot-air balloons the French are sailing now, the automobile won't last long at all."

Lacey didn't know how to respond to that. He seemed to know more about the subject than she, so she asked instead, "Did you get your crate loaded into the baggage car?"

"Oh, yes. No problems. I'm about ready to board now. Come see me off."

Feeling like Peter's dutiful daughter—for she was young enough to be—she followed him down the length of the platform until they reached the car to which he had been assigned. Steam rose up from the brakes of the locomotive, blowing dust and loose dirt into the air. Lacey shook out her lilac skirts, not wanting any of the nasty soot to cling to her dress. It was her newest frock, and it would be a shame to have it ruined on her first outing in it.

Peter stopped and took her in his arms. She allowed him to kiss her upturned cheek, the wide brim of her Gainsborough hat making it impossible for him to successfully kiss her mouth.

"Try and miss me while I'm away, will you?" he asked.

"I won't have to try." She smiled. "I *will* miss you."

"I wish I could believe that, my dear."

Something in the timbre of his plea pulled at her conscience. She touched his cheeks and began, "Peter, don't—"

But his gloved fingertips quickly covered her lips, silencing her. "Shh! Don't say anything more. I'm content with what we have."

"'BOARD!" cried the conductor. "ALL ABOARD!"

"Good-bye, my dear." He planted a kiss on her glove-covered palm before turning away and bounding up the steps into the car.

Lacey stood there for a moment until his head appeared in one of the windows, then she walked toward it, smiling at him. It would be nice if she could feel something other than friendship for him, but at times even that sentiment seemed to pall.

The huge engine began to churn, billowing great puffs of smoke out of its stack as steam hissed again from the brakes. The enormous wheels turned slowly at first, then gained momentum, pulling the multicar train out of the depot and down the tracks.

Lacey watched it until the caboose disappeared, then she turned and retraced her steps back down the platform to the stationmaster's office, where the exit lay. The days Peter would be away from Austin were not going to be empty ones for her; she had already decided that. She would have Nicole to occupy most of her time, and the few remaining hours she did have free, she intended to spend them doing work with Mrs. Fellowes, her neighbor, and the local charity organization.

Mrs. Henrietta Lange would be proud of her if she knew of all the good work she had done recently. In fact, Lacey decided to write the Dallas society matron a letter, as soon as she got home, to let her know what she had been doing. With a smile, she thought that while she was at it, she would write to Hattiebelle, too, and find out how everyone was faring, now that they no longer lived in Gallagher House.

Nearing the baggage car of the newly arrived train, Lacey's thoughts were centered on what she would write. But at the sound of a familiar voice nearby, she turned, sure that her ears were deceiving her, and saw a young black man, who was unloading two large trunks onto a small handcart.

"William?" Though soft, her voice penetrated through the noise and confusion, and William turned.

Spying her, he grinned a brilliant smile that split across his face. "Lacey!"

Giggling with delight, she rushed over to him, threw her arms about his neck and let him sweep her off her feet, much to the surprise of the startled onlookers.

"Oh, William! It's so good to see you!"

"It's good to see you, too! You're lookin' mighty fine," he beamed.

Patting his brown-suited shoulders, she remarked, "I believe you've grown some since I last saw you. It must be Hattiebelle's cooking."

"You know I never turn down Momma's meals."

She laughed, looping her arm in his. "Where is she, by the way? Outside the depot, waiting for you?"

"No, Momma's back home, stayin' with some friends."

"She is? Then what are *you* doing here in Austin?"

"Oh, I came down with—"

"He came with me, Lacey."

Her head jerked up at the sound of the low-pitched voice in front of her. "Nick!" His name was spoken on a whisper so soft, it almost went unheard. *Dear God, he hasn't changed at all,* she thought, savoring each detail of him with an indescribable hunger. And she hadn't changed either, for one look was all it had taken for her to want him with that old, familiar, frightening need.

She started toward him, watching as his arms slowly came up from his side, parting to receive her in an embrace that she longed for desperately. The feel of his body next to hers, even though their many layers of clothing would separate them, was something she had sorely missed over these last, long, barren months. The touch of his hand, the brush of his lips against hers, the taste of his kiss were cravings she had to assuage, and all the bitterness between them be damned!

"Mr. Gallagher?"

Hearing his name called, Nick reluctantly tore his eyes away from Lacey even as she continued to close the distance between them. Catherine Ainsworth, the diminutive auburn-haired actress he'd met on the train, swished over to him and placed her delicate hand on his arm, a slightly devious smile playing about her rouged mouth.

"I do want to thank you for your . . . mmm, help, Mr. Gallagher."

223

Out of the corner of his eye, Nick became aware that Lacey's progress toward him had stopped, and she was now standing, rooted to the platform, not three feet away from him. *Oh, shit!* he cursed inwardly. *Of all the damn rotten luck.* He managed, however, to reply. "Uh, my pleasure, Miss Ainsworth."

Turning to look at Lacey, he noted her tight-lipped, glacial scowl. Well, dammit, he'd come so close this time, he wasn't going to admit defeat now. He would get that warm smile back on her face, even if it killed him. After all, wasn't that what he was here for?

Lacey glanced first at Nick, and then at the petite woman who stood proprietorially beside him. The stupid ass! she seethed. The dumb, ignorant, stupid ass! Chasing after one bottle redhead hadn't been enough evidently; but this one did look to be of a little higher class than the other, and she assumed that his dalliances were improving in quality.

She finally turned to William, wanting to break the heavy silence that hovered about them. "Tell me, did Hattiebelle get the package I sent to her last Christmas?"

"She sure did." He grinned. "I'm supposed to tell you that the seeds took root right away. She was gonna write to you herself, but with the way things have been lately and all, it just sorta got away from her."

"Oh, that's all right. I never expected her to answer my letter anyway. But I didn't want her to worry; that was my main concern, really. By the way, where will you be staying while you're here?"

"Uh . . ." Unable to answer, because he wasn't sure, William turned to look at Nick.

"We'll be at the Capitol Hotel until we can arrange for permanent accommodations elsewhere," he supplied.

Lacey wondered what he meant by "permanent accommodations," but before she could ask him the other woman's preemptive exclamation cut her short.

"The Capitol Hotel? Why, that's where I'm staying! My goodness, isn't that a coincidence?"

"Yes, isn't it?" grumbled Lacey, her eyes fastened on Nick. They had probably planned it on the train.

Turning, she walked with William as they left the now less-crowded platform for the exit, where she intended to hire a waiting cab. She would worry about what to do about this new development once she was at home. Now wasn't the time. But when William asked her how to get to the hotel, she paused a moment and told him. It wasn't too far, quite near the Capitol Building, as a matter of fact, which was clearly visible in the distance.

One moment she was standing there, conversing with her old friend, and the next she felt herself being lifted and placed into the coach that Nick had hailed when she hadn't been noticing.

"Just what do you think you're doing?" she hissed when he thrust her into the corner of the seat. "Let me out of here!"

"Just sit tight, Red, and mind your manners."

"Mind *my* manners! Why, you—"

"Hush up!" he ordered, then turned to help the actress in.

225

Catherine Ainsworth took the seat across from Lacey, smoothing her skirts aside so that Nick would have plenty of room to sit next to her. She gave Lacey an arched smile that was just short of being smug, and Lacey, feeling quite benevolent, returned it. Nick crawled into the coach then and closed the door behind him.

Lacey didn't know whether to laugh out loud at the woman's disconcertion, or be mad as hell when Nick sat down beside her, dropping his arm possessively around her shoulders. Of all the nerve! Wasn't one woman enough for him?

Nick stuck his head out of the window and hit the side of the coach, shouting, "You can go now, driver."

The coach jerked into motion and they were off.

Lacey tried her best to sit still, not wanting to touch Nick any more than she had to. It was impossible not to brush against him, though, because the road they traveled over was full of bumps, dips and large potholes. She could feel the weight of his hand on her shoulder, holding her steady each time the cab swayed, and she could smell the heady scent of his bay rum which seemed to permeate the very air she breathed.

For her sanity's sake, the journey from the depot to the hotel was fortunately a short-lived one. They soon pulled to a stop in the hotel's forecourt and activity ensued as two bellboys began to unload their many trunks and bags.

"Aren't you getting out?" Nick asked her when the final bag had been placed on the hotel steps.

"No, I've got to go home," she answered, her eyes riveted on the actress, who stood beside him.

"Where's that?" Nick queried.

"Ask William," she snapped. "He knows."

Continuing to hold the door so that the driver couldn't pull away, Nick looked at her for a long, silent moment, admiring the heightened color in her creamy cheeks and the dark sparkle of her eyes. Sensing that the actress was moving away from him, he said, "We've got to talk, you know."

"No, Nick, I don't know."

"There's a helluva lot I need to say to you, Red, and you know it."

"Don't call me Red!"

"Does he have red hair like yours?"

Caught totally by surprise at his query, she blinked down at him in confusion, a frown wrinkling her brow. "He, who, Nick?"

"Our son."

"Our . . . *what?*" A harsh, uneasy laugh passed through her parted lips. *"We* don't have a son, Nick."

His disappointment was instantly evident. "So, Darcy *was* wrong. It wasn't you after all. She'd heard that you—"

"Maybe one of your other women had your *son*, Nick. But I didn't. *Driver!* Take me home, please."

Nick didn't stop to analyze the cause behind her sudden angry outburst; but then he didn't need to. He knew jealousy when he saw it, and she positively burned with it! Making his way into the hotel, he couldn't help but think how lovely she was when she was angry. Her eyes glittered brilliantly and her cheeks bloomed with color. She was, and always would be, the most beautiful woman he'd ever seen in his life.

When he had registered at the busy front desk, he turned and saw Miss Ainsworth, standing nearby, apparently waiting for someone—him, as it turned out.

"Are you going to be in Austin long, Mr. Gallagher?"

"Longer than I'd thought, ma'am," he muttered.

"If you don't mind me saying so, your sister-in-law did not look at all as pleased to see you as you thought she would be. You said on the train, coming down, that your trip here was to be a surprise, yet she was at the station waiting for you."

"No, she wasn't waitin' for me. I 'spect she was seeing someone off."

"Mmm." She nodded understandingly and followed him toward the grand staircase in the center of the room. "Well, I've learned over the years that it is never a good idea to visit family unless there's an absolute necessity. That's why I left the train here rather than journeying on to San Antonio."

Reaching the top of the stairs, she gave him a teasing little smile and asked, "Are you *sure* you couldn't take time out from your busy schedule to visit me in Houston? I'll be playing there for the next month."

"I'm afraid not, ma'am," he replied. "My business here is too important to be interrupted." Knowing what Lacey's attitude was now, it was going to take all the work he could put into it just to get her to come around again. If the actress hadn't come up to him at the depot, he knew, without a doubt, that he and Lacey would have been back together again by now, son or no son.

Tipping his chin respectfully, he mumbled, "'Day, ma'am," and ambled off in the direction of his room.

William was already inside the suite, helping the porter with their trunks and valises. Nick dug down into his pocket and produced a coin, flipping it in the porter's direction.

"Thank *you*, sir!" the boy beamed, backing out.

When the door was closed, Nick stripped off his coat and tie and dropped dejectedly onto the bed, stretching out full length. William gave him a long look, then muttered, "Yeah, that's all right, you just lay there and take yourself a little rest. I don't mind, unpackin' for the both of us. After all, there ain't much here." He turned pointedly to look at the two trunks and three valises, then glared back at Nick, who hadn't been listening.

"Something's bothering me, William. I can't put my finger on it, but I know somethin' ain't right."

"A little physical activity would get your blood to flowin'. Maybe you could think then."

"Lacey was upset about something . . . something I said."

"Momma always told me that a man did his best figurin' when he was on his feet, doin' somethin'."

"What could I have said to make her so mad at me? I only asked if our son had red hair." At the instant sound of William laughing, Nick looked over at him, a frown twisting his features. "What tickled your funny bone?"

"*You!*" William informed him, laughing again and forgetting about the unpacking.

"Me?" Looking at the younger man as if he had

suddenly sprouted a second head, he asked, "What's the matter with you?"

William sobered momentarily, his laughter coming out now in short, intermittent chuckles. "If I was you, I'd buy me a ticket on the next train bound for Dallas and forget all about trying to get Lacey back. You done played hell with that lady, and only a miracle from the Good Lord Himself is gonna help you out of the mess you've got yourself into."

"What're you talking about?"

"You and Lacey! That's what I'm talkin' about."

Nick sat up, a look of comprehension slowly crossing his face. "Look, I didn't have nothing to do with that little actress on the train, if that's what you're—"

"I ain't talkin' about that woman," William retorted impatiently. "I'm talkin' about what you said to Lacey, when you asked her about your son. She didn't have a *boy*, you fool. She had a little girl!"

The wrinkles of confusion cleared from Nick's forehead as his dark eyes widened. His bottom lip, visible beneath his moustache, dropped open as a low, guttural groan vibrated in his throat. Dear God, he *had* played hell!

Lacey had more than enough time to think about her confrontation with Nick. The further she rode away from him, the angrier at him she became.

"How dare he!" she cursed into the emptiness of the coach. "How dare he assume that I had his son! Never a thought of a daughter. *No,* only a son! Oooh! The arrogance, the unadulterated conceit of that man is . . . is outrageous!"

When the cab finally reached her house, she paid the driver and rushed inside, mounting the stairs to her bedroom. A warm breeze fluttered the curtains at the opened windows, as it usually did this time of day. And from the confines of her little crib, Nicole was watching her as she removed her richly adorned hat and violet jacket.

"Your father is the world's biggest bastard," she announced to Nicole as she moved about the room, putting her things away. "In more ways than one! So he thought I'd had his son, did he? Well, I'd like to tell him a thing or two about that!"

After hanging her jacket in her wardrobe, she crossed over to the crib and lifted her daughter out, pressing her cuddly little body close to hers. As she had known it would, her ire began to abate almost instantly. She could never stay angry for long when holding her child.

"Oh, darling," she whispered softly. "You're so precious, so sweet. I don't care if he doesn't know about you, or that he only wants a son, because I want you more than anything in the world."

She sat down in the rocking chair before the windows, placing the baby in her lap, and continued to talk to Nicole. They discussed the silliness of the male gender and how unfair it was to the women in the world to have to depend on them. Of course, their conversation was a bit one-sided, with Lacey doing all of the talking, but the little girl's eyes widened in fascination as Lacey's mouth continued to move. Nicole's tiny lips opened in her attempt to speak to her mother, but a spate of gurgles and coos erupted instead of words.

Thinking it the most wonderful sound she'd ever heard, Lacey began to laugh. Soon Nicole was laughing with her, showing her mother pink gums that were devoid of teeth. It was their combined laughter, unfortunately, that was their downfall, because it masked the sound of footsteps that came running up the stairs. And it wasn't until Lacey heard the quick, heavy breathing, coming from her bedroom doorway, that she quickly turned and gasped at the sight she saw there.

Nick leaned against the doorjamb, disheveled and red-faced. His coat and tie were gone, his vest and shirt buttons were unfastened and the celluloid collar and cuffs he'd worn earlier were gone, too. His sleeves were rolled up past his elbows, and it looked to Lacey as if he had been in the process of undressing when he suddenly decided to pay her a call.

All of his attention, she noticed, was centered on the smiling baby girl in her lap. But when he began to cross the room toward them, she inhaled sharply, wondering what he intended to do.

Nick knelt beside the rocking chair and accused softly, "You should have told me, Lace. Why the hell didn't you tell me?"

Lacey swallowed, but the lump of rage in her throat would not be suppressed. "How did you find out?"

"William had to tell me. Why did you lie, Lace?"

"I did not lie!"

"Dammit, I nearly came apart at the seams when you said we didn't have a baby. Don't you think I have a right to know about my own child?"

"Don't raise your voice at me, Nicholas Gallagher!"

"You deserve to be yelled at, woman! You keep my daughter's birth a secret and—"

"I did not! Hattiebelle and William knew!"

"—then decide on your own that I shouldn't know about it. How long have Hattiebelle and William known?"

"Since she was first born," Lacey replied, lifting her chin defiantly. "I wrote Hattiebelle, telling her what I had named *my* daughter as well as all of the other particulars that would only interest another mother."

"And she didn't tell *me!*"

"Maybe she thought you wouldn't be interested."

That dart hit him precisely where she had intended it. Nick's ruddy complexion turned an even darker shade of red as his teeth ground together angrily. Fury pushed him to his feet and he began to pace the distance of Lacey's room. "And all this time . . . all this whole damn time, while she's been on my back about coming to get you, she's known!"

"Well, you can't blame *me* for that. It was her decision not to tell you; not mine."

He stopped his pacing and glowered down at her. "Why didn't *you* write and tell me?"

Lacey was unable to answer him immediately. All she could think about were those dozen or more times when she *had* started to write him, only to end up tearing the letters into tiny bits as waves of frustrated anger washed over her. There was their final parting, hanging between them still, and she could not get it out of her mind.

Finally, shaking her bright head as she pressed Nicole closer to her, she responded, "You didn't need to know."

"Didn't *need!* Good God in heaven, Red, that's my daughter you—"

"So was the one in the Yukon, Nick. Or have you succeeded in forgetting all about her?"

Her quietly spoken accusation had the effect of a swift kick in Nick's midsection. He looked down at her, paling noticeably under her unwavering stare. Of all the things that had happened between them, of all the things he had told her, she had remembered that one, sordid, painful detail of his life.

"This . . . is different," he objected weakly.

"How can it be?" she retorted instantly. "Both of your children were born to women you weren't married to. Why should I consider *my* daughter any more special or different from the other woman's? You didn't even mourn your first little girl when she died at birth, Nick. Why should I think you would care that your second . . . bastard was healthy?"

A muscle twitched in Nick's jaw. "Well, it *is* different, that's all! Dammit, Giselle had been with so many men before I came along, I couldn't be sure that the kid was really mine. On the other hand, Red, I was your first. You can't deny that."

Lacey's skin tingled at the memory of their shared passions. Embers of desire, long dormant, began to smolder in the pit of her stomach, warming her blood. But determined not to let her lustful craving get the better of her, she blocked out the thoughts and asked pointedly, "Was Giselle's baby your daughter?"

Nick groaned and sank to the side of her bed, wearily resting his head in his hands. "Hell, honey, I don't know. She could've been. It's been so damn long, though, and—"

"Time shouldn't have anything to do with it. The loss of a baby is . . . is catastrophic. Time can never erase a catastrophe; veil it, maybe, but never erase it." Smoothing the baby-fine curls away from Nicole's forehead, she added softly, "I don't think I'd want to live if Nicole—"

"But *she's* healthy!" Nick asserted, leaving the bed to kneel beside the rocking chair once again. He touched his daughter with a long, calloused finger. "Just look at her. You can see right off how healthy she is. Giselle's baby was a tiny, sickly little thing that was . . . that was malformed. She only lived for about an hour before she just stopped breathing. I don't think the Lord meant for her to be born."

Lacey became increasingly aware of the haggard look on Nick's face. Without wanting it to, her heart went out to him and she felt instinctively the agony and pain that he had so carefully hidden for so many years. He wasn't the unfeeling, callous brute she'd thought him to be. He had cared, honestly, for that tiny bit of misshapen life that hadn't had a chance to live. No matter that the little girl had or hadn't been his, he had cared for her.

"Giselle," he went on quietly, "well, she was beyond my helping her. Her fever was so damn high there wasn't nothing I could do to get it down. And with a blizzard goin' on outside the cabin where we were, there wasn't any way I could go riding off for the doc.

"Toward the end, she started calling out for some

man. She rambled on and on, like people with high fever do, talking in French. She called, 'Albert, Albert,' till I thought I'd start ramblin' crazy myself. *Any* man in my place would get the notion the kid wasn't his. And . . . I guess it helped, thinking I'd been duped, that the baby I'd helped bring into the world and bury when it died wasn't mine.''

Lacey gazed at the crown of Nick's lowered head, just a fraction of an inch from his daughter's. The sunlight, pouring into the room, cast reddish glints in his thick brown hair. As if they suddenly became possessed of a will of their own, her fingers reached out and wove through the crisp, masculine hair. They smoothed back the vibrant strands from his forehead as his heavily lashed lids lifted to look up at her. His eyes were dark, emotional pools of brown, and she found herself drowning in their depths.

Examining her lovely, compassion-filled features, Nick noted the clarity of her green eyes and the moist opening of her pink mouth. "Lace," he whispered on a ragged groan, bending closer to her. "Oh, God, Lace! I've been only half a man without you."

Words of censure and rebuke were forgotten as her fingers began to move again, exploring the long-forgotten texture of his skin. She caressed his wide forehead, following the indentation of a shallow wrinkle that led to the bridge of his beaklike nose. She traced a line down it, past the tip and on to brush the top of his moustache before feeling the deep groove beside his wide mouth. As she started to cross the dividing line of his lips, he turned his head slightly and captured her fingertips in his mouth, gently licking them with his rough, wet tongue.

An age-old tempo began beating within her breast as the blood sang in her veins; a duet which caused her head to spin. Her lips, dry from breathing raggedly, were moistened with the tip of her tongue, and she released a slight moan in her throat as she felt Nick's large, warm hand move to rest on her sheerly covered thigh.

His mouth moved closer and closer to her own as the anticipation of the kiss that was soon to be swelled within her. She wanted him so badly it hurt, but now he could take away all of her pain and she would welcome it.

"Miz Gallagher?" From the doorway, Daisy's voice shattered the tenuous link that bound Lacey to Nick. "Momma said to tell you that the tea will be ready soon. Uh, will the gentleman be stayin'? I'd like to know so I can set another cup."

Sanity returned to Nick and Lacey instantaneously. Lacey's darkened green eyes blinked rapidly as she felt her face grow hot, then cold.

"Uh, yes, Daisy," she choked out convulsively. "Mr. Gallagher will be staying for tea."

"Mr. Gallagher? Oh, is he your family, then?"

"Daisy," Lacey intoned firmly, noting Nick's look of pained frustration. "That will be all, thank you. And, *yes,* Mr. Gallagher is family."

The girl shrugged her plump shoulders and turned, leaving them with "Well, I'll go tell Momma then."

"My God!" Nick slowly rose to his feet, not bothering to hide the very obvious bulge in his trousers. "Of all the dimwitted . . . where'd you dig her up at?"

Lacey didn't take immediate offense at his irritability; she knew he was suffering. "She and her mother, my cook, happen to be the best housekeeper-and-maid combination in the neighborhood. Peter and I were darn lucky to find them when we did."

Hearing the other man's name, Nick glowered down at her. "I've been meaning to talk to you about him, Lace."

But she gave him a quelling, sidelong glance and stood, shifting Nicole in her arms as she crossed the floor to her wardrobe. "Not now, Nick. I have to change."

Eyeing her slim figure as it passed by him, all thoughts of Peter Thorne escaped him. "Don't go to no extra trouble on my account. Whatcha got on looks fine to me."

"Yes, I'm sure it does, but I still have to change. Someone might decide to call on me, and while this dress is suitable for one thing, it is not appropriate for receiving guests."

"Guests?"

She noted the slightly suspicious tone in his voice and clarified her statement with an indulgent smile. "Friends, Nick. You see, I belong to a very active charity organization here in Austin. There are times when the members find it necessary to drop in unexpectedly. Here, hold Nicole while I change."

Nick took the baby from her, then turned to stare back at her as her words finally registered. "Nicole?"

"Yes, Nicole," she retorted, lifting her chin a notch. "Nicole Rochelle . . . Gallagher."

"Well, I'll be damned!" he grinned lopsidedly. "You named her after *me.*"

"And after my mother!"

Watching him hold their daughter, she witnessed a dramatic change occur. No longer did he possess his usual strength and self-assurance. With the baby, he was awkward, uncertain and totally at a loss as to what to do next.

"M—maybe you'd better take her back. God knows, I'm afraid I might drop her."

"Oh, for heaven's sake! Sit down on the bed and get acquainted with her."

"Sit down?" he repeated stupidly. "But she ain't heavy. She's as light as a feather."

"Hold her long enough and you'll swear she weighs a ton." Lacey delivered this bit of dry advice as she disappeared behind a tall, folding silk screen that shielded her wardrobe from Nick's vision.

Staring in amazement, Nick couldn't believe that the tiny little thing he held was really a part of him, created from one moment of his lustfulness. Her green eyes, so like Lacey's peered up at his with saucerlike roundness. *I don't know what to think of you, either, sweetheart,* he thought with a grin.

Nicole's tiny, starfishlike hands circled one of his rough fingers and, as was her instinctive habit, she tried to taste it. But Nick gently moved the digit away from her mouth, feeling the strength in her tiny grasp, and turned her hand over to examine it. Miniscule, paper-thin nails graced the tips of her delicate fingers. And when he gingerly felt of her wrist and arm, he was astounded at the size of her little bones. Proudly he had to admit that there was nothing sickly or malformed about this baby. She was perfect in every way . . . except maybe for her nose, which looked a lot like his.

It was then that Nick sensed the tension that had suddenly grown thick in the room. Hairs on the back of his neck literally stood on end. He turned his head and saw Lacey, standing next to the folded screen, her blouse still covering her shoulders, but parted and gaping down the front as her hands, clenched into fists, were jammed firmly on her hips.

He swallowed nervously. "Wh—what's the matter, babe?"

Her green eyes narrowed, her mouth taut and unyielding. "That . . . that woman!"

"Woman?"

"That *floozie* from the train."

He released his breath. "Oh, her!"

"You come bursting in here, accusing me of unwarranted crimes and I forgot all about her."

"Well, good! She didn't mean nothing anyway."

"The audacity . . . the utter gall you have in coming in *my* home and insinuating that *I* . . . oh! Nick Gallagher, if you're not out of this house in one minute, I'll start screaming at the top of my lungs and have you thrown out!"

"What the hell for?"

"You will not come waltzing back into *my* life! Not after all that you've done!"

"I haven't done a damn thing, Red." But he wisely put the baby down and rose to his feet before slowly backing toward the door as she continued to advance toward him predatorily.

"Don't lie to me! I bought your lies once before and look where it got me. But no more! I wouldn't believe you if you told me darkness followed daylight."

"Look, that woman don't mean nothing to me, Red! Honest to God, she don't! Why, I only met her this morning."

"Ha! That's a likely story, if I've ever heard one. You've always had a fancy for loose women. You obviously haven't changed, either. Well, *I* have. I won't be taken in with your deceitful vows of innocence *ever* again. I've got two good eyes and they weren't lying to me when they saw the look on your face when that . . . that *hussy* rubbed up against you. Well, you can tell her for me that she's more than welcome to you!"

And with that, she slammed the door in his face. He winced as he heard the bolt being shot home, but he continued to stare at the panel in disbelief for a moment before giving his head a quizzical shake. What had brought all that on? he wondered. One minute she was as sane as he was, then the next, she wasn't.

Scratching his head in bewildered confusion, he loped easily down the stairs and found the buxom little maid, standing in the hall below.

"The tea's in the parlor, sir," she informed him.

"Well, good! But I ain't staying . . . now," he growled.

Just before he slammed the front door behind him, he thought he heard her mutter, "Pity!"

Up in her room, pacing back and forth, Lacey took deep gulps of air, hoping that one would have the calming effect she badly needed. The nerve of that man. Thinking he could just breeze back into her life and take up where he'd left off as if nothing had ever happened between them. Well, if he thought that, he certainly didn't have his head screwed on right, because she would sooner have the plague than get mixed up with him again! Their first union had brought her nothing but unhappiness and pain. No, she would never willingly suffer that agony again.

Her pacing slowed somewhat and she found herself standing before her window. Looking down at the treelined street, she saw Nick's tall figure, striding toward a horse that was tied to the front hitching post. The gaze she threw him would have bored through solid granite.

There was nothing about him even remotely attractive, she tried to convince herself. He was stubborn, hardheaded, opinionated, uncouth, barbaric, not in the least good-looking, and there were times when she seriously doubted his intelligence. But with all those faults, why did she still feel drawn to him? What was it about him that made her lose all semblance of control whenever he was near?

Nick. She focused her attention on him, seeing that he had stopped now, and was just standing on the walk near the horse, as if in deep thought. Then she saw his head tilt to a cocky angle and his shoulders relax. He tossed a quick look over his shoulder, forcing her to draw away from the window, then he began to laugh; a deep, self-assured rumble that sent chills up her spine. She didn't like the sound of it one bit.

"The fool," she whispered. "And he called Daisy dimwitted!"

Chapter Twelve

FASHIONABLY DRESSED MEN AND WOMEN MINGLED about the elegant drawing room, drinking champagne from fluted glasses and eating dainty sandwiches served to them by fancy-coated waiters. They had been assembled here tonight at the special request of Mr. and Mrs. Herbert R. Talmadge, art patrons and university trustees, for the unveiling of Peter Thorne's latest works. Many of the guests had previous knowledge of the artist and were looking forward with great enthusiasm to seeing what his most recent efforts looked like. The others were here merely as observers or were members of the charity committee who would benefit from the large gathering as well.

Standing on one side of the room, Peter couldn't stem the surge of pride that welled up within him as he looked around the crowded room. Tonight was the pinnacle of his career to date, one that he'd been looking forward to most of his adult life. Now that it was finally here—his big night!—he couldn't help feeling just a little bit cocky and arrogant. He had done it all on his own, and hadn't relied on anyone else's talent but what God had endowed him with.

Standing beside him was Lacey. Her cream-colored silk gown, with its high-necked lace bodice, seemed to bring out the healthy luster in her peach-and-porcelain complexion. Her glossy copper-gold hair, worn twisted and coiled with a strand of pearls at the crown of her head, gave her natural, ethereal beauty a regal quality. She was, in his proud estimation, one of the most beautiful women in the room.

But her outward appearance was in direct conflict to the turmoil she felt inside. Nervous and anxious, she was just plain scared that something was going to go wrong before the night was over. She had tried to overcome the fears, but with Nick Gallagher back in her life again, she knew she had just cause to be apprehensive.

Taking a deep breath, she silently reflected over the past few weeks, back to the day that Nick had reentered her life and discovered that he had fathered a child . . . *her* child. He had seemed pleased, almost thrilled over Nicole's existence then. For days afterward, he had called on them, bringing little dolls and trinkets for the baby, and flowers for her. But without warning, his visits had suddenly begun to taper off to a lesser frequency, causing Lacey to wonder just what he was up to. Lately she had been surprised if he happened to come to her house at all.

She tried not to let it annoy her. Nick was his own man, after all, so what else should she expect? There was hardly any way she could predict what his actions would be. But the reality that she couldn't see him, even on an irregular basis, was very painful for her to accept. This only reaffirmed that which she had tried for so long to deny, that she was still in love with him.

"Not nervous, are you, my dear?"

Lacey flashed a false smile up at Peter, unaware of the lovely pink glow that bloomed in her cheeks. "No, of course not," she lied. "Should I be?"

Peter chuckled and shook his head. "Not at all. After tonight you will probably be the most sought-after young woman in the state. Every young buck within a two-hundred-mile radius will be camping outside your door to get a look at your exquisite beauty, and you will probably be jealously envied by all the young women as well."

A faint smile twisted her lips. "I seriously doubt that, Peter."

"Mark my words, Lacey—the unveiling of my paintings tonight will make you world-famous." In the crowd gathered about them, Peter had seen art critics from New York, Boston and Philadelphia, and he had even seen a couple from as far away as London and Paris, if their accents were anything to go by. Not only would *she* be famous, but *his* name would be on the lips of those around the globe as well.

Sensing that there was something unspoken in Peter's flowery platitudes, a tiny frown formed between Lacey's brows. "Peter? Have you done something that I'm not aware of?"

"Of course not!" he denied immediately.

But she continued to gaze at him in a sidelong, speculative manner, questioning his hasty, glib reply. "Then why do I get the feeling that you're not telling me everything?"

"Lacey, darling! I thought you had more trust in me."

"Oh, I trust you," she assured him, deadpan. "About as far as I can throw you. I know your reputation for deviousness almost as well as I know the back of my own hand."

"Devious! Me?" He issued an uneasy chuckle. "Why, I'm merely a poor, starving artist who is only trying to make a living and a name for himself. If I have done things in the past that are, shall we say, less than honorable, I've only done them because it was expected of me. I don't like all this harum-scarum existence any better than you do, but we creatively blessed individuals are expected to be a little out of the ordinary." He shook his head firmly. "But I wouldn't call the pride that I have in my work 'devious.'"

"Yes, well, we'll just see about that, won't we?" she murmured suspiciously.

Peter coughed uncomfortably and gave a disdainful sniff. There were times when Lacey was aware of more than what was good for her. Her woman's intuition reared its disturbingly nasty little head at the damnedest of times, like tonight, but he wasn't going to let its presence worry him. He was sure that she wouldn't be *too* disappointed with the slight alterations he'd made in the paintings of her. She was, after all, a woman of the world, having been Gallagher's mistress. And though she was still more than a little conventional, she would probably agree with him that the alterations he'd made were done in good taste. . . . At least, he hoped she would.

Lacey's voice, heavily tinged with misgiving,

broke in on Peter's thoughts. "Oh, my Lord! Who invited *him* here tonight?"

Peter glanced in the direction she was staring and saw Nick Gallagher step into the drawing room with the next wave of newly arrived guests. Dressed in elegant black evening clothes, Peter had to admit that the man looked almost respectable for a change. In fact, inspecting Nick's appearance more closely, he looked almost like a member of the upper class, and nothing at all like the coarse, redneck ruffian he actually was.

"Peter? You didn't ask Mrs. Talmadge or Mrs. Fellowes to send him an invitation, did you?"

"Well, Lacey—"

"Oh, you did! Why?"

"I simply took the advice that my banker gave me. Gallagher does have money, you know, just like everyone else here tonight. In fact, he probably has more."

"Oh, you're right in assuming that; he does have money. But the one thing you didn't consider is his taste in art. Naked women hanging behind a saloon bar is more in his line, not classic Greek Muses."

Peter turned from the flushed and seething Lacey to see that Nick was approaching them. He hurriedly extended his hand and gave the lanky Texan a smile that was almost sincere. Why not? he questioned himself. This man's money was as good as any other man's. "Glad you could make it, Gallagher."

"Thanks for the invite. Wouldn't have wanted to miss this little shindig for the world," Nick grinned. Eyeing Lacey, he asked, "How are you?"

"I'm just fine," she retorted tersely.

His brown eyes, dancing with hidden amusement, traveled over her slender body insolently. "Yeah, I can see that." Then, turning back to Peter, he said, "Say, I hear that them pictures you're gonna show us tonight are up for sale. How much you asking for 'em?"

"Five thousand each," Peter responded smoothly. "With a matching donation to the charity's scholarship fund."

"Whooeee!" Nick winced. "Ain't that kinda steep?"

"Merely a fraction of what they're really worth, Gallagher. Why, I predict that in years to come they will be worth ten times that paltry amount."

Nick scratched the back of his head before giving it a rueful shake. "I ain't never seen a picture that was worth *that* much money. They sure must be somethin'!"

Lacey forced herself to stand there and listen to the ensuing conversation between Nick and Peter. In a matter of minutes, though, when Nick's nearness began to grate on her composure, she knew it was time to make herself scarce. It was almost time to feed Nicole, she thought, who was upstairs in one of Mrs. Talmadge's guest bedrooms. She wouldn't have been able to come tonight if the gracious hostess hadn't insisted that she bring the baby with her. But then, being the mother of three grown children herself, Mrs. Talmadge knew firsthand how constricting a young mother's social life could be.

Politely asking to be excused, Lacey smiled at the two men and left them among the press of important people before making her way up the winding front stairs to the small bedroom at the back of the house.

Daisy was holding her daughter, walking up and down the length of the small room, trying to quiet Nicole's crying.

"It's past her feedin' time, Miss Lacey," the girl scolded.

"Yes, I know. I'm sorry I couldn't come sooner, but it was difficult for me to get away. Here, let me have her."

Lacey quickly unfastened the top of her gown and stepped out of it before taking her hungry daughter from Daisy's arms. Then, sitting down in a chair in a quiet, dark corner, she exposed her full breasts after cradling Nicole in the crook of her arm. Her daughter instantly found the protruding nipple and latched onto it hungrily, sniffling and grunting at the same time.

"Why don't you go down to the kitchen and get something to eat?" Lacey suggested to the young girl. "I'm sure you must need a break."

The hint needed no second bidding. Daisy was more than willing to leave her fretful little charge with Lacey. She hurriedly extinguished the lamps at Lacey's request before closing the door softly behind her.

With a sigh, Lacey leaned her head back carefully against the cushioned chair, not wanting to muss her coiffure any more than she could help. She would still have to look presentable later on at the unveiling, and didn't want to spend any more time than was necessary on her appearance. Taking a deep breath, she savored the silence surrounding her.

But Nicole continued to wriggle and grunt, obviously dissatisfied with the tiny amount of milk she was receiving.

"It won't come any faster, darling, if you don't settle down," Lacey chided gently. She shifted Nicole to a more comfortable position, moving one of the small feet that persisted in pushing against her rib.

"Maybe I can help," came Nick's husky voice from out of the darkness.

He had followed her, she realized as she tried to shield her bared breast with the small scrap of lace from her unbuttoned camisole. Pulling on it with her free hand, she discovered to her horror that it had twisted behind her and would not come free. A warm flush crept up her throat as he walked over to her, and she demanded quietly, "What are you doing here?"

"I came up to see my daughter."

"You could have seen her earlier at my house. Why choose now?"

"'Cause it's the first chance I've had. I've been . . . busy," he explained evasively. "My, my! She sure has grown, hasn't she?"

"You saw her just two weeks ago, Nick. She hasn't changed all that much."

"Well, like I said, Red, I've been busy."

"I can imagine," she muttered. He knelt down beside her chair then, his nearness causing her to feel slightly uncomfortable. "Nick! I don't want to sound rude, or anything, but I'm having a difficult enough time as it is, trying to get her to nurse, without you making it worse by butting in."

Ignoring her, Nick extended a hand and patted Nicole's chubby thigh, chuckling, "It don't look like she's been missin' many meals. The little dickens is gettin' fat."

Ribbons of moonlight from the undraped window illuminated his rugged features, casting his face into a mask of sensual shadows. Lacey's discomfort increased and her heart began to pound erratically. Her stomach muscles constricted and her breathing altered irregularly as Nick's hand moved from Nicole's leg to brush Lacey's exposed breast. The sound she tried so hard to repress could be contained no longer, and she heard herself moan, a quiet, almost erotic sound that seemed to echo loudly in the room. The warmth from his fingers penetrated her cool skin when he caressed the breast his daughter held, and it was at that moment that Lacey's milk came down.

Nicole instantly became still and began to gulp noisily, having finally gotten that which she'd been rooting for, her last meal of the day.

"You see?" Nick intoned softly. "I told you I could help."

His hand moved again, slowly, surely. Lacey was unable to stop his fingers from trailing across the bareness of her chest to the other breast that gleamed like pale ivory in the moonlight. His thumb and forefinger drew a circle around the darkened aureole there, feeling the raised bumps that had appeared on the surface the instant his hand had touched it. When his fingers gently drew out the nipple, rolling it between them, it hardened into a point and milk suddenly dripped from its pores.

"Nick, stop it," she demanded breathlessly.

"Why? You like it, don't you? You used to like for me to do this. I only had to touch you this way before you would open up to me like a flower, Lace."

Wincing at the painful memory of how they once had been, she gathered together all the strength she possessed and pushed his hand away. "Why are you doing this to me, Nick? Does it give you some sort of twisted pleasure to see me squirm?"

Nick moved away, chuckling drily beneath his breath. "You know something, Red? You've lived like a nun for too long."

"Whereas, *you* certainly haven't lived like a monk, have you?"

"Never said I did. I ain't monk material."

A myriad of retorts floated through her head as she glared at him. "And just what makes you think I've lived like a nun?" she countered, smiling at the disturbed look which flashed across his face.

"If I thought for one minute, honey, that there was any truth in that, I'd—"

"You mean, it's all right for *you* to have other women, but it isn't right for me to have other men?"

"Damn right!" he barked, knowing that she had been the only woman in his life for years now.

"What a stupid, archaic philosophy! I'm over twenty-one now, Nick, and no longer subject to your guardianship. I can do *what* I please with *whom* I please. If I should choose to take a dozen lovers, I'll do it!"

"That ain't likely, though. I learned a long time ago just what kind of lady you are. You ain't got the nerve to climb between the sheets with some other man. Hell, you had to battle your conscience when you gave yourself to me!"

"Then if I'm such an unappealing prude, why are you here with me now? Why aren't you with your little actress friend?"

Nick's mouth quirked to an odd angle. Her jealousy was so obvious. "I don't know what you're talking about, honey."

"Don't play the innocent with me, and I'm not your honey!"

His shoulders vibrated with amusement. Lord, she was positively green with jealousy! Tossing back his head, he released a roar of laughter that split through the quiet room.

Startled by the unexpected laughter, Nicole's little head twisted sharply, turning toward the sound. But her little gums, dotted with tiny, razor-sharp teeth, still retained a tight hold on her mother's nipple. Pain ripped through Lacey, and she shrieked out in agony.

Nick sobered instantly. "Whatsa matter?"

Inhaling in a long, loud hiss, Lacey gently loosened the suction Nicole had on her breast, then released her breath slowly. "Your daughter bit me!"

"Geez, I'm sorry! I didn't know that was gonna happen, Lace. I—I didn't mean for it to."

Blinking back unbidden tears of pain, Lacey ground out, "Yes, I know, Nick. You don't *mean* to do a lot of things, but you do them just the same."

"What's that supposed to mean?"

"You figure it out!" Settling the baby at her other breast, she added crossly, "Why don't you go back downstairs? Daisy will be up in a few minutes, and I don't want her to start asking a lot of embarrassing questions."

"Hell, Lace, that kid ain't got enough sense to know what questions *to* ask," he mumbled sarcastically. "I doubt if she's got any brains at all in her head. . . . They're all in her chest."

Lacey gasped, outraged. "That is a despicable thing to say! Daisy happens to be one of the sweetest, most gentle little girls I've ever known."

"Little! Her?" Nick threw back his head and laughed again.

"There's much more to that child than the size of her breasts, but of course *you* wouldn't see it. And just for your information, Nick, she's only fourteen."

"Lord!" Nick gave his dark head a disbelieving shake. "She looks a lot older than that. I thought she was at least eighteen or nineteen."

"Well, she's not! And her life hasn't been a bed of roses, either. Her father used to beat her and her mother regularly, from what I've heard. And I expect that the only reason they are both alive today is because the old fool was killed when a bull went wild and kicked him in the head. So, if she happens to be a bit dull-witted, you can put all the blame on her father, and not the size of her mammaries."

"Look, Lace," he began, shamefaced, "I'm sorry I made fun of the kid. I didn't know she had a daddy like that."

"And you didn't bother to ask either, did you? No, you just made up your mind beforehand and disregarded all the other possibilities that might have existed. Well, what should I expect? You men are all alike."

"No," he disagreed with a firm shake of his head, "we are *not* all like that girl's daddy."

After a thoughtful moment, she conceded, "Maybe not *all* of you . . . just most of you!"

Cursing beneath his breath, Nick turned and wrenched open the door. "One of these days, Red honey, you're gonna find out just how wrong you are about that."

"Ha!" she snapped, and watched the door close behind him. "Like hell I will."

Crimson velvet draped one wall of the long gallery, shrouding the unseen framed canvases. Along the other wall, where Lacey now walked, open floor-to-ceiling windows allowed fresh air into the otherwise stale-smelling room. She inhaled deeply, hoping that the fresh air would somehow hold down the mounting anxiety within her. If she had been scared earlier, her recent scene with Nick had caused her to feel positively petrified. Her sense of impending disaster was sharper at this moment than it had been before.

Across the room, Peter beckoned to her with a wave of his upraised hand, and she started through the crowd of guests to reach his side. There was no sign of Nick, but she knew he wasn't far away. The fingers of apprehension that crawled up her spine only reaffirmed her suspicion.

"Are you ready, my dear?" Peter asked as she stopped beside him.

"As ready as I'll ever be, I suppose." She twisted her gloved fingers together and breathed deeply.

"Ladies and gentlemen!" Peter announced loudly, pausing for a moment as a hush fell over the assembled throng. "I am honored by your presence here tonight. Before I unveil my latest works for you to see, I would like to thank Mr. and Mrs. Herbert Talmadge for allowing us the use of their beautiful home. And I would also like to thank those of you who are involved with the University Scholarship

Society for lending your support and your names to this event. I am sure that the contributions you receive tonight will greatly add to the benefit of some well-deserving young students.

"In my meager attempt to promote great beauty and refined culture in this rapidly growing state of ours, I have tried to capture on canvas my interpretation of the nine Greek Muses. The Thorne Muses, as I hope they will be known in the future."

He turned to Lacey and extended his hand, a silent indication for her to join him. "With me tonight is the woman whom I perceive to be the epitome of the classic Greek female in both face and form. She has worked with me diligently over these last months, and without her I fear I would not be where I am now. Ladies and gentlemen, may I present to you Mrs. Christopher Gallagher, my beautiful model."

Muffled applause erupted at this point, followed by a murmur of hushed voices. Peter moved toward the draped canvases and Lacey stepped back, feeling tension coil tightly inside her stomach.

"Urania," Peter called out, whipping back the drape and revealing the first canvas. "The muse of astronomy!"

Like the other guests, Lacey had to admire the way in which Peter had depicted her in the painting. In a voluminous, all-concealing gown of gray chiffon, she stood beside a doric column, studying a small globe of the world in her outstretched hand.

"Polyhymnia, the muse of sacred poetry!"

Another burst of applause erupted as Lacey was this time shown depicted as an ancient Greek saint, posed in a tranquil, prayerlike stance.

The paintings of Clio, Calliope and Euterpe all received equal amounts of applause and praise, as did the painting of Melpomene, the muse of tragedy. Lacey began to relax and enjoy herself then, realizing that she might have been a bit hasty in worrying over the outcome of the evening. Peter was really a very good artist and deserved the recognition he was receiving.

But then Peter exposed the seventh painting, announcing, "Thalia, the muse of comedy!" and all of Lacey's fears came flooding back over her.

Thalia's gown, which Lacey could swear had been quite modest, was not painted modestly at all. In fact, the gossamer fabric clung to her slight curves so closely, it gave those who viewed it the impression of much more pale skin than was socially acceptable for a lady.

"Terpsichore, the muse of the dance!" Peter called out.

Lacey felt heat rush to her face. This muse's dress was even thinner and more revealing than the ones before it had been. Her bare arm was outstretched, her hand holding a beribboned tambourine, obscenely outlining the fullness of her breasts, and the expression on her face would have tempted any mortal male with its bewitching smile.

"And last, but not least," called Peter, "Erato, the muse of love!"

Women in the room actually gasped as Peter pulled the last drape aside. One look at the painting told Lacey all that she needed to know, forcing her to turn away ashamed and much too embarrassed to face the ogling crowd.

Reclining on a chaise, holding a book of love

poems, Lacey had been painted all but nude. A gauzy, diaphanous veil softened somewhat the explicitness of her endowments, but the sensuous, beguiling expression on her face made it appear to the onlookers that she was in the throes of passion.

Leaving the last painting, Peter walked over to her side, positively beaming with unabashed pleasure at the adulation he was receiving. The men in the room were going wild with their approval, while the women were still speechless from their shock.

"Well?" he asked her. "What do you think?"

Lacey managed to look up at him, her face a cold mask of fury. "I wish I had a gelding tool on me right now, Peter. I would dearly love to use it on you."

If she had slapped him outright, he couldn't have looked more stunned. "You—you don't like them?"

"How can I?" she countered. "They're not me. They're . . . lewd! My God, and you're actually proud of the way you've humiliated me!"

"Humiliated! My dear girl, I've made you famous!"

"*In*famous!" she corrected scathingly, then turned and started out of the room.

She could feel every head turn and look in her direction as she made her way toward the gallery doors, but she kept her eyes straight ahead, not bothering to acknowledge their stares. With her chin held high, she ascended the stairs to the second floor, and when she finally reached the quiet seclusion there, she lost the last shred she had possessed of her self-control and dropped to her knees, weeping openly. All this time she had trusted Peter, and this was how he repaid her. What a fool she had been . . . again! She had falsely assumed that he respected her. Some respect! He had made her to look like a common trollop in those gowns, gowns which she knew for a fact were far less revealing than he'd painted them. Well, it was easy to see now where his mind had been while they had been working together all those months.

Slumping dejectedly against the cold, paneled wall behind her, she let the tears course unheeded down her cheeks. At least, she told herself, there was one thing he hadn't done to humiliate her further; he hadn't captured her pregnant belly on those canvases. He had clearly defined everything else, though; her uptilted breasts with their darkened tips, the curve of her inner thigh, even the slight darkened area at the apex of her legs, but her distended belly, thank God, had been concealed.

"You ain't got nearly half the flesh to show off that Little Egypt does, but it sure comes across like you do." Nick came trudging up the stairs, one hand on the banister to help his ascension. "Yeah," he drawled, "old Pete could sure make himself a tidy little fortune if he could fit them pictures inside a nickelodeon machine and make 'em move."

Lacey, wanting to remove herself from his cutting jibes, pushed herself weakly to her feet. His sarcastic words had hit her right where they hurt the most, and she covered her face as more tears began to flow.

"Oh, come on, Red. Don't tell me you didn't know what that pantywaist was doin' when he painted you."

"I *didn't* know," she quickly denied. "Honestly, Nick, I had no idea that he was painting me like that. The gowns that I wore . . . well, they weren't anything like those in the last three paintings. They weren't thin or obscene. And if you don't believe me, I've got them in a trunk at my house to show you that I'm telling the truth."

Nick looked at her for a long moment, then finally conceded, "Yeah, I guess I do believe you. But I doubt that the rest of the folks downstairs will. Poor Red. You ain't never gonna make it to the top of the society heap . . . not after tonight."

"Must you gloat over it?" she whimpered.

"Honey, I ain't gloating." A nerve ticked in his jaw as his dark hooded eyes narrowed to menacing slits. "You think I'm proud of the way that bastard has embarrassed you? Well, I'm not! Right now, I'd like nothin' better than to go down there and punch his teeth down—"

"No!" she cried, reaching out to stop him. "No, Nick. Don't make a spectacle of yourself on my account." *I'm not worth the effort anymore,* she thought bitterly, feeling another wave of humiliation wash over her.

Hearing her pathetic whimpers, Nick reached into his pocket and produced a snowy handkerchief. He thrust it into her hand, murmuring, "You about ready to go home now?"

She nodded, unable to answer.

"Well, what do you say we go get the baby and head out?"

Wrapping his arm about her quivering shoulders, he led her down the hall.

Chapter Thirteen

PETER ARRIVED AT LACEY'S HOUSE JUST MOMENTS after she awakened from a very restless night. Her bedclothes were tangled about her, caused by all the tossing and turning she had done during the night. But when Daisy entered her room to announce that Mr. Thorne was downstairs in the parlor and was adamant about seeing her, she kicked her legs free of the covers and hopped out of bed with the agility of a well-rested person.

She didn't even take the time to dress. She merely threw a wrapper on over her cotton nightgown and stormed down the stairs, prepared to confront the man who had degraded her so. She wasn't going to let him get away with ruining her so carefully built reputation!

"I want to know why the devil you ran out on me last night?" he demanded angrily the instant she stepped into the room.

"*What?* Peter Thorne, you've got some nerve, coming here and expecting *me* to supply the explanations, especially after what you did to me last night!" Why, the way he was behaving, anyone would think that *she* was the one to blame for all that had happened. "Don't you realize that I'll never be able to show my face in public again, because of those . . . those hideous lies you unveiled."

"Lies!" He stared at her incredulously, an angry stain mottling his skin, and expelled a harsh, mirthless laugh. "Why you hypocritical little bitch! What right have *you* got to sit in judgment? *You* of all people."

"I have every right!" she countered furiously. "You've ruined me, Peter! You invited the most important people in the state to the Talmadges', then publicly humiliated me with those lewd monstrosities. My Lord, even Nick was there to witness my disgrace."

"Ah!" The word came out on a long, slow breath. "That's it, isn't it? That's been it all along."

"What are you talking about?" she queried, stiffening with indignation.

"You still love him, don't you?"

Lacey laughed uneasily. "You're talking nonsense, Peter."

"No, for the first time I think I'm beginning to make a great deal of sense. You're still in love with Nick Gallagher, though only God knows what you see in him. I seriously wonder if you've ever stopped loving him."

Holding her wrapper tightly to her, she walked over to the window and stared out blindly. "I'd have to be a fool to do that," she rasped, recalling only too clearly the way Nick had comforted her last night. His gentleness toward her had almost been her undoing. If Nicole hadn't awakened when he began to kiss her, distracting them both back to reality, she might possibly have begged him to stay the night with her. And what a mistake that would have been!

"I thought you were old enough to accept life for what it is, Lacey," Peter remarked behind her, "not for what you fantasize it should be. But evidently I was wrong. Well, if you're so besotted with the man, why in heaven's name don't you try and put aside the differences you've had with him and make a fresh start?"

"Fresh start!" Whirling about, she glared at him. "You mean, become his mistress again?" She hadn't kept any secrets from Peter—with Nicole's presence, she couldn't. He knew from the beginning just what her relationship with Nick had been, and he hadn't condemned her for it, either.

"If that's what you want, yes! There's nothing wrong with being a man's mistress. *You* should know that. In some cases it's much better than being his wife!" Waving aside her confused expression, he asserted, "At least you would be with him. And don't try telling me that that isn't what you want, because I can see that it is. I know how you feel about Nick Gallagher. My God, it's written all over your lovely face each time I mention his name."

He paused a moment to draw in a deep breath, then he resumed, "You know something? More than anything else, I think your biggest problem is denying the truth when you don't care to admit it. You're afraid to, I think. But you would be a lot better off—you *and* your damn conscience—if you would just admit what you really feel for him. And, just for the record, even though I don't like his brand of gentleman very much, he's not the completely unfeeling brute you seem to think he is."

Lacey crossed to the fireplace and fingered a vase of flowers there on the mantle, feeling an array of emotions conflict within her. "Oh, I'll agree with you," she retorted stiltedly, "Nick does have some admirable qualities, but they're too far outweighed by the bad. I'd be an utter fool if I tried to love him and not recognize his faults, too. You see, the man doesn't know the meaning of the word 'fidelity.' He's much too much like his father in that respect ever to be faithful to one woman." And he was like his younger brother, too, she thought silently.

"Oh?" Peter queried innocently. "I wasn't aware that your mother's life with Maxwell Gallagher had been such a horrible one."

With her back to him, Lacey didn't see the slightly amused smile that came to his lips. "It certainly wasn't pleasant, I can tell you that."

"The old reprobate beat her regularly, did he? Never gave her a penny and always kept her in rags?"

"No!" she denied, whirling about to face him. "No, it wasn't like that at all. In fact, I don't think Max ever raised his voice in anger to Momma the whole time we lived with him. Not that she ever gave him cause to be angry with her, mind you. And we always had more than we needed, because he wasn't tight-fisted at all. But it wasn't his mistreatment of us, or his generosity that was so bad, it was the constant humiliation we were forced to endure that hurt so much."

"Ah, humiliation." Peter said the word slowly with a nod of his head, as though it carried a wealth of information.

"He *could* have married Momma," she continued, "but he wouldn't. He had the means and more than enough opportunity to make her an honest woman, but he didn't. And there was no wife in the background to stop him from marrying her, either. His wife, Lillian, had died long before we ever moved into his house . . . but you know that already."

"Maybe they didn't need, or want, any legalities to bind them. Have you ever considered that? No, don't stare at me like I've uttered an obscenity or something! Stop and consider what their relationship was really like. You know about it far better than I. Did he ever openly flaunt another woman in your mother's presence? Did he ever, to your knowledge, maintain another mistress while he kept your mother?"

"No! He didn't need any other woman when he had Momma," she responded huskily. "She was the warmest, the kindest . . . the most loving woman in the world . . . and she had his highest regard."

"Then it would be safe for us to assume that he was faithful to her."

Lacey nodded, sure of that fact now, but unsure of where Peter's train of thought was leading. Somehow they had gotten away from their original argument, but she was at a loss as to how to return to it.

"And, of course," he was saying, "your mother was faithful to him."

"Yes!" she cried, outraged at the notion. Her mother may have been Max's mistress and a less

265

than honorable woman because of it, but she was not and never had been a whore. Rachel had been a lady . . . always!

"Well, it sounds to me like they made their own vows of fidelity and stuck to them. Lacey darling, *those* vows—the ones made before God with honesty and forthrightness, and not the ones professed before a crowd of gathered witnesses—*those* are the ones that really mean something. In the eyes of God, my dear, your mother and Max Gallagher were man and wife!

"They refused to compromise their integrity, the way I see it. They allowed each other the freedom to remain what they initially were, yet joined together in a union that, perhaps, had more strength and more credibility than any proper ceremony ever could give them. So, for heaven's sake, stop condemning them for the love and happiness they had and try to find a little of it yourself! They got more out of their brief life together than you and Nick are obviously getting out of yours."

By the time Peter had finished speaking, Lacey was feeling profoundly miserable inside. For the first time, she had to admit that, perhaps, she *had* been misjudging Max and Rachel all these years. Perhaps she had been wrong about them all this time and had been too stupidly biased to see it. But whatever else she was being forced to acknowledge, she knew, without a doubt, that what her mother had shared with Max could in no way be compared with what she had shared with Nick. It couldn't!

"But don't you see, Peter," she said, turning misty green eyes up to him. "Don't you see that that's where Nick's similarity to his father ends? Max, at least, had a certain degree of respect for Momma. Nick has absolutely no regard for me at all! That's what hurts so much—I love him, and he doesn't give a damn about me!"

It was such a shock to hear herself confess her love for Nick, all of her former restraint vanished in the blink of an eye. Having kept the truth bottled up within her for so long, the pain she'd kept buried came gushing out in torrents of bitter tears. She wept openly now, crying out all the disappointments and anguish she'd quietly suffered the past year, and all the years before that. In the end, she felt as though she had no pride left at all, only sadness and empty desolation.

After a while, when her sobs began to diminish, Peter came to her side and tried to comfort her. "You're so wrong about him not loving you, my dear. You've never been more wrong in your life. Gallagher, even though he is uncouth and just barely civilized, has more regard for you than you've given him credit for."

But she continued to disagree with him, shaking her head firmly as she rummaged through her wrapper pocket for her handkerchief. Angrily mopping her wet cheeks, she countered, "If that were so, Peter, he would have come more than the handful of times he's been here to see his daughter."

"I think, maybe, he's still unfamiliar with the position of fatherhood. God knows, I'm certainly no authority on the subject myself, but even I can sense the certain degree of pride that Nick has in his child."

"Well, I wouldn't know!" she sniffed. "I'm ignorant myself on the matters which concern father/daughter relationships."

Peter took her pale hands in his and gave them a gentle, reassuring squeeze. "I know that not having a father as you were growing up was painful, my dear, but you did survive. We can't go back and change what has already been; the past is completely out of our hands now, and it would be better for you if you could put it aside and forget it."

"There are some things, Peter, that are impossible to forget."

Looking at her understandingly, he said, "You mean Nick."

"*And* his other women." She then elaborated further by telling him about the actress who had arrived on the train with Nick.

"He *is* a man, Lacey, and he does have needs."

"Well, of course, you *would* condone his whoremongering."

"No, I wouldn't. I'm just trying to get you to see the situation from a man's point of view. However wrong his actions may have been, it is not your place to sit in judgment! If you love him, as you say you do, then forget the other women he's known or will know and just love him! As strange as it may seem, it is quite possible for a man to have an ongoing affair with a woman and not feel a thing for her. A man's head and his heart are two, entirely separate entities."

"Oh, I'm well aware of that!" she responded scornfully.

"Lacey, no matter what you say, I still believe that

he has a great deal of affection for you. If he didn't, he would have left Austin long ago. In fact, he wouldn't have come here at all if he hadn't truly wanted you."

"He came because he thought I'd had his son!" she insisted. *"That's* why he came, Peter! Not because he had an undying sense of love for me, but because he wanted his son!"

"Oh, Lacey," Peter groaned, shaking his head.

"Don't 'Oh, Lacey' me! If Nicole had been a boy, Nick would've been here every day to see her. Instead, he's only been half a dozen times since he got here. Girls don't mean much in this world; we never have and never will. If I'd been born a boy, Max would not have hesitated a moment in marrying Momma and adopting me."

"You're so bitter, my dear," Peter observed, moving away.

"Well, I've got a lot to be bitter about!" she cried, unleashing all of the rage that remained within her. Once it began, the flood of hurt could not be damned up again. She poured out her anger and her frustrations onto Peter's shoulders, draining herself of all the wrongs and slights she'd experienced in her young life. "Every person who ever meant anything to me has either left me or hurt me," she said, drawing to the end of her tirade. "All except for Momma, that is. She didn't leave of her own free will; she was killed. But even my own husband wasn't faithful to me long enough to consummate our marriage. He went to another woman before the ink was dry on our license."

Peter's head snapped up and he frowned at her

incredulously. "But Chris didn't go to another woman!" he announced forcefully. "I thought you understood that."

Her self-pitying maledictions interrupted, she could only blink at him stupidly. "But—but he was at—"

"*At* the house, yes, but never *in* it. I should know—I was with him that day . . . or rather, *he* was with *me. I* went to the bordello to pay off a debt I owed. Chris stayed outside and waited for me. *That's* when he was hit by that wagon."

Feeling her knees begin to buckle beneath her, Lacey stumbled over to the settee and fell onto it weakly. All of her former anger seemed pointless suddenly, without meaning. "Oh, my God!" she groaned, reliving that awful day over and over again in her mind. But instead of being overjoyed in learning that her young husband had not been unfaithful to her, she felt overwhelmed with guilt—guilt for what she had thought of Chris all this time, and guilt for what she had done to him. "Oh, my God!"

The silence in the room stretched between them like an ominous black cloud. When Lacey finally lifted her head to Peter, she saw his unbridled contempt for her mirrored in his twisted frown.

"I'm disappointed in you, Lacey. Very disappointed indeed. You actually believed all of those vile rumors that were told about Chris, didn't you? Good God, woman, he loved you! He spoke your name with almost every breath he took. He would never have done anything as sordid as they all claimed. How could you possibly think he could?"

"I—"

"No!" He stopped her with a firm shake of his head. "Don't bother trying to explain. You're obviously not the woman I thought you were, if you could believe that about the man who loved you." His upper lip had turned back in a disgusted snarl. "You and Nick Gallagher deserve each other; and maybe Chris *is* better off dead. At least he doesn't have to know what a contemptible little hypocrite you are."

Slowly he turned and began to gather up his discarded hat and gloves, which he had tossed into a chair when he had first entered. "You won't be hearing from *me* anymore, so don't bother looking. I don't want to have anything more to do with either you or Nick. You both disgust me so much that I no longer care what the two of you decide to do with your twisted lives."

Pulling on his gloves, he added beneath his breath, "The only thing worthwhile to come out of this is the fifty thousand dollars I received for the Muses."

"Fifty thousand . . . !" Suddenly reminded of *his* duplicity, she glared up at him, her face full of concern. "Who bought them, Peter? I have to know who bought those paintings!" Heaven knows, she didn't have much pride left, but she wasn't about to allow her nearly nude likeness to remain on view for just anybody. And though fifty thousand dollars was an awful lot of money—money that she didn't have —she would have to try and buy them back, somehow.

Peter snorted, unaffected by her concern. "I

haven't the faintest idea, Lacey. An agent approached me with a bank draft last night at the unveiling and I accepted it. As far as I know, or care, your pictures could be hanging in a barn or . . . or an outhouse!" And with that, he turned and walked out of her house . . . and out of her life.

Chapter Fourteen

THE WEIGHT THAT WAS PRESSING AGAINST NICK'S midsection caused the churning gorge in his stomach to rise in his throat. He was almost afraid to open his eyes and face the light of day, for the pain in his head was throbbing unbearably. He knew that the moment he lifted his grit-lined lids, the pain in his head would go out of control and he would be in agony. Hadn't he learned anything from the last time he had overimbibed? Evidently not!

Slowly he became aware of the sounds and movement around him. Outside his bedroom window, the usually calm morning breeze had taken on the sound of a wind reaching gale-force velocity. And the gentle rustling of branches against the side of his house sounded like someone was using a battering ram against the walls. Everything, every sound, had increased in intensity, even the vibrating roar atop his chest. It was as if God, in all His infinite majesty, had decided to bring about the end of the world on this particular morning when He knew Nick was close to death anyway.

It was his thought of his Creator that reminded

273

Nick just how long it had been since he had last prayed. About to meet his Maker anyway, he didn't know of any better time to talk to Him than the present.

"Lord!" he began in earnest. "I'll never do it again, I swear. I'll never drink another drop as long as I live, if You will just let me make it through the next few minutes. And, uh, Lord? If You don't want me to live—if You've decided already to send the Angel Gabriel after me—please send him soon before this pain in my head gets worse. Please! Uh, amen."

He waited, almost too afraid to breathe. Even the sound of air passing over his nostril hairs sounded like a wind piercing through the slats on a shuttered window.

The weight pressing against his chest shifted suddenly. Startled, Nick opened his eyes and stared in amazement at what had been sitting atop him.

A calico kitten, sitting directly dead-center on his breastbone, washed her paws with a lazy thoroughness. Her tiny, rough tongue paused a moment in its chore as she looked into Nick's narrowed, confused, red-rimmed eyes. Her emerald green orbs blinked arrogantly back at him, then she returned, almost boredly, to her grooming.

It was then that William's strident voice preceded the sound of his lead-weighted feet as he stomped down the hall. "Where you at, you stupid, mangy critter?" He threw open the door and spied the cat, sitting on top of Nick.

"Do you have to be so damn loud?" Nick glowered up at the young black man before turning a baleful frown on the kitten. "And where'd you find *this* noisy little monster?"

"Me! You was the one that brung her in here last night. Said her eyes looked like Lacey's and Nicole's and you was gonna keep her since you couldn't have the others. Looks to me like she's done made herself at home."

"Well, get her off me!" he roared. "And how do you know it's a her?"

"Calicoes is almost always female." In two long strides, William crossed the room and removed the featherweight kitten from Nick. Curling his lip into a disgusted snarl, he said, "After what you done last night, I'm surprised you'd want to get out of bed at all."

Nick was in no mood to play games this morning. People on the verge of death seldom were. But the note of sarcasm in William's voice was just too obvious for him to ignore. "What do you mean?"

"You don't remember? Jesus Lord, you must've been drunker'n I thought."

"Oh, hell, William! What'd I do?" he bellowed, then winced as a pain shot through his head.

"You done gone and bought yourself an automobile—that's what you've done! What you plan on doin' with it, God only knows, 'cause you sure don't know how to drive it."

"You're beginning to sound more like your momma every day," he growled. Shoving the covers aside, he sat up and felt short, powerful bursts explode through the roof of his skull.

"Well, I got a right to complain! You go spendin' all our money, we ain't never gonna get back home to Dallas. And this place is just too damn wet for my likin'. My joints ain't used to all the damp around here; they squeak when I get up in the mornin's."

Nick jerked his wrinkled trousers up over his lean hips, not bothering to fasten the fly. "How your momma," he grumbled, "as smart as she is, could have a son as dumb as you, is beyond me. Did you ever stop to think that since I *have* bought an automobile, we won't be stuck here? We can go home anytime we like."

"I ain't dumb," William countered. "Leastways, when I buy myself somethin', I don't pay out the cash money till I seen what it is I'm buyin'."

"Who says I haven't seen it?" Nick challenged over his shoulder as he made his way out of the room.

William, curious and not about to be left dangling by his cryptic remark, followed Nick down the short hall and out the back door to the little house down the path. "You mean, you've seen the automobile?"

Nick had the door to the outhouse open and was ready to step inside when he turned and looked back at William. "Course I seen it!"

"When?"

Nick snorted impatiently. "Look, I ain't about to hold no discussion with you here and now. I *need* to go! And since this here ain't no two-holer, you're gonna hafta wait outside till I'm done. It'd be mighty hard for the both of us to fit in it together. You savvy?"

William grumbled to himself and leaned against the corner of the small building until Nick had finished answering nature's urgent call.

But when Nick stepped out the door, looking

considerably more relieved than when he had awakened, he asked brusquely, "You got any breakfast cooked?"

William's dark head shook negatively, forgetting momentarily about Nick's newest purchase. "Didn't know when you was gonna get up. Last drunk you pulled, you slept most of the day."

"Must've been that beer I drank on top of all that champagne. It didn't set well at all."

"You want me to see if I can rustle up some eggs for you? Maybe I can find a clean skillet to fry 'em in. That cleanin' woman you hired ain't showed up yet, and if she sees that man all sprawled out in the parlor, she ain't likely to come back neither."

Nick frowned in confusion at William as his fingers continued to fasten his fly. "What man?"

"The one you drug in with the cat."

"I don't remember bringin' in any man with me last night." Truth to tell, he didn't remember much of anything after he dropped Lacey off at her place. He'd gone to the saloon to meet his business contact and—

"Well, you did!" William proclaimed, gaining Nick's attention. "He's about your size with a nose spread across his face that'd make a turnip envious. He come a sashayin' in the house before I could even shut the door."

A tall man with a big nose! Nick's aching head wouldn't let him think clearly. "And he came in with me?"

"Yep! He come a reelin' in, a singin' the same song you was."

Turning toward the house, Nick grunted, "I don't sing."

"I know," William agreed. "Y'all sounded more like a pair of wild coyotes in heat than carolers with all that caterwaulin' you two done."

Nick stopped dead in his tracks just inside the kitchen, turning to glare coldly at the young black man. "You know somethin', William? I was all wrong about you a while ago. You ain't nothin' like Miss Hattiebelle at all. She's got better taste than you, for one thing . . . and for another, she ain't near as ugly."

It was only after Nick had swallowed down his scorched and tasteless breakfast—William's revenge, he suspected—that the identity of the man in the parlor came to him. He had to be Steven Penrose, and Englishman who had been down on his luck and in need of money when Nick had met him. It was his automobile that Nick had bought the night before.

Entering the parlor, he found the Englishman hopping around on one leg as he tried to pull his trousers on. It was such an unexpected sight, Nick had to stifle the urge to laugh out loud.

"How are you this morning, Penrose?" he asked soberly.

Penrose fell against the wall and leaned there until he succeeded in covering his sticklike legs. "Rather hung over I'm afraid, old man," he admitted at last. "I'm not ungrateful though, mind you. I do appreciate your letting me sleep here on your sofa. Considering my state of intoxication last evening, I'm not sure that I could have made it safely back to my boardinghouse."

He staggered across the room to retrieve his

wrinkled shirt from one of the armchairs. After he pulled it on, he paused a moment before buttoning it to stare in puzzlement at Nick.

"I say, I did sell you my Daimler last night, didn't I?"

"Is that what it was? A Daimler? Yep, you sure did." Nick grinned proudly. "She sure is a beauty, too! I hear tell that your King What's-His-Name got him one not too long ago."

"Oh, King Ted. Yes." Penrose nodded. "We both bought ours from the same German chap, as a matter of fact."

"You don't say! I didn't know you was on speaking terms with royalty."

"Well, I'm not, actually," Penrose admitted. "His Majesty doesn't frequent the same social circles that I do."

"Oh," Nick responded, nodding as if he understood . . . which he didn't. "Oh! By the way, before I forget—I really do appreciate you doing me that little favor last night."

"Think nothing of it, old man. I was glad I could be of some help to you, considering all the help you've been to me." He stuffed his shirttails into his trousers and asked, "Er, ah, you wouldn't by chance have a pot of tea on the premises, would you?"

"Tea? Nope, 'fraid not. All we got's coffee . . . if you can call it that."

"Coffee, hmm? Well, I'll probably have developed a taste for it by the time I leave for London, so I don't suppose it would hurt to have a cup."

"London?" Nick repeated, leading Penrose out of the parlor and down the hall to the kitchen.

"That's right."

"What brought you all the way to Texas?"

"Mainly curiosity, I suppose. I've always heard such interesting stories about this wild and wooly land of yours. I promised myself that if I ever had the chance, I would come see it one day. When a great-uncle of mine happened to pass away last year, leaving me a small legacy, I decided to shed my academic mantle and cross the great ocean to have my adventure."

Not everything Penrose said made a whole lot of sense to Nick. "You shed your mantle of what?"

Penrose flushed, then issued an embarrassed chuckle. "I do beg your pardon, Gallagher. I really didn't mean to sound so pompous. You see, I am a . . . or I *was* a science teacher at a boys' school before I resigned my position. Nasty little buggers." He shuddered. "It's been quite a relief, let me tell you, just getting away from them for a while. Always muckin' about with my fossils and disturbing my experiments. Can't keep their hands off a damn thing!"

Nick poured the Englishman a cup of William's stout coffee, but when Penrose had finished speaking, he was suddenly hit with an idea. "You wouldn't by any chance be one of them gee-olo-gist felluhs, would you?" he asked, pushing the filled cup toward him.

"Well, yes, as a matter of fact, that's exactly what I am!" Penrose announced, looking surprised as he picked up the cup. "How did you know that?"

"You see," Nick began, watching Penrose sip the coffee, "I got me a parcel of land just north of Beaumont and—"

Penrose choked on his sip of coffee. It spewed out of his lips and across the table.

Nick whacked him soundly between the shoulderblades, saying, "I knew it was too strong when I poured it. Damn, I should've warned you not to gulp it down."

Penrose sputtered and coughed for a while longer, tears coming to his watery blue eyes, until he finally caught his breath. When he was once again under control, he looked over at Nick and gasped out, "It wasn't the coffee, old man."

"It wasn't?"

Penrose shook his head, his thick blond hair falling down into his face. He took a deep breath and retorted, "My God, man! Do you have any idea what happened in Beaumont last January? A—And then you can just sit there as though it's an everyday occurrence."

"You ain't by any chance talking about Spindletop, are you?" Nick inquired, wiping up the coffee with a corner of the tablecloth.

"That's *exactly* what I'm talking about. Why, it's—it's the biggest geological discovery of the century!"

"Yeah, that's what they been sayin'. But, you see, Spindletop's on Anton Lucas's spread, not mine. Course, my place ain't too far away, but—"

"But there's a possibility that oil could be on your land as well!" Penrose pointed out excitedly.

"Them folks over at Magnolia Oil have been tellin' me and Jake that, but we thought it over and decided it'd be best if we waited to see if Lucas's venture is gonna pay off or go bust before we dig any holes on our property. Ruins the hell out of grazin' land!"

Penrose just sat back in his chair, looking thoroughly astonished by Nick's casual attitude. "My God, man, you don't honestly intend to put cattle on that land, do you?"

"Yeah, I'd thought about it," Nick nodded. "But when you said you were a gee-olo-gist, I thought, since you don't seem to be tied down to a reg'lar job or nothing, I thought I'd ask you to do one more favor for me . . . if you don't mind, that is. I'd be willing to make it worth your while."

Penrose's eyes lit up as if he'd just been presented with the chance of a lifetime . . . which he had. "Anything you want, Gallagher. Anything! I can be on the next train to Beaumont. . . . That is, if trains go there."

"Oh, they do!" Nick assured him. "I was just there myself last week to meet my lawyer, Jake Goldstein. But if you've already got plans made, I wouldn't want to interfere with 'em."

"I have no plans! Why do you think I sold my automobile? I was trying to scrape enough money together so that I could get to Beaumont! I've been trying to get there since last February, when the news of the oil discovery reached San Francisco, where I was staying."

"But didn't you say something a while ago about going home to London soon?"

"If all else failed, yes! But I won't be leaving now. . . . Not for London, at least."

Slowly absorbing all that Penrose had told him, Nick nodded his head. "Well, when do you think you could start work for me?"

"Right now!" Penrose cried. "I can begin immediately. All I need to know is what you want me to do first."

Nick reiterated then the discussion he'd had with Jake when they had met in Beaumont. He verbally listed all that needed to be done before digging for ore samples could commence. "Of course, you'd be in charge of the operation," he informed Penrose finally. "But you'd still have to answer to Jake or me. No, come to think of it, you'd answer only to Jake. I won't be here. You'd notify him if any problems came up."

"Oh, are you planning a holiday?"

"Yeah, sort of." Nick grinned boyishly. "You see, if I can get the lady to agree, I'm thinking about getting married. If she says yes, I'd most likely be on my honeymoon when all the work starts. But you don't have to worry none about Jake. He's real easy to get along with."

"Who is the fortunate young lady, may I ask? Did I meet her last night?"

"I don't know if y'all were introduced or not, but you saw her pictures."

Reality dawned on Penrose, and he stared once again in astonishment at Nick. "Your fiancée is the young lady who posed for the nine Muses?"

"That's right! Course, I'd be much obliged if you'd just forget what them pictures of her look like, even though you did buy 'em for me as a favor an' all. A man could get a might uncomfortable, thinking someone else was acquainted with his wife's . . . er, form, if you get my meaning."

"Oh, I do!" Penrose nodded. "And I agree with you wholeheartedly, Gallagher. You did the right thing in purchasing those paintings. And if I may be allowed to say, she is a lovely young woman. Very lovely indeed."

"Yeah, I think so," Nick grinned proudly.

"When is the wedding, by the way?"

"Oh, I don't know that yet. You see, we gotta get on speaking terms before I can ask her."

Chapter Fifteen

IT WAS ALMOST LAUGHABLE, THOUGHT LACEY, HOW AN incident so terribly humiliating to her could blow over and be nothing more than a minor embarrassment to all the others in such a short span of time. Yet here she was, sitting in Mrs. Eleanor Talmadge's drawing room, participating with the other charity committee members as though that night had never occurred here three weeks ago. Oh, the committee members had been justifiably outraged at first, but when the contributions started rolling in, they looked on the whole affair as something of a godsend.

Mrs. Fellowes, her neighbor, had come to her house personally just days after the unveiling, beaming with pride over the good news she had to tell. "We can actually support and educate ten students now, my dear."

Lacey, still feeling raw from what had happened, was much more reticent. "But, Mrs. Fellowes, are you sure you want me to continue with the organization? I mean, I have brought a lot of shame and embarrassment upon the group."

"Don't be silly!" the older woman had scoffed. "You said in your letter of apology that you had no idea Mr. Thorne was portraying you in that unseemly manner. Of course we want you to remain a member! Why, my dear, *we* would be the hypocrites if we held you responsible for a situation that was obviously not of your making."

Still, even with the support and assurance the group had given her, it was difficult for Lacey to attend the monthly meetings with the other women and not feel ill at ease. She had the uncomfortable feeling that they were merely enduring her presence, even though nearly everyone had gone out of her way to demonstrate just the opposite.

"Motion made and carried," announced Madam President with a resounding rap of her gavel.

"I move that we adjourn the meeting," Mrs. Fellowes suggested, rising to her feet beside Lacey. "I have supper to cook for Mr. Fellowes, and it's almost four o'clock right now."

There was a low twitter of laughter among the other ladies, but no one objected. And when the motion was seconded and they had all agreed, Madam President, who was Mrs. Talmadge, called the meeting to an end. They all stood then, gathering their hats and gloves together, before making their way out of the drawing room.

Mrs. Fellowes turned to Lacey and asked, "You are riding home with me, aren't you, my dear?"

"Oh, yes, if you don't mind."

Mrs. Fellowes let out a patient sigh and shook her silvery gray head. "You really must stop thinking badly of yourself, Lacey. Shouldn't she, Eleanor?"

A very gracious woman in her late fifties, Mrs.

Talmadge turned at the mention of her name. "Shouldn't she what, Rebecca?"

"I said, shouldn't Lacey stop thinking badly of herself for what happened last month?"

"My Lord, yes!" came Mrs. Talmadge's stern agreement. "Are you still brooding over that incident, child?"

Lacey was unable to answer, a thick knot having suddenly formed in her throat. Knowing she didn't deserve these women's kindness, she did manage to nod her head.

"Good Lord, that's water over the dam," Mrs. Talmadge insisted with a wave of her hand. "Why, if I were to feel embarrassed over all the situations I've been in in my life, I'd go to my grave red-faced."

Mrs. Fellowes chuckled at that, her laugh coming out high-pitched and girlish. "Oh, Eleanor! Do you remember the time we went skinny-dipping in the springs at San Marcos?"

Mrs. Talmadge groaned, rolling her eyes heavenward. "Trust you to remember that, Rebecca."

Now that the entrance hall was nearly empty of the other committee members, Lacey listened intently as the two ladies looked back over their girlhood days together. And the longer she listened, the more her worries dwindled.

"Remember all those lovely Yankee soldiers who were camped just up the hill from the springs?"

"They were a bunch of nosy rascals, and you know it," the other woman snapped. But her wrinkled cheeks developed a pair of deep dimples as she began to smile. Then laughter erupted into the cavernous hallway. "All except one or two, that is. I'll never forget the look on poor old Aunt Hettie's face when that dashing Yankee captain brought the two of us back to her house, dripping wet. Lord, she was fit to be tied!"

Rebecca Fellowes's eyes glittered brightly. "Yes, wasn't she. But he was such a handsome captain."

"Yes," Mrs. Talmadge agreed. "Almost as handsome as his lieutenant."

Both ladies sighed deeply, rousing Lacey's curiosity even more. "Well, what about them?" she urged. "The captain and his lieutenant, I mean. What happened to them?"

"Oh, my dear," Mrs. Fellowes twinkled. "Why, we married them, of course."

"Yes," Mrs. Talmadge nodded. "We married them. I married my Herbert not long after Rebecca married her Edward. Of course, both of us almost died from swimming so often in that cold water, but after about a month of doing it, it finally dawned on the two fools that we were trying to attract their attention. They proposed to us just in the nick of time, too! We almost caught pneumonia."

Lacey was hard pressed not to laugh at the audacity of the two women. It was difficult to imagine them as anything other than what they were now; staid and quite respectable. She couldn't, for the life of her, envision them as young girls hell-bent on attracting a couple of men. The thought, as humorous as it was, kept coming back to her as she and Mrs. Fellowes drove home later that afternoon.

"Tell me something," she said as their carriage turned onto their quiet street. "Who was the captain, and who was the lieutenant?"

Looking like a plump little hen, Mrs. Fellowes

admitted with a reminiscent glow in her eyes, "Oh, my dear—my Edward was the captain. Such a handsome young man he was then."

She left Mrs. Fellowes still smiling as she walked across the street to her house, and she chuckled to herself most of the way. But as she entered the house, her humor died abruptly when Daisy told her who had been to call while she was out.

"What do you mean, Mr. Gallagher has just left?" Ripping off her hat and tearing at her gloves, she glared angrily at her young housemaid.

"J—just that, ma'am," Daisy answered. "Uh, he drove up not long after you left for your meeting."

Entering the parlor, Lacey was at a loss for the reason behind her anger. My God, she thought, she would probably be the talk of the neighborhood again, if she wasn't that already. "What in heaven's name did he want?"

"He, uh, he just wanted to play with the baby, ma'am," Daisy explained. "Like he's always done."

"What? Do you mean to tell me that he's been here before? Just how long has he been coming anyway? And why haven't I been told of his visits before?"

"Well, ma'am, to tell you the truth, you've been kind of moody here of late, and Momma and me didn't think there was really any harm in letting him come in, so we just didn't bother telling you. We know, you see, that y'all don't get on real well."

"You should be blaming me, Miz Gallagher," Mrs. Edwards spoke up from the doorway. She entered the parlor, wiping her hands on her apron, and confessed, "I'm the one who let Mr. Nick in the first time; not Daisy. I didn't think there was any harm in it, seein' as how he's little Nicole's fa . . . er, ah, uncle, I mean."

Lacey was instantly aware of the blush that colored her housekeeper's neck and cheeks. So, another of her misdeeds had come to light, had it? But had Mrs. Edwards drawn her own conclusions, or had she been told of Nicole's parentage . . . by Nick?

"How long has he been coming here without my knowledge, Mrs. Edwards?" She asked this on a much calmer note, not wanting her housekeeper to feel more intimidated than she already did. If anyone was at fault, it was she and Nick, not Mrs. Edwards.

"Not long, ma'am," the woman admitted. "Just a couple of weeks. The first time he came around was about a week after Mr. Thorne paid you that early-mornin' call."

Lacey nodded and reflected back to that particular morning. Nothing had seemed out of the ordinary then. She had gone out to run some errands and had come home only to find Nicole was taking her nap later than usual. The baby had slept, and had slept, causing the milk in Lacey's breasts to become painfully uncomfortable. But as soon as Nicole had awakened and had nursed, everything was back to normal again. Now Lacey knew the reason why her daughter had slept so long that day: Nick had tired her out.

"Do you want me to not allow him in the house if he comes around again?"

After a thoughtful pause, Lacey shook her head.

"No, Mrs. Edwards, that won't be necessary. I'll make it a point to be here from now on." If necessary, she would send Daisy out on her errands. Whatever it took, she would most definitely be here the next time Nick Gallagher decided to pay a call on their daughter.

Later that same day, as Lacey sat in her bedroom feeding Nicole, she looked down into the baby's sweet, cherubic face and felt a pang of pride mingle with one of regret. With each passing day, the likeness Nicole bore to Nick was becoming more and more obvious. She could see it; had Nick detected the likeness, too?

How could he not? she wondered. The man would have to be blind not to see the similarities between Nicole's precious little face and his more rugged one. Even as close as she was to the situation, she could discern an almost exact likeness between the two—except perhaps for Nicole's emerald green eyes and her pale, porcelain complexion.

"Oh, my little angel, what does he say to you when you're together? Does he ever mention my name?"

He probably didn't, she concluded. Even though she had meant something to him at one time, it didn't necessarily mean that she meant something to him now. After all, a lot of water had flowed over the dam—to misquote Mrs. Talmadge—since the last time he had expressed his feelings for her. There were a lot of barriers keeping them apart, not the least of which was the memory of Sally O'Donnell and Lacey's own pride.

"Dear Lord, was I wrong in not trusting him

291

more? I wish I *could* trust him—I wish it with all my heart, but I'm so afraid."

She hadn't been afraid, though, when she gave herself to him the first time so brazenly. But she had been someone else then, someone who had been freed from the torturing confines of conventionality, someone who had rushed headlong into her lover's arms without shame or regret. She had never felt more secure and protected than she had then. But she had rejected Nick when she discovered him with Sally O'Donnell and she had refused to listen to him when he tried to explain about the prostitute. If anyone was at fault here, it was she—she and no one else.

She still loved Nick, though. No matter what he had or had not done, she loved him more than anything . . . except, perhaps, for Nicole. The thought of him sharing his affections with another woman, giving to someone else what she herself wanted so badly, hurt more than she could say.

In the pit of her belly an ache spiraled out and fed into her blood. It was the kind of ache that could be assuaged by only one thing—Nick Gallagher's touch, *his* brand of possession. If he were to come upon her at this very moment, she would throw convention aside and go to him wantonly without restraint. Maybe, after all was said and done, that was what she was—a wanton. Perhaps she'd been one all along and it had taken Nick to awaken that dormant side of her nature. For only God knew how empty and barren her life had been before he had entered it. Her cloak of respectability had been more like a funeral shroud, or a nun's habit. But

Nick had ripped aside that false veil of values and had shown her her genuine self. He had made her feel sensations so astounding, she could only marvel at their existence. He had taken her into a world of such sensual delight that she longed with all her heart to go there again and again . . . but only with him.

She wanted Nick Gallagher, perhaps more now than before. Not only did she want his nearness, his touch; she wanted his intimate possession and his love. For over a year now she had lived without seeing him or hearing his voice with any regularity, and she longed for those sensations with all of the intensity of a person who was crazed with thirst. Like a sponge, she wanted to absorb Nick into her being and be made whole again.

Peter had been right, so right, she acknowledged painfully; she had been afraid to face the truth. But now, having faced it, what was she to do? There were only two options open to her; the first, quite obvious and completely out of the question, and the second, much too painful even to consider. She could brazenly go after Nick and suffer the consequences of her rashness, or she could learn, all over again, to live without him. The second option would be sheer hell, and she knew it. If she couldn't have Nick, have his love, she would sooner not live at all.

If Rachel could put aside her conventional beliefs for Max, why couldn't she do the same for Nick? After all, she *was* her mother's daughter . . . in more ways than one, she was beginning to believe. To hell with what the gossips might think, and to hell with morality! Anything was worth the risk, if she could just have Nick.

She just prayed that it wasn't too late.

Lacey didn't leave the house for the next few days. She remained at home and anxiously waited for Nick to arrive on her doorstep as he'd done before.

With no clear plan formulated in her mind, she had only a sketchy idea of what she would do or say to him when he did arrive. She would tell him, to the best of her ability, that her affections for him had not really changed, that she still loved him. Then, if his response to that was positive, she would attempt to find out just where she stood in his affections. But she didn't want to frighten him off by being too outspoken or too forward, and she most certainly couldn't come right out and ask him to marry her! *He* would have to do that . . . if he was interested in marriage, that is. But if he decided to make her his mistress and nothing more . . . well, she would deal with that problem when she came to it.

Nick did not come to visit that day.

Nor did he come the day after.

Lacey waited a whole week and didn't hear from him once. By the time the week finally drew to a close, she felt more confused, hurt and lonelier than ever before. In fact, she was almost certain that her last, remaining chance for happiness had been taken from her.

Coming to grips with the loss was a painful exercise for her. But she knew she would have to accept it and learn to live with it, no matter how hard it was. Nick, by the looks of it, just wasn't a part of her life anymore.

By the following week, when some of the numbness had worn off, she knew she could stay at home no longer. Just because Nick was gone, it didn't mean that her life had to cease completely. There were errands that she needed to run, and her fitting at the dressmaker's was a week overdue. Not only that, Nicole was beginning to teethe again, and Lacey wanted to buy her a new little silver ring to chew on. All perfect examples of how life was still going on about her.

As always, before going out, she dressed with care. Austin might not be a fashion capital, but it was the capital of Texas and its residents were conscious of their appearance. They weren't snobbish about it by any stretch of the imagination, but they were concerned with how others perceived them.

Checking her appearance in the tall cheval mirror, she turned to peer at her back, looking over her shoulder. Her voile gown, a bright robin's egg blue, draped enticingly over her derriere. Thank goodness she had no need of a bustle form. In fact, she wished that those ungainly contraptions would go out of style altogether. What nature had endowed her with was curvaceous enough, in her opinion.

Turning to examine her front reflection, she ran a hand down the bodice of her gown, following the cream-colored lace insert which plunged all the way down to the top of her satin waist sash, then back up again to where it covered her long, swanlike throat. The matching voile waistcoat, when slipped on and buttoned, made the entire ensemble appear quite subtle and enticing.

At her throat, Lacey wore her mother's modest

three-strand pearl necklace, and on her ears were tiny pearl drops. Her copper-gold hair was pinned into a simple coil at the top of her head with wispy ringlets left free to curl at her ears.

The crowning touch to her tasteful ensemble was her hat. A fashionable Gainsborough, the wide, stiff organza brim swept down on one side to touch her shoulder and partially hide one eye, while the other side flipped up, exposing her saucy profile. The crown was embellished with silk flowers of every color and held intact with a satin ribbon the same shade as the one worn about her waist.

All in all, the effect was an arresting one, she conceded with an approving nod of her head. Then, hearing the gurgle which came from Nicole's bed, she left the mirror and went to her daughter's side. Scooping up the scantily clad infant, she hugged her moist little body and kissed her sweet, talcum-scented neck. She was so precious, this child of hers, that she took great delight in holding and cuddling her at every opportunity.

"Momma's going to go out this morning, darling," she informed her daughter, as though the child understood her perfectly. "But I shouldn't be gone too long."

For a reply, Nicole ground her two bottom teeth against the pearly nub that had just recently penetrated her topmost gum. Her little face twisted into a grimace as she grunted out her pain and frustration.

"Are they hurting you, precious? Well, maybe Mrs. Edwards can find something for them until I can get back with your new teething ring."

When she had changed Nicole's diaper, she sauntered down the stairs with the baby in her arms and found the housekeeper in the kitchen. "I think she's having a problem cutting her newest tooth," Lacey explained as she entered the sunny room.

"I've got just the thing for that," Mrs. Edwards remarked before turning toward the cupboard.

Lacey watched as the woman opened the door and then closed it again, an ominous-looking bottle held in her hand. "Is that *gin?*"

"Yep. Now you know I don't hold with havin' liquor of any kind in my house . . . for drinkin' purposes," the housekeeper asserted defensively. "Lord knows, after what my mister put me and Daisy through with his drinkin', I'd be crazy as a loon to try it myself. A shot of this, though, when you're feelin' peaked, is the best medicine I've come across."

Mrs. Edwards came toward the baby, uncorking the bottle, and Lacey asked cautiously, "You aren't thinking of letting her drink that straight, are you?"

"Lor-dee, no, girl!" the woman laughed. "Just you watch. This'll take away her pain quick as a flash."

She inserted her clean, work-roughened finger into the mouth of the bottle, then tilted it until the tip was well coated with the clear, potent brew. Wiggling her fingers inside Nicole's mouth, she ran it back and forth over the baby's sensitive little gums. "There now," she soothed at last, patting Nicole's chubby thigh. "Feels just a whole lot better, don't it, honeybun?"

Nicole tasted the foreign substance, her little mouth working eagerly, but never once did she screw up her face into a distasteful grimace. In fact, from where Lacey stood, the baby actually savored the whiskey's numbing effect.

"Anytime you need this," Mrs. Edwards said, returning the bottle to the cupboard, "it'll be right here. Feel free to use it."

"Thank you, I will," Lacey promised.

"My, my, you sure look spiffy this mornin'!" the older woman observed, coming back to stand beside Lacey. "You goin' to the dressmaker again?"

"Yes, but I shouldn't be gone too long. You won't mind watching Nicole for me, will you?"

"No, course not. Take your time." She took the baby from Lacey, adding, "Me and Miss Nicki here'll spend our mornin' bakin' some tea cakes. She just loves my tea cakes."

Lacey left the house, wondering just how much help her young daughter would actually be. Not a lot, she surmised with a smile. But at least she was being well looked after. Thank goodness that both Mrs. Edwards and her daughter were fond of Nicole. Lacey didn't know what she would have done if they weren't.

The trip to the dressmaker's shop was a short one since it was on the outskirts of Austin's business district and not in the center. Lacey had no sooner stepped out of the carriage she'd hired than she saw a familiar face near the entrance to the dry-goods store nearby.

"William?" she called out, and watched as the young black man turned. He flashed her a glowing smile as she closed the distance between them. "What are you still doing here? My goodness, I thought you had gone back home to Dallas ages ago." It was a natural assumption—William usually went wherever Nick did.

"Oh, we went, but we didn't stay," he explained. "Fact is, we got back from Beaumont just last night."

"Beaumont!" Then she recalled the land she and Nick jointly owned there; land that had been surveyed long before Spindletop had become so famous. "Oh, yes, Beaumont! Has, uh, Nick discovered something that I should know about?"

"Not yet, he hasn't," William confessed dryly. "Of course, now that he's got that geologist felluh working for him, you never can tell what'll happen. Penrose seems to think we might have something, though."

"Really?" She shook her head in amazement. "So that's where you've been for the past week."

"No, not exactly. We went to Dallas first, like you said, then we went on to Beaumont. I wanted to see how Momma was doin' and Nick . . . well, he wanted to see how far along that architect had got with the house."

"He's building a house?"

"Yeah," William nodded. "Not where the old place stood; he sold that land to some speculators. But he's got him a spread farther on out and it appears as though it might be a real nice spot, too. Water and lots of trees all around it."

At least Nick wasn't just sitting around, doing nothing, she thought. She felt a twinge of jealousy and, rather than deny its existence, she acknowledged it for what it was. If Nick could give his attention to the building of a new house *and* to the development of the acreage in Beaumont, why couldn't he devote some of his time to her and Nicole?

Repressing her anger, she turned to William and smiled. "Where *is* Nick, by the way?" she asked with feigned innocence.

"When he left the house this mornin', he said he was on his way to see his daught . . . uh, I mean, the baby."

"He *what?*" Her first day away from the house and *he* decided to call on her!

"That's what he said. He took off just a few minutes ago, right after we got up. I suppose we shouldn't have slept so late this mornin', but after gettin' in so late last night . . . hey! Where you goin'?"

Lacey didn't answer William's question. She was too concerned with getting home before Nick could leave again.

Imagine! Staying away, without a word, for over a week, then deciding out of the blue to pop in on her . . . and she wasn't home!

All the way back to the house, she seethed silently, her face mirroring the conflict that warred within her. She gave no thought to her former resolution, which was to approach Nick humbly and tell him of her love. She had forgotten about that altogether. Now her only thought was to confront him and tell him what she thought of his thoughtlessness, his total lack of consideration for her or their daughter's welfare.

But Nick wasn't in the house when she stormed into it minutes later.

Daisy, coming down the stairs with her arms full

of soiled linen, looked up and greeted Lacey with a cautious smile.

"Where is he?" she demanded.

"Who, ma'am?" Daisy asked, stopping before she reached the bottom of the stairs.

"Nick . . . uh, Mr. Gallagher, that's who! Where is he?"

Daisy shrugged her plump shoulders. "I dunno. He took the baby and went out a minute ago."

"He did *what?*"

Daisy started to back away from her just as Mrs. Edwards appeared in the kitchen doorway. Lacey looked at the older woman and demanded, "Why did you let him take my baby?"

"But Miz Gallagher," Mrs. Edwards began, "he only—"

"He only kidnapped my daughter!" she accused shrilly, not considering any other possibility. "He stays gone for an eternity, then comes back as pretty as you please and *takes* Nicole! Why, I'll have his neck in a noose for this! So help me God, I will!"

Whirling around, she stormed out of the house and down the steps, unaware of her housekeeper's and Daisy's puzzled looks. Lacey vaguely heard Mrs. Edwards say something about Nicole being taken out for a stroll, but her irrational mind refused to acknowledge it. She could only think of finding her baby before Nick got too far away with her.

"Just how the hell does he think *he* can take care of a baby?" she asked no one in particular, stalking past the automobile that was parked in the street. "*I'm* her mother, dammit, he's not!"

She reached the corner and started to cross the

301

street, but, turning her head, she spied a familiar-looking figure at the other end of the block, coming toward her. Tall and well-dressed in a summer white business suit and hat, Nick should have looked dashing and very handsome. Instead, he looked totally ridiculous, because in front of him he pushed an elaborate, white wicker baby carriage.

"Oh, my Lord!" Lacey laughed, feeling more than slightly ridiculous herself. She had flown off the handle at Mrs. Edwards for nothing, it seemed. Nick hadn't kidnapped Nicole. He had merely taken her for a stroll, as Mrs. Edwards had tried to tell her.

Lacey slowly began to walk toward him, knowing that meeting him halfway would be something of a precedent for her. The closer she drew to him, the louder his words became, and it took a moment for her to realize that he was talking to the baby, who was inside the carriage.

". . . when you get big enough, I'll get you your own pony to ride, too! There's a real nice little creek close by so you can swim in it when the weather's warm, but don't worry, 'cause I'll teach you how to swim when the time's right." His daughter, wide-eyed and captivated with all his promises, listened intently, receiving a foolish, lopsided grin from him as he continued to explain, "Yeah, I will! And not only will I teach you how to ride and swim, I'll show you how to dig for worms and how to make a fishin' pole so we can catch our dinner in that creek. Don't that sound good?"

The carriage stopped abruptly, having bumped into something. Nick lifted his head to see what he had hit. Directly in front of him stood Lacey, her green eyes glittering with an emotion that he thought never to see again. A sensation of desire mingled with embarrassment overwhelmed him, and he found himself stuttering, "Uh . . . uh, mornin', Red." Lord, help him! For the first time in his life, he was at a loss for words. Her appearance, so sudden and unexpected, caused him more anguish than he cared to admit.

Lacey didn't say anything. She just stood there for a few moments, giving him a smile that melted his insides. Then she took a deep breath and stepped closer to him, placing her gloved hand alongside his smoothly shaven cheek.

"She's just a little girl, Nick," she muttered huskily, one finger teasing his moustache. "Little girls aren't supposed to go fishing or dig around in the dirt for worms."

Nick's voice was thick with emotion as he responded, "Our daughter may be more like her mother than you want her to be, Lace."

Sooty lashes blinked over emerald eyes. "What?"

His wide mouth quirked at one corner. "The day I paddled your butt, you and Chris were fightin' over his fishin' pole and his can of worms. You didn't want to dig for your own, as I recall; you wanted him to give you his. And you would've pushed him into White Rock Creek if I hadn't come along and stopped you."

"I remember now," she smiled, the event becoming clear in her mind. "I thought, at the time, that you were the meanest person I'd ever met when you turned me over your knee and wounded my pride . . . not to mention my backside. If my memory serves me right, you then told me to leave your little brother alone and that if I wanted worms, I would have to dig them up myself. Then you got on your horse and rode away."

She looked at him silently for a long moment, her eyes filling with moistness. "Were you serious?"

"About what?" His hand left his side to push an errant copper-gold curl off her cheek, his fingers coming to rest on her neck as his thumb caressed her smooth jaw.

"Were you serious about teaching Nicole how to ride and . . . and all the other things you said?"

"Yes, I was serious," he nodded. "I wouldn't lie about somethin' as important as that, Lace."

"You . . ." She stopped, took a deep breath and began again. "You want to be her father?"

His mouth twisted into a lopsided smile as a laugh rumbled through his broad chest. "I think I'm that already, babe."

Then the question that had plagued Lacey for so long suddenly demanded to be answered, and it burst forth from her on a breathy sigh. "And what about me, Nick?"

"Well, I sure as hell don't want to be *your* daddy," he growled huskily, his other hand coming up to cup her face while his eyes fastened hungrily on her opened mouth. "I'd rather be your friend . . ." He kissed her lips. ". . . your companion . . ." He kissed her cheek. ". . . your lover . . ." He caressed the all-too-sensitive spot below her ear with his tongue. ". . . your mate." Then his lips worshiped at her neck for a long moment before traversing the path back to her mouth. "I want to be with you, Red, any way I can."

Nearly mindless at this point from the effect of his

kisses, Lacey felt a brief moment of regret that she would be nothing more than his mistress. But that was better than nothing, and she chose not to object . . . just now. Her fingers dug into his back, propelling him closer to her as she whispered, "Yes, Nick, anything you want. Anything, just as long as we can be together."

His head moved away and he looked down at her passion-drowsed face. A puzzled frown marred his forehead, but it soon vanished as a smile crossed his lips, and his head dipped toward hers once again. But this kiss, to her regret, was not a long, lingering one. Nick merely sipped the nectar from her lips, muttering between nibbles, "I mean it, babe. I'm not just some horny stag in rut, you know. I love you! I love you so much I burn inside whenever I think of you."

Lacey's lids fluttered open. "Nick?" Was he telling her the truth? Or was he just mouthing platitudes because he knew it was what she wanted to hear?

"Hell, Lacey, you started a fire inside of me years ago that'll burn forever."

"But why didn't you tell me all of this before when we were in Dallas? Why did you wait until now, when it was almost too late?"

"Because . . . I couldn't."

"Yes, you could have!" she insisted, putting distance between them. "This past year never would have happened, Nick, if only you had told me how you felt. I would never have left Dallas. I would have stayed and—"

"*That's* why I couldn't!" he admitted, rubbing the back of his neck. "We had to get you out of town,

Lace, don't you see? Stratton tried to kill you once, and I sure as hell wasn't gonna let him get to you a second time."

Looking at him, puzzled by what he meant, she gasped as a thought registered. "There *was* a connection then, wasn't there?"

"Huh?" he frowned.

"Yes, there had to have been. There was a connection between you, Jake, Marshall Stratton, Jamieson Crawford and that poor prostitute, Sally O'Donnell. You were all in something together."

"Not by choice, I can tell you," he confessed, pushing the baby carriage again at the sound of Nicole's fretful crying. She had grown bored with her immobility and everyone ignoring her, but when her conveyance began to move again, she soon quieted down.

"You see," Nick continued, "I didn't know the whole story myself until we got Stratton into court and got the truth out of him. All I knew was he was trying to get rid of us."

"Us! You mean, you and me?"

"No, it was worse than that," Nick admitted with a grimace. "He was trying to get rid of *all* of us. Every last Gallagher in Dallas."

"But why? What did we ever do to him?"

"Not a damn thing! Pa did some business with the man once that I can remember and I thought that was the end of their association. But it came out in the trial that Stratton wanted that land down in Beaumont and Pa got to it first. Stratton's diseased brain made him crazy when Pa bought it, and we were the unlucky ones to receive his sick punishment."

"What kind of disease did he have?" Lacey asked, her frown mirroring her inability to imagine an ailment that would make a man go insane.

Nick hesitated before he muttered, "He had syphilis."

"Oh!" Her grimace was much like Nick's earlier one.

"Yeah," he nodded. "I don't know much about it—"

"Thank God!"

"—just what Jake's cousin, the doctor, told us. He said that sometimes, if the disease isn't gotten rid of soon enough, it can destroy the brain. Some men get a notion into their heads to do something and they don't let go of it until they've accomplished whatever it is they've set out to do. In Stratton's case, it was to get rid of us Gallaghers . . . and he damn near succeeded."

He explained then, to Lacey's horror, all of the terrible accidents and near-accidents that had befallen the Gallaghers, from the first attempt on his own life in the Yukon, to Max's and Rachel's deaths, to Chris's, and even to the accident that Hattiebelle and William had been in on New Year's Eve.

"It should have been you and me in that buggy," he disclosed raggedly, "not them. God knows, I never stopped once to think what the consequences would be that night. All I knew was that I wanted you and I had to have you. The thought never entered my mind that my lust would put someone else in danger."

"Then I'm as guilty as you are," she admitted.

"Hell, you can't be!"

"Yes, I can, too. I wanted you as much as you wanted me . . . I still do!"

He placed his hand lovingly alongside her neck and smiled. "You didn't always. That day you walked in on me and Sally at Cora's, you hated me enough to try and kill me."

"I didn't try and kill you! I merely hit you over the head with the water pitcher."

"And kicked my shins and beat me with your parasol and kneed me in the groin!"

"Well, I was angry!" Her chin tilted defiantly. "You had been leading me on, or so I thought, making me believe one thing while something entirely different was going on. When I saw you with that . . . that poor, unfortunate woman, what else could I do? Sit back and pretend it didn't matter?"

"But she *didn't* matter, never! Sally had been gettin' information from Crawford, who was workin' with Stratton, and she passed it on to me and Jake. You could've listened to me. My God, do you know that I couldn't show my face in public for nearly six whole months after that blasted day at Cora's? Talk about public animosity! I could close down a saloon just by walkin' into it. I would venture a guess that half the good wives in Dallas followed your example that day and delivered punishment to their husbands, guilty or not, if they were so much as suspected of visitin' Frogtown or Boggy Bayou."

"Well, let me tell you something, Nicholas Gallagher, the beating you took on Cora Noble's front porch is mild compared to what you *will* get if I ever find you looking at another woman. And God have mercy on your soul if you *touch* one!"

Nick stopped and stood there, staring at her for a

moment. Fire glittered in her green eyes and heightened the color in her creamy cheeks. She was the most beautiful woman in the world, and she was all his! Then, tossing back his head, he laughed heartily at his good fortune, nearly losing his hat in the process.

"Listen to us, Nick," she said soberly, bringing his laughter to a halt. "We haven't been together for more than fifteen minutes and we're already arguing."

Nick cocked his head to an angle and shrugged. "That's all part of life, ain't it? The laughing, the crying, the fighting, and the loving?"

They had finally reached her house and were standing on the walk below the porch. Lacey, feeling a million doubts and questions race through her mind, could only sigh as she looked up into Nick's craggy, hawklike face. "Where do we go from here?" she queried softly.

"Where ever you want us to go, Lace. It's up to you."

"But what do *you* want?" she asked reluctantly, girding herself for what his answer would be.

"I want you," he stated simply. "And our daughter, and any other kids our union might produce."

Lacey swallowed the lump that had risen in her throat and tried to blink back the tears welling up in her eyes. "We're all bastards, you know. You, me and Nicole. Will the next Gallagher be a bastard, too?"

Nick released a long, low breath. "Not if I can help it. If I'd known about her, my daughter wouldn't have been a bastard, either."

"You do realize what you're saying, don't you?"

With an amused grunt, his mouth tilted at one corner. "Well, hell, Red! Don't you think it's about time I ended my bachelor days and spent a while being a husband and father? How 'bout it? Will you marry me?"

It certainly wasn't the most romantic proposal in the world, she told herself wryly, but it was the one she wanted. She loved this man more than she could ever admit, and he had said that he loved her. That, after all, was all that really mattered. She had things to tell him, of course—things that he probably knew already—but those explanations and confessions would have to wait a while.

"Yes, darling," she said finally, stepping into his outstretched arms. "I'll marry you anytime . . . anywhere . . . anyplace."

From the confines of her baby carriage, Nicole Rochelle Gallagher let out a yelp of displeasure. She was wet and hungry and tired of being on her back. But her cry for attention was not answered immediately—her mother and father were too busy sealing her future and theirs with a very fiery, very passionate, very long overdue kiss.

About the Author

CAROL JERINA, a native of Dallas, Texas, began her publishing career with *Lady Raine*. When she isn't creating new books with colorful plots and characters, she spends her free time acting as head cook, housekeeper, chauffeur, and referee for her four sons and her husband, Drew.

Tapestry
HISTORICAL ROMANCES

Next Month From
Tapestry Romances

FRENCH ROSE
by Jacqueline Marten
PROMISE OF PARADISE
by Cynthia Sinclair

____DEFIANT LOVE
Maura Seger
45963/$2.50

____FLAMES OF PASSION
Sheryl Flournoy
46195/$2.50

____LIBERTINE LADY
Janet Joyce
46292/$2.50

____REBELLIOUS LOVE
Maura Seger
46379/$2.50

____EMBRACE THE STORM
Lynda Trent
46957/$2.50

____EMBRACE THE WIND
Lynda Trent
49305/$2.50

POCKET BOOKS

____FORBIDDEN LOVE
Maura Seger
46970/$2.75

____SNOW PRINCESS
Victoria Foote
49333/$2.75

____FLETCHER'S WOMAN
Linda Lael Miller
47936/$2.75

____GENTLE FURY
Monica Barrie
49426/$2.95

____FLAME ON THE SUN
Maura Seger
49395/$2.95·

____ENGLISH ROSE
Jacqueline Marten
49655/$2.95

____DESIRE AND DESTINY
Linda Lael Miller
49866/$2.95

____WILLOW WIND
Lynda Trent
47574/$2.95

____IRISH ROSE
Jacqueline Marten
50722/$2.95

____BOUND BY HONOR
Helen Tucker
49781/$2.95

____ARDENT VOWS
Helen Tucker
49780/$2.95

____MASQUERADE
Catherine Lyndell
50048/$2.95

____PIRATE'S PROMISE
Ann Cockcroft
53018/$2.95

____ALLIANCE
OF LOVE
Catherine Lyndell
49514/$2.95

____JADE MOON
Erica Mitchell
49894/$2.95

____DESTINY'S EMBRACE
Sheryl Flournoy
49665/$2.95

____FIELDS OF PROMISE
Janet Joyce
49394/$2.95

____FIRE AND INNOCENCE
Sheila O'Hallion
50683/$2.95

____MOTH AND FLAME
Laura Parker
50684/$2.95

____LADY RAINE
Carol Jerina
50836/$2.95

____LAND OF GOLD
Mary Ann Hammond
50872/$2.95

____DAUGHTER OF
LIBERTY
Johanna Hill
52371/$2.95

____CHARITY'S PRIDE
Patricia Pellicane
52372/$2.95

____BANNER O'BRIEN
Linda Lael Miller
52356/$2.95

____GALLAGHER'S LADY
Carol Jerina
52359/$2.95

Tapestry

Pocket Books, Department TAP
1230 Avenue of the Americas, New York, New York 10020

Please send me the books I have checked above. I am enclosing
$_____ (please add 75¢ to cover postage and handling. NYS and NYC
residents please add appropriate sales tax. Send check or money order—no
cash, stamps, or CODs please. Allow six weeks for delivery). For purchases over
$10.00, you may use VISA: card number, expiration date and customer signature
must be included.

Name _____

Address _____

City _____ State/Zip _____

959

☐ Check here to receive your free
Pocket Books order form

Home delivery from Pocket Books

Here's your opportunity to have fabulous bestsellers delivered right to you. Our free catalog is filled to the brim with the newest titles plus the finest in mysteries, science fiction, westerns, cookbooks, romances, biographies, health, psychology, humor—every subject under the sun. Order this today and a world of pleasure will arrive at your door.

POCKET BOOKS, Department ORD
1230 Avenue of the Americas, New York, N.Y. 10020

Please send me a free Pocket Books catalog for home delivery

NAME _____

ADDRESS _____

CITY _____ STATE/ZIP _____

If you have friends who would like to order books at home, we'll send them a catalog too—

NAME _____

ADDRESS _____

CITY _____ STATE/ZIP _____

NAME _____

ADDRESS _____

CITY _____ STATE/ZIP _____